An
Evil Eye

a novel

JASON GOODWIN

SARAH CRICHTON BOOKS
Farrar, Straus and Giroux
New York

SARAH CRICHTON BOOKS
Farrar, Straus and Giroux
18 West 18th Street, New York 10011

Library of Congress Cataloging-in-Publication Data
Goodwin, Jason, 1964–
    An evil eye : a novel / Jason Goodwin. — 1st ed.
        p.   cm.
    "Sarah Crichton books."
    ISBN 978-0-374-11040-6
    1. Yashim (Fictitious character : Goodwin)—Fiction.   2. Detectives—
Turkey—Istanbul—Fiction.   3. Eunuchs—Fiction.   4. Defectors—Fiction.
5. Women—Turkey—Fiction.   6. Harems—Fiction.   7. Istanbul (Turkey)—
History—19th century—Fiction.   I. Title.

PR6107.O663E94 2011
823'.92—dc22

2010039938

Designed by Cassandra J. Pappas

www.fsgbooks.com

1   3   5   7   9   10   8   6   4   2

For Harry

Life is a comedy for those who think,
& a tragedy for those who feel

—HORACE WALPOLE

An
Evil Eye

Istanbul, 1836

THE yali *is made of wood silvered by the sun, dry as tinder.*

As evening falls, the timbers begin to cool. Beams settle; boards contract. Cracks ease around the window frames, whose latticed glass flames orange with the setting sun.

The pasha's two-oared caïque skims like a cormorant up the Bosphorus toward it, away from Istanbul.

He leans into the cushions, his back to the setting sun, and lets his mind rove idly across the water, over the surface of his ambitions and his desires.

He checks himself. He is not a superstitious man, but praise and pride attract the evil eye; certain thoughts are better left unframed.

Almost guiltily, he turns his head. The yali stands so beautifully at the water's edge, looking out across the Bosphorus to the hills of Asia beyond. The evening meal has been taken, and he imagines the murmur of voices as his household prepares for sleep. He can almost hear the yali settling, its old bones composing themselves for the night, wooden joints creaking and crackling in the dusk.

He turns his head—and puts out a hand, as if it were in his power to stop what is about to happen. As if he could fit the house in his own palm, and keep it safe.

Between his outstretched fingers, the yali is ablaze.

It burns so beautifully, as if a wild spirit were dashing through the rooms. A window explodes, and against the evening sky the sparks fly up like shooting stars. Galaxies twist from the staircase; suns blaze in every room.

The pasha screams. The rowers glance back. They miss a stroke.

Over the crash of falling timber and the snapping of the flames, the pasha hears screams from the harem apartments, upstairs.

When the caïque touches the marble stairs, the pasha flings himself onto shore. His mouth is open, sweat rolling down his face.

He races from one end of the burning house to the other, moaning. He feels the heat on his face. He can no longer hear the screams.

But he hears, instead, someone call his name.

"Fevzi Pasha! Pasha!"

Two arms thrust a bundle from a window. The pasha reaches up.

The roof sags, dropping a sudden flurry of flaming shingles, which spin to the ground. The pasha leaps back. The figure at the window is gone. The window is gone.

The flames are driving a firestorm: the pasha feels the wind snatch at his cloak, drawing him back toward the yali.

He cradles the bundle to his chest and stumbles away.

The gate bursts open, and a crowd of men surges in with buckets, hooks, ladders. But it is far too late. As the men run by, the pasha hears timbers break and the sky is lit up.

He does not turn back.

Summer 1839

CANNON boomed across the Bosphorus. White smoke, the color of mourning, billowed low over the water.

Sultan Mahmut II was dead. He had come to the throne of Osman as the turbaned ruler of a medieval empire, and had died in a frock coat and a fez. In his long reign he had given the Ottoman Empire French saddles, a constitution of sorts, modern drill and percussion rifles. He had destroyed the ferocious Janissaries, as an obstacle to progress, and he had lost Greece to the Greeks and Crimea to the Russians and Egypt to an Albanian adventurer called Mehmet Ali Pasha. He had built himself a modern palace, at Besiktas, where he maintained a harem like sultans of old.

The harem was in pandemonium.

"You are the Kislar aga, Ibou. You must help them to leave," Yashim said quietly. "The sultan's harem is your domain. The sultan has died, and the women must move on."

The Kislar aga, the master of the girls, shut his eyes and pressed his fingers against his smooth cheeks. "They—they do not want to go, Yashim."

"Abdülmecid is sultan now. Any moment he may arrive here, at Besiktas, and he will bring his women." Yashim gestured to the staircase.

The Kislar aga took a deep breath and started up the stairs. "You must come with me. We must get the women away."

Yashim followed reluctantly as the Kislar aga bustled through the gallery, clapping his hands. "The carriages are come, ladies! To the carriages!"

Not one of the women paid him the slightest attention. They had spent years learning how to behave, how to speak, how to be beautiful, devoting their lives to the service of the sultan. Now the sultan was dead and carriages were to take them away.

They wanted to wail and scream, and to mourn.

To mourn the sultan, their youth, their hopes.

And grab what they could, while there was still time.

ABOVE the gardens of the palace, in the smaller quarters reserved for the crown prince, Elif leaned at a window and watched the pigeons through the lattice. Each crump of the guns shook the heavy air and sent clouds of birds fluttering from the domes of Istanbul. From the leads of the Süleymaniye they rose high above the Golden Horn; clapping their wings from the low rotunda of Ayasofya, where the Horn bled into the waters of the Bosphorus; billowing from the domes of the Grand Bazaar, and from the single hemisphere of the Grand Mosque on Üsküdar. Again and again the pigeons clattered into the sky, and then fell back.

"It will not be long, Elif." Melda lay on the divan, twisting a lock of black hair between her hennaed fingers. "The aga will call for us very soon."

Elif murmured a lazy assent. She had known that the old sultan had been about to die. Everyone knew. When he went, he went: a day and a night before they put him in the ground. You couldn't wait longer; not in this heat. Dead, buried, and the cannons booming out to tell the world that Abdülmecid was sultan now.

High in the sky, something moved: the whirling speck caught Elif's attention. She raised her chin a fraction.

She heard the distant thump of the cannon, and watched the hawk drop. She saw its talons extend, and the spurt of blood and feathers as it struck.

As the hawk sailed to the ground, clutching its prey, Elif saw the imperial caïque approaching from the Golden Horn. Under its fluttering canopy sat the new ruler of the empire, Abdülmecid, sixteen years old, fresh from his investiture at Eyüp, at the tomb of the Companion of the Prophet.

She turned from the window.

"Abdülmecid has been girded with the sword of Osman," she said. She ran her hand across her stomach. "It's time we joined him, don't you think?"

ABDÜLMECID'S girls ran as a herd, sweeping past a black eunuch on the steps, across the polished marble floors, streaming up the wide shallow staircase to the harem.

At the top of the stairs, the girls paused.

The wailing and keening for the departed sultan had given way to tantrums and the gnashing of teeth. Doors flew open, and slammed. Women dashed in all directions. Children were running aimlessly from room to room. The black eunuchs stood about wringing their hands. Matrons bawled, while slender Circassians squealed, their blond ringlets all askew; somebody was dragging at the curtains in a little room. Bags and boxes were piled pell-mell in the hallways. A girl sat on a box, crying into a broken mirror.

Abdülmecid's girls paused, pretending astonishment: eyebrows arched, fingers to horrified lips.

"It's disgusting," Elif said.

"*Süyütsüz,*" Melda corrected her: *undignified.*

Elif nodded. *Undignified* was better. It was a proper harem word. The harem had a language that was all its own: words and phrases that you had to learn unless you wanted to look like a novice. It went with a way of speaking that was softer and more sibilant than the street language of the ordinary Turks, grander, more easygoing. That harem lisp was like having soft hands: it showed your rank. The voice of a harem girl was like a caress.

But not today.

Elif stuck with Melda, who seemed to know where she was going.

THE lady Talfa stepped out of the room, hand across her mouth, the sound of cannon and the screaming in her ears.

She saw women sweep down the corridor, hammering at the doors, dragging at each other's clothes, and baring their teeth, like wolves.

A vase wobbled on its stand, between two windows. As the lady Talfa watched, a skirt brushed against the stand. A woman flung back her hand and caught the rim of the vase as it circled. It swung wide and went over with a smack, shivering to pieces on the wooden floor.

Slippered feet trampled over the fragments.

Two girls ran past, hand in hand, laughing. The lady Talfa saw the color in their cheeks, the sparkle in their eyes.

She stepped forward.

"Who are you? Where do you think you're going?" she hissed.

Elif's head whipped around. She saw a woman in the doorway. "It's our turn now, auntie," Elif spat. She laughed at the shock on the older woman's face and her pretty blue eyes narrowed. The woman was jowly and pallid and she had lost her waist.

Elif cupped her hands beneath her breasts. "We're the pretty girls."

She saw the look of hesitation on Talfa's face, and her glance shifted over Talfa's shoulder. "What's this room, Melda? What's in here?" she said, tugging at her friend's hand.

But the other girl drew back impatiently. "I know where to go, Elif. Don't waste time."

Elif shrugged. "All right, you lead." As she sped off she half turned her head: "Better get packing, auntie!"

Talfa blinked. She had seen the carriages drawn up in the courtyard, and the women stuffing the sultan's treasures into little bags. It was all they had, whatever they could carry off.

But they could have been allowed to leave the harem in peace, with dignity.

It was a serious blunder for which Ibou, the chief black eunuch, should be made to pay.

The lady Talfa gripped the door frame as another burst of wild laughter rang down the corridor, followed by an anguished scream.

ELIF and Melda reached the stairs at the end of the corridor and scampered up them, giggling and breathless.

At the top they had a corridor to themselves. They chose a door and burst into a room that overlooked the Bosphorus.

A woman was shoveling the contents of a small table into a bag.

They all stared at one another. Then the woman screamed and Melda sprang at the woman and slapped her on the cheek.

"Stop that! Stop it! What are you doing with that bag?"

The woman tightened her grip on the bag. "This is mine! Get out!"

Melda made a grab for the bag. The woman yanked it back and the table went over.

"Now look!"

Elif snatched at the woman's scarf. Melda kept her eyes on the bag. "What's in there? What are you stealing?"

They heard running footsteps in the corridor and one of their girls put her head around the door, then withdrew it again.

The woman with the bag seemed to have trouble breathing. Her eyes bulged and her face went red. Elif gave the scarf a last savage tug and Melda went for the bag. The woman staggered and let it go. "It's mine," she choked.

"Drop it, auntie. If it was yours you'd have packed it by now. Go on, get out!"

They shoved the woman into the corridor. She was wringing her hands, but there were two of them and there wasn't much she could do. Melda and Elif put their backs to the door and watched the handle rattle.

After a while they heard more people running in the corridor. The handle went still.

The two girls turned to each other and burst out laughing.

Later they looked into the bag. It was pathetic what those women tried to carry off—right down to their kohl, and half-used bottles of rose-water, and little paper talismans. The woman they'd surprised had obviously thought she could get away with the coffeepot! Even if she'd been the coffee kalfa, it didn't belong to her. The rest of the stuff in the bag was almost certainly stolen, too. All that money—and she wasn't even pretty.

Elif shrugged. Those women were old and their sultan was dead. She thought of the woman they'd frightened on the floor below. Perhaps they should have seized her room.

It is our turn now, she thought, as she examined the scarf. It wasn't even torn.

But Elif had made a serious mistake.

The woman on the floor below was the lady Talfa. She was neither particularly young nor particularly pretty. But she had no plans to leave. She took no orders from the chief black eunuch.

The lady Talfa was not one of the late Sultan Mahmut's slaves.

She was his sister.

New girls could come in. Her nephew Abdülmecid could move into his new palace chambers. But for now, and always, this harem was her home.

She stamped her foot. Where was Bezmialem? The sultan's mother should have been here, taking control of her son's girls. The young valide.

Talfa glared down the corridor and saw a familiar figure in a brown cloak.

"Yashim!" she cried. "Can't you do anything? Can't you stop all this—this noise?"

YASHIM ordered the halberdiers to move the baggage to the carriages: the new girls were already beginning to paw at it themselves. The soldiers moved slowly, with infinite gentleness, eyes down: the women lunged and clung to their arms.

The women who served the late sultan were to leave for Eski Saray, the old Palace of Tears, for centuries a home for the harem beauties whose sultan had died. Some—the lucky ones, maybe—would marry, entering the harem of some Ottoman officer of the guard, or a pasha of the civil bureaucracy. The rest could hope for little more than to drag out their existence behind the walls of the Palace of Tears, forgotten and ignored.

Getting the luggage away made things easier: the women followed their belongings. Others—dragging their fingernails down their cheeks, or cramming their things into little sacks—felt suddenly resigned to do what Yashim suggested. They were drawn to him, just as the lady Talfa had been; they relied on him, as Ibou the chief black eunuch relied on him, instinctively. Against the bright plumage of the harem women, Yashim's brown cloak was modest almost to invisibility. He spoke quietly, in a room that rang with shrieks and tears; his gestures were restrained. There was a stillness in Yashim that made the women pause and listen. His low voice wearied and fascinated them, as if it carried an echo of the burdens of life. It was the voice of a man, perhaps: yet Yashim was not, quite, a man himself. Yashim was a eunuch. By evening the women had taken to the carriages, and gone.

Upstairs, in her new room, Elif picked up her oud and began to play.

Farther along the corridor, a pale woman reclined on her divan, shading her eyes with the back of her hand.

Bezmialem had heard the pandemonium and locked her door. She sought only peace and seclusion.

At her moment of triumph, when her son returned to the palace as sultan, Bezmialem had a headache.

"Yashim efendi?"

The halberdier swung back the door of the gatehouse. Outside Yashim saw a small closed carriage, with another soldier holding the door.

"Please, efendi."

"Where are we going?"

"We must be quick, efendi."

Yashim climbed into the cab and the halberdier slammed the door. Yashim heard him shout something to the driver and then, with a lurch that shot him back into the buttoned leather seat, they were off. The carriage squeaked and swayed; Yashim wound his fingers around a leather strap in the dark. The windows of the cab were tightly curtained, but he could feel the drumming of the wheels on the cobbles and the slick lurch when they left hard ground for muddier, unpaved streets.

Yashim peeled a curtain aside and peered out. At first he could make nothing of the high, blank walls, until the carriage veered to the right, flinging him back again, and they rolled under the High Gate, which gave its name—Sublime Porte—to the Ottoman government.

The driver pulled on the reins; the cab's pace lessened; the door was flung open and a young man in a Frankish uniform and cap saluted Yashim. As they bustled up the steps the young man's sword clinked on the marble; then they were through the front door, scurrying down corridors where anxious faces peered at them in the candlelight, where doors opened noiselessly at their approach.

Yashim knew exactly where they were going. He'd been there before, to the private chamber of the grand vizier, the man who held the reins of the empire for his sultan's sake.

The cadet threw open a door and ushered him in with a sweep of the hand.

A lamp was burning on a great mahogany desk.

"Come."

The rumble of the vizier's voice came from the divan, placed in an alcove at the far side of the room. Yashim half turned, in puzzlement.

"Husrev? Mehmet Husrev Pasha?"

As he approached the divan, he could make out a heavy figure sitting cross-legged in the half-light, wearing a Circassian shawl and a tasseled, brimless cap.

As the pasha gestured to the edge of the divan, his ring caught the light. It was a sign of office, but until now Yashim had seen the ring of the grand vizier on someone else's hand.

"Changes, Yashim efendi," the old pasha growled, as if he had read Yashim's mind. "A time of change."

Yashim settled on the edge of the divan. "My pasha," he murmured. He wondered how the change had been made, what had become of Midhat Pasha. "I was detained at the palace. I offer you my congratulations."

Husrev fixed him with a weary stare. His voice was very deep, almost a whisper. "The sultan is very young."

"We must be grateful that he can draw upon your experience," Yashim replied politely.

The old pasha grunted. He pressed his fingertips together in front of his face, brushing his mustache. "And at the palace?"

"Sultan Mahmut's women were slow to leave." Yashim bit his lip; it was not what he should have said. Not when Husrev himself had moved so fast.

Perhaps Husrev Pasha thought the same, because he gave a dismissive snort and slid a sheet of paper across the divan. "Report from the governor of Chalki. A dead man, in the cistern of the monastery."

"Who was he?"

The pasha shrugged. "Nobody seems to know."

"But—he was killed?"

"Perhaps. Probably. I want you to find out."

"I understand, my pasha." For the second time that day, he was being asked to do someone else's job.

Husrev Pasha's heavy-lidded eyes missed little. "Have I said anything to displease you, Yashim?"

Yashim took a deep breath. "Is it not a matter for the governor, my pasha? The *kadi*, at least."

"Would I send for you if it was enough to direct the *kadi*? The governor?"

Yashim heard the anger in his rumbling voice. "Forgive me, my pasha. I spoke without thinking."

To his surprise, the old vizier leaned forward and took his knee in his massive paw.

"How old are you, Yashim?"

"Forty."

"I have seen what may happen when a sultan dies. When you were a little boy, Yashim. We thought the sky was falling on our heads. Bayraktar's Janissaries stormed the Topkapi Palace. In the provinces there was fear—and fighting on the streets of Istanbul. The Muslims afraid of the Greeks."

Yashim listened, and said nothing.

"The city is quiet today," the old pasha continued. "But the weather is hot, and the sultan is young. I am a little afraid, Yashim. Men have hopes I do not yet understand. Some have demands. Between demand and threat you cannot pass a horsehair. And the state is weak. Russia, as you know, gains every day at the expense of our people. Moldavia and Wallachia are occupied by the tsar's troops, to the mouth of the Danube. Serbia rules itself, with their aid. Georgia and the Armenian lands are under Russia now."

He cracked his huge knuckles. "Egypt is strong. Long ago, we could count on Egypt; that time is past. Mehmet Ali Pasha is not to be trusted. We are caught, Yashim, between hammer and anvil."

He picked up a pile of documents at his elbow and let them drop heavily onto the divan. "With these, I must govern this empire. I must keep the peace." He shrugged. "This is a dangerous time for all of us, Yashim, and I do not know exactly where the danger lies. Perhaps from a corpse in the Christians' well."

"I understand, my pasha," Yashim replied. "Your eyes must be everywhere."

"If not, Yashim, they would fill with tears." He rubbed a massive thumb and finger over the bridge of his nose. "Tomorrow morning will be sufficient," he said.

9

STANISLAW Palewski, Polish Ambassador to the Sublime Porte, put up a hand to steady his straw hat as a light wind threatened to tip it by the brim.

"This," he remarked, "is better than Therapia."

Yashim, beside him on the bench, grunted assent. When Istanbul lolled in the dog days, under the summer sun, the other European ambassadors liked to retreat to their summer residencies at Therapia, up the Bosphorus; only Palewski remained in town. He lacked funds; he lacked a summer residency; he lacked, in point of fact, a country.

It had been Yashim's idea to invite Palewski to spend a cooling day out on the water, traveling to the island of Chalki and back. Yesterday's work in the harem had exhausted him, and the cannons booming out across the water had sounded like the blood pounding in his own head. The breeze at Marmara blew as well as the breezes of Therapia, and at a fraction of the cost: a ticket to the island could be had for a sequin—a seat on deck, a view over the water, a chance of seeing dolphins, and a glass of sweet tea into the bargain.

Palewski was Polish, from his tongue to his heart, and represented a country that no longer existed—at least, it was not recognized by any of the Christian courts of Europe. The Ottomans sustained the notion that their old proud foe existed still; they accepted the credentials of an ambassador whose country had been swallowed by its neighbors. They even sustained the ancient custom of paying the ambassador a stipend for his maintenance, for magnanimity was the mark of a great empire, and old habits died hard; but the stipend was small and did not stretch to summer residencies.

They made, perhaps, an unlikely couple, Palewski and Yashim; though anyone who had seen them together on the deck of the felucca might have noticed that both, in their way, were conservatively dressed. Palewski's coat was well cut, in the old fashion, if slightly shabby, and his waistcoat was more colorful than the age prescribed; while Yashim's embroidered waistcoat and white pantaloons belonged to a style that was fast disappearing in the capital. Most Ottoman gentlemen followed the lead of their late sultan in adopting dress coats and tight black trousers, beneath a scarlet fez. Yashim wore a fez, but it was swathed in a strip of linen, some twelve feet long, which he wound tightly around his head as a turban. On his feet he wore the comfortable leather slippers that the Ottomans had always worn, before the sultan persuaded them into tight-laced boots and woolen socks.

An odd couple, then, but with more in common than might have at first appeared—not least a shared desire to escape the summer heat and enjoy the breezes out to sea.

The largest of the Prince's Islands advanced swiftly over the sun-pricked waters. The sails were furled, one by one; the canvas slapped, the chain ran out, and soon the boat was drawn alongside the quay. The Greek sailors stepped ashore with coiled rope and lazy familiarity.

A few minutes later, Yashim and his old friend had exchanged the sea breeze for the equally welcome shade of the ancient limes that flanked the path up to the monastery of Hristos. The air smelled of charcoal and roasted meat where the kebab vendors had set up their braziers in the shade; the cool white walls of the island houses and their ocher pantiled roofs, peeped through the trees. Others shared their path: veiled women in long striped coats, a sailor in a shirt without a collar, a Greek priest in high canonicals, little boys on errands with bare feet, and a stout woman in a headscarf who rolled along after her donkey, its panniers stuffed with reeds.

Close to the gateway of the monastery, set back from the avenue, stood a small café.

"Sherbet, Yash. They'll do a pear syrup here, too," Palewski suggested, steering his friend gently by the arm toward the café path.

Two men swerved past them, running up the hill.

"So hot," Palewski murmured, raising an eyebrow.

Cushions were scattered on carpets spread beneath the boughs of an enormous pine, whose resinous fragrance perfumed the air. A boy in a waistcoat took their orders: he seemed distracted, glancing now and then through the trees toward the avenue of limes.

"Pear, not apple," Yashim corrected him. "Pear for my friend, and coffee, medium sweet, for me."

The two friends lay in companionable silence, watching the sky through the boughs of the tree. Rooks cawed in the upper branches; farther off, Yashim could hear a murmur of indistinct voices like wind soughing in the pines.

Palewski dipped into his pocket. He brought out a slim volume bound in soft red leather, which he opened and began to read.

Yashim struggled for a few moments with the curiosity that comes over anyone when they watch someone else with their nose in a book. Then he gave up.

"*Pan Tadeusz*—again," Palewski replied, with a smile.

"The national epic," Yashim murmured. "Of course."

"Really, I never tire of it," Palewski said. "It is the Poland I represent. Poland in the old days." He sighed. "I wrote to Mickiewicz, proposing a French translation."

"The poet? And did he reply?"

Palewski nodded. "Of course, he could do it himself. He lives in Paris. But he said he'd be delighted if I'd like to try."

"And you've begun?"

"Awfully hard, Yashim." Palewski leaned back and closed his eyes. He flung up a hand toward the trees and began to recite:

> *"Litwo! Ojczyzno moja! Ty jesteś jak zdrowie.*
> *Ile cię trzeba cenić, ten tylko się dowie,*
> *Kto cię stracił. Dziś piękność twą w całej ozdobie*
> *Widzę i opisuję, bo tęsknię po tobie."*

Yashim could not understand the words; he had stopped listening. He could hear a sound like angry bees, buzzing farther up the avenue; now and again he heard shouts.

"I've made a start, Yash, but it's picking the words. And matching the rhyme—"

Yashim bent forward and touched his knee. "Don't go away," he said.

"But I haven't given you my translation yet."

Yashim had scrambled to his feet. "I'll listen later."

"Your coffee's coming."

"I'll be back."

He went to the avenue and turned up the hill. A few hundred yards ahead he could make out the wooden gate of the monastery. The gate was shut, and outside it a few dozen men were standing in a semicircle, their backs toward Yashim.

"Unbelievers!"

"Open the gate!"

A man stooped and picked up a stone, which he threw against the wooden gate. Soon the whole crowd was hurling stones, which thunked against the heavy wooden planks.

Yashim moved to the edge of the circle.

"What are you doing?"

The man beside him turned his head sharply. "The unbelievers, efendi. They have the body of a Muslim in there. They are hiding him."

Yashim frowned. "How do you know that?"

"At night, they will feed him to the dogs!"

Yashim put up a hand. "How can you know so much? Have you talked to them, inside? Have you seen this Muslim?"

The man turned angrily. "Open this gate! We are Muslims!"

Yashim glanced back. More men were surging up the avenue; some were shaking their fists.

Ever since the Greeks of Athens had secured their independence, Greeks and Turks had been like flint and steel, striking sparks that threatened to set the empire alight. Husrev Pasha was right, these were uncertain times. The weather was too hot—and a man was dead.

Yashim put his hands in the air and stepped out in front of the gathering crowd.

"Listen to me."

The men paused, curious.

"Listen to me. I am from the palace."

A bareheaded man stepped forward. "The unbelievers! They treat the Muslims like dogs!"

Yashim laid a hand on the man's shoulder, and invited him to sit down. He opened his arm, gesturing along the line. "All of you, please. Sit down."

The men began to form knots. After all the noise, the quiet voice of the stranger seemed almost hypnotic. Some squatted, and one or two of them actually sat, crossing their legs.

"We will find out what is going on here," Yashim continued. The name came to him at that moment. "Where is Mullah Dede?"

The men looked around. Mullah Dede was not there.

"Fetch the mullah. Go."

"Who are you?" It was a fat man in an open shirt. He had his hands on his hips and he was glancing right and left. "Who are you, from the palace?"

"I am Yashim." He spoke quietly, but loud enough for the men to hear. A wary look appeared on the fat man's face. "And your name?"

"I am . . . Hasan."

Men are driven by fear: and they fear only what they do not know.

"Will anyone else give me their name?"

Men looked away, feeling the ground with their eyes.

Yashim could see the figure of the mullah climbing briskly up the avenue. "When Mullah Dede comes we will all sit quietly, while he and I discuss the matter."

The mullah walked in slowly through the ring of men, looking from right to left. He saw Yashim, and salaamed.

"What is this gathering, my son? They say the monks have taken the body of a Muslim. Can this be true?"

"We will ask the monks," Yashim replied.

"Yes, that is the best way." Mullah Dede nodded slowly. "We will enter, and speak with the abbot." He turned to the men squatting on the ground. "Go, all of you. Go in peace, and if we have need of you again, I will call."

Yashim glanced at Hasan. He was swaying, as if uncertain what to do; eventually he turned away and began to go down the hill. Many joined him; a few, however, only moved farther off, and squatted under the trees, planning to see what happened next.

"And now," said Mullah Dede, "we will knock on the door, and hope that we are answered, inshallah."

"Inshallah," Yashim echoed.

AT the sultan's palace at Besiktas, the lady Talfa was jingling an enormous bunch of iron keys threaded onto an iron loop.

"Some of you girls," she announced, "will receive keys yourselves as you settle in to your duties. That will be a matter for the Kislar aga to arrange, with my help, naturally."

They were on the ground floor of the palace, where the windows were shuttered on the inside with diamond-shaped lattices to prevent anyone from looking in.

The girls avoided one another's eyes, anxious not to be thought overbold. Many of them hoped to receive a key and to be allotted an important task. They had already inspected the laundry, under the lady Talfa's direction: there would be a laundry kalfa, maybe two. They had looked into rooms containing the coffee sets for the coffee kalfa to manage; a silver room, stacked with plates, trays, and ewers; a china room, whose china kalfa would preside over the proper storage and cleaning of the Chinese porcelain.

The lady Talfa had familiarized them with each part of the building she knew so well. Baths had a key; so did the dressing rooms, where the sultan's linen would be stored, properly folded and stacked away, and his frock coats, brushed every day and inspected for any sign of moth or dirt, with lengths of silk and muslin for his turban. There was even a slipper room, to which a slipper kalfa would possess the key.

The girls who followed the lady Talfa were used to luxury, but the scale of Besiktas bewildered them; the number of potential responsibilities and duties excited them. Some of them had forgotten their training and wandered openmouthed, eyes darting from precious silks to the immaculate polished parquet and marble on the floors. All of them were feeling weary, and slightly overawed.

Which was just how the lady Talfa wanted it, as she turned a key in the cellar door.

"Bring the lantern," she said, "and follow me."

They descended a stone staircase. Some of the girls reached out to clutch each other: it was quite dark, and the shadows that raced across the vault overhead seemed sinister and demonic. Somebody tripped and squealed.

At the bottom of the steps, the lady Talfa turned and held the lantern at her shoulder. Her face was plunged into dark shade. The girls, feeling the cold, shivered; they wondered why they had been brought down here.

"I have a duty, as the senior lady in the palace, to pass on a warning. The harem has many rules, as you know, and many traditions. Some of these ensure the smooth running of the sultan's household. Some are upheld for your comfort and protection."

The girls stood still, listening.

"There is one rule above all that you will be expected to obey, and that is the rule of silence. We are a family. We will have our disagreements and our rivalries, no doubt, as a family will. But what goes on here, in the sultan's harem, is a matter for us and for no one else. You will see and hear things that will surprise you. Perhaps they will even upset you. But these are for us, and for us only. Do you understand?"

The girls murmured assent. They understood they had to keep their secrets.

Now, they hoped, the lady Talfa would lead them all upstairs, out of this dank cellar.

But the lady Talfa had turned, swinging the lantern. "The penalty for a girl who talks, or infringes the most serious regulations, is severe and horrible. Look."

The lamplight settled, and the girls craned their heads, peering into the gloom.

"Do you see the table?" Talfa demanded.

They nodded. It was a plain wooden table with four stout legs. On the table lay several coils of thin cord.

"Can you see that the table stands on a block of stone?"

Talfa crossed to the table and set the lantern down.

"A girl who disobeys the regulations here will soon find herself on this table. She will be strapped down, unable to move. Then, one of the eunuchs will engage the engine."

The girls were wide awake now. They shuffled closer together, unwilling to come too close to where the lady Talfa stood behind the table like a priestess at the altar.

"The engine, hanum?"

"A turning engine. When the lever goes down, the table will start to spin. Around and around, faster and faster. The stone here"—she tapped her slippered foot—"slides back, and as the table turns it begins to sink down through the floor."

She paused, as if she expected a question: but the girls were far too nervous to ask it.

"Under this floor there is a tunnel, from the Bosphorus." She held up a finger and rotated it in the air. "Once it is set in motion, the engine cannot be stopped. The table sinks into the water, and the girl is drowned."

The girls stared at the table wide-eyed.

"Some of you may have heard about this place already. It would be better that you had not: the girl who spoke of it—well." She pursed her lips; there was no need to spell it out. "None of you, I am sure, would want to make the same experiment."

She picked up the lantern and walked back to the steps. The girls behind her jostled for position, each of them trying to climb hard on the lady Talfa's heels. No one wanted to be the last to leave that cold, dark vault.

WHEN Mullah Dede knocked on the wicket gate, a hatch slid back instantly. Eyes surveyed them through the grille. A moment later, the door opened and they stepped inside.

The monk quickly shot the bolts home and leaned back against the door.

"I am Brother Palamedes," he gasped. "I will take you to the abbot."

Brother Palamedes led the way through a door in the side of the gateway, and they entered a large, cool room with a flagged floor and a vaulted ceiling. In the middle stood a long oak table, flanked by benches, and at its head stood the abbot.

"You are most welcome," he said. "You will take coffee?"

Mullah Dede smiled. "I do not touch stimulants," he said. "But if my friend Yashim wishes . . . ?"

Yashim shook his head. "Thank you, no."

The abbot leaned on the table. "For several days, my friends, the brothers have been falling sick. They have stomach pains, vomiting. One of our oldest monks has died."

Mullah Dede murmured an invocation.

"In the end, I had to suspect the water. So yesterday we sent a monk down the well to investigate. He found the body of a man."

The mullah raised his eyebrows.

The abbot nodded. "He was—far gone, efendi. It was by no means easy to bring him out of the well, and so—" He wrinkled his nose and snorted, as if expelling an unhappy memory. "We are at a loss."

"But you informed the civil authorities?"

"We sent word to the governor, but at a time like this . . ." The abbot spread his hands, and shrugged. "The sultan has died. Perhaps this death seems small. We need to bury him, God rest his soul."

Mullah Dede coughed. "The people are saying that the man is a Muslim."

"We do not think he is a Muslim, mullah," the abbot said. "If he were to be a Muslim, that would cause difficulties. It would be out of our hands."

The mullah nodded, and stroked his white beard. "I am thinking of the man's soul."

Yashim said: "You have taken steps to determine the man's faith?"

The abbot glanced at Brother Palamedes. "It is—indistinct, Yashim efendi. He must have been dead for quite some time."

Yashim squared his shoulders. "It would be better if you let me see."

"It is not a good sight."

"I imagine not." Yashim paused. "A riot on the island would not be pretty, either. Anger feeds on speculation."

The abbot nodded. "Very well," he said, in a low voice. "Mullah Dede?"

"You understand my position," Mullah Dede said. "If the dead man is a Muslim, he must be buried with the appropriate prayers, and in the proper place. While there is doubt, speaking as a man of faith, this seems to me to be the safest course. But we will let Yashim efendi decide. I do not wish to make trouble for the monastery, but neither can I allow a Muslim to go unburied."

The sun beat down mercilessly on the first court, bleaching it almost to invisibility as they stepped out of the dark gateway.

"I told the abbot we should have dealt with this ourselves," the monk burst out. "I am sorry, Mullah Dede, but it is true."

12

BROTHER Palamedes turned the key in the lock, and stood back.

"Once, efendi, is quite enough."

Yashim reached up and tugged the end of his turban loose, unwound it several turns, and wrapped the length of cloth over his mouth and nose. He pushed the door.

On the floor of the empty room, lit by a shaft of sunlight streaming through a barred window, the corpse lay on its back in a puddle of water. It seemed, at first glance, to have melted into the floor. Loose skin sagged around its legs and arms, the head a deliquescent lump.

Yashim squatted down by the body, trying to see a division where the skin met the clothing. The man's face was like a cauliflower streaked with pale hair: it told Yashim little. There were fair Muslims, and fair Christians; on balance, perhaps, more fair Christians. His skin had wrinkled in the long immersion under water, soft and ridged like the white brains of sheep laid out for sale in the butchers' market. A line of tighter skin ran from the dark mass of the man's mouth toward his eye, and the flesh had bulged over it. It looked like an old scar.

Yashim gritted his teeth and pushed his fingers quickly into the base of the man's neck. He breathed shallowly, each breath bringing the sweet odor of decay into his mouth. The skin was soft. He made his mind a blank, working his fingers toward the nub of a stitched hem. As far as he could see, the man was wearing underclothes—a sleeveless vest and a pair of drawers. He felt a seam and dragged at it, loosening the cloth from the soft flesh that spilled over it.

From his belt Yashim drew a small knife, took hold of the triangle of cloth in his left hand, and slid the blade beneath it, working from the man's neck along the top of his shoulder. The cloth parted easily.

As he worked to undress the corpse, he gagged: once he went back to the door and leaned against it, sweat prickling his eyes, to draw breath. The monk stood with his back to the doorway; only the mullah regarded him sorrowfully, the corners of his mouth firmly turned down in sympathy for Yashim's plight. Yashim held up a hand to tell him to wait a little longer.

As he was cutting away the cloth along the man's ribs, the arm rolled slowly back. Yashim stared for a few moments, frowning.

When it was done, he came out into the sunshine and felt instantly nauseated, the heat seeming to suck at his stomach, so that he heaved and retched.

The monk brought a basin and a clean cloth. Yashim scrubbed his hands.

"As far as I can tell, he was a Christian," he said finally. He rinsed the knife and polished it hard on the cloth, until it gleamed, and stuck it back into his belt. "Fair-haired, uncircumcised. Not more than forty—maybe a lot younger. Fit, too. A big man."

The concern on the mullah's face faded slightly. "I am happy to accept your judgment, Yashim efendi. At prayers, I can tell the believers, and the hubbub will die down." He turned to the monk. "I am glad, for all our sakes."

At the gate Brother Palamedes peered through the peephole.

"There are still some men outside, mullah."

"I will speak to them, then." Mullah Dede stepped out into the sunshine.

"I'll trouble you for a drink of water," Yashim said.

In the kitchens, lit by high windows, the monks were preparing the evening meal. They looked at Yashim curiously, but said nothing. Brother Palamedes fetched him a beaker and filled it from a jug with a long spout.

Yashim accepted the beaker, then hesitated. "Not the same well?"

The monk shook his head, unsmiling. "This is from the inner well, efendi."

Yashim drank. "There is one thing I do not understand, Brother Palamedes. May we speak, privately?"

The monk hesitated. "I can take you to my cell, efendi."

The cells were built in two rows facing a narrow, sunless courtyard: as soon as he saw them Yashim recalled the apartments set aside for eunuchs in the imperial harem. Brother Palamedes's cell contained a narrow bed, a desk, and a wooden stool. On the desk lay a thick book bound in cracked leather, with a flimsy notebook beside it. Beside the notebook lay a quill pen. A bottle of ink stood at the far corner of the desk, beside an earthenware jug and an empty glass. On the wall above the bed hung a crucifix mounted on wood, with a small plaque beneath it. There was nothing written on the plaque. The tiled floor glowed a dusky pink, worn into hollows by the passage of feet over many centuries.

"Who was he?"

The monk spread his hands. *"Then xero."* I do not know.

"An utter stranger."

"We live a secluded life, Yashim efendi, but of course this island is our home. The dead man is not a priest, nor a monk. He is not a Muslim or a Jew, as you have established. We know of no one of the faith—I mean, our faith—missing on the island, or indeed on any of the islands."

"How did you bring him out of the well?"

"We made a sling of canvas. Brother Andrew guided the man's body into the sling, and then we drew him up. And we put him where he is now."

"Someone examined the body?"

Brother Palamedes puffed out his cheeks. "Examined? We could see he was dead."

"We?"

"Brother Andrew and I laid the body on the floor."

"And since then? Who else has seen the body?"

"I'm not sure what you mean, efendi. We sent to the governor, that's all. We haven't had a reply."

"I understand. You laid the body on the floor, and since then no one has opened the door, until I came?"

"The body of a man is not a spectacle," the monk replied, stiffly. "No one knew him."

Yashim nodded, slowly. "You have not answered my question."

The monk blinked. "Efendi?"

"Who saw the body, apart from you and Brother Andrew?"

Brother Palamedes wetted his lips. "I—I do not understand."

"Your head may be weak—or not. But I think you have a strong stomach, brother."

The monk was still.

"You cut a small patch off the man's skin, from under his arm."

Brother Palamedes sat down abruptly on the little bed. "I wanted—only—to avoid a scene," he said in a small voice, folding his hands on his lap.

"A tattoo, perhaps?"

"Something like that."

"Show me. Please."

The monk shook his head. "I threw it away."

Yashim bit his lip. His mouth felt dry. He reached for the earthenware jug.

Brother Palamedes snatched at the jug. "I will fetch some more water."

But Yashim had already gripped the handle, and as the monk lunged he pulled away. Water slopped out of the mouth of the jug and splashed his wrist.

He splayed his fingers and tipped the jug upside down. The water cascaded onto the tiled floor.

When Yashim set the jug down, he was holding the flap of skin in his hand.

BROTHER Palamedes put his fingers across his face.

"Someone came to us, a week ago, maybe longer. Asking about a friend who had gone missing. I thought—perhaps . . ."

He trailed off.

Yashim said: "Someone? *Ortodox*?" He meant someone of the Orthodox faith, the usual description for a Greek: the empire recognized people by their confession, not their race.

The hesitation was momentary. "A type of *Ortodox*, yes."

Yashim widened his eyes. "A type of Orthodox," he echoed. It could mean Armenian, or Serbian. A glance at the monk's face told him it was none of those. "Russian," he said.

Brother Palamedes clasped his hands together. "Please, Yashim efendi. At Hristos we are men of the church. We do not seek the friendship of the Russians. Believe me. We welcome the friendship of all men but—we must be careful."

Yashim glanced at the pale slip of skin lying on the table, and shuddered. For years, Russia had been stirring up the Greeks, encouraging them to rebellion, disturbing their age-old compact with the Ottoman state.

"Who did you intend to tell?"

The monk twisted his fingers in his lap. "No one. That is—we want no trouble, Yashim efendi. These days anything may be taken amiss. You understand."

Yashim grunted. He picked up the monk's pen and pushed the skin flat against the tabletop.

"It's not a tattoo."

"No, efendi. I do not know what it is. But a mark, of some kind."

YASHIM found Palewski fast asleep, with *Pan Tadeusz* across his face.

"I can't believe it, Yash," Palewski said at last. "You seem to have prevented a sectarian riot, identified a corpse, and thrown suspicion on the Russians, all while I was drinking my pear syrup. Incredible."

Yashim unwrapped his handkerchief. "Do you know what this is?"

Palewski raised his eyes to Yashim's. "No. But after all that, you're going to tell me that it is a piece of human skin."

"You don't believe me?"

"Oh, Christ," Palewski said. He sagged back against the cushion. "I'm sorry, Yashim. That's the most disgusting thing I've ever seen."

"It was taken from the man's underarm. It shows something, I'm not sure what. A scar, maybe."

Palewski was silent for a while. "Or a brand."

"A brand?"

"A jail brand. Either that, or Russian army—which comes to much the same thing. Regimental badge, so to speak. Germans go for facial scars. Your Janissaries—they carried tattoos, didn't they? The Russians can be pretty crude, as I think I've mentioned."

"Under the arm?"

"Why not? The right people will always know where to look."

"The monk cut it out, Palewski. Either because he wanted the body to remain unidentified, or—"

"Or the opposite. I don't suppose he put it in his water jug to improve the taste."

"He meant to preserve it." Yashim frowned. "I should go back to Istanbul. Perhaps I can identify the mark."

They sauntered down the avenue of limes and arrived at the quayside just in time to see the Istanbul ferry pull out.

Yashim kicked the ground.

"A couple of hours won't make any difference," Palewski said equably. "Let's take a stroll and look for something to eat."

They wandered off along the track that lined the shore, overhung with Judas trees. Small fishing boats with painted eyes were drawn up on the beach, watching them as they passed. On the rocks, fishermen sat mending their nets or cleaning the day's catch.

Yashim sniffed the air.

"That smells good, my friends!"

A group of fishermen were sitting around a fire and dipping bread into a cauldron. "You are very welcome, kyrie. Join us. Take some bread, and have a little wine."

An older man, with a fine crop of white curls, grinned and winked at Palewski. "For the Frankish kyrie, the wine is good."

Yashim squatted gravely by the fire. Palewski settled like a cormorant on a rock. A boy was sent to the sea with a couple of tin plates. He presented them, clean and fresh, to the newcomers. The old fisherman ladled out some stew, and someone passed them a loaf of round bread, from which they broke pieces.

Palewski held his thimble of yellow wine to the light. "To your hospitality." He drank; the men murmured their approval; his glass appeared refreshed.

Yashim was curious to taste the fishermen's stew. He took several mouthfuls: it was strong, flavored with the wild thyme that grew farther up the shore, beyond the track.

"Tomato!" he exclaimed.

One of the younger men nodded. "I've seen them growing it, kyrie. It grows like a weed, when you know how, and it tastes good. Even raw."

The old fisherman put up a stubby finger. "Raw, it's no good." He passed his hand across his belly. "It lies here, very cold. And gives my wife headache."

"She always has headache."

"Not like this."

"What do you think, kyrie?"

"I think tomato is good to eat." Yashim picked out a little mass of bones with his fingers, and cast them toward the sea. "But like an eggplant, it is dangerous raw."

The old man nodded. Palewski said, in his workmanlike Greek, "I have read that it is safe to eat it raw, but you should not eat the . . . the little seeds."

"The pips, that's right. That's where the trouble lies."

The younger man shrugged amiably. "I eat it, pips and all." He touched the knuckle of his thumb to his belly. "I feel good."

"Why not? You're young."

Yashim smiled and buried his head in his plate. Greeks always had some opinion, and they adored novelty. Their conversation never flagged.

"You grow the tomatoes yourself?"

The young man laughed. "It is better to have friends, kyrie. My cousin works in the pasha's *konak*, his mansion on the island. As a gardener."

The old man frowned. "Enough. You talk too much."

"The pasha?"

The young man scratched his chest. "He's gone away," he said vaguely. "It's not a crime, when he's away."

"Eh, time to mend." The old man slapped his thighs. "Then a rest."

"You'll go out again later?" Palewski was curious.

"Best time for us, early evening. It's the light," the young man said.

"I don't know about that," another man countered. "My old man always swore by the tide."

Later, as they walked back along the track to the quayside, Palewski gestured to the fishing boats.

"The Greeks were painting eyes on their ships in Homer's time," he said. "I've read somewhere that the practice is universal. Even in China. I wonder what we should make of that?"

Yashim did not reply.

"Splendid fellows, those sailors," Palewski remarked. "The wine wasn't bad at all. Ship a barrel to the residency, maybe." He yawned. "Good stew. I think we have time to take coffee, and then home."

But he was wrong: a ferry had already docked. They took seats along the port side, for the view returning to Istanbul. A sail went up and filled in the wind; the rope was cast off. Palewski went to find some coffee.

Yashim was watching idly for dolphins.

"May I?"

Yashim glanced around to see a tiny man in foreign dress bending toward Palewski's seat. He wore a wide-brimmed flat black hat and carried a cane.

"I'm afraid it's taken," Yashim said.

"Everybody wants to drink coffee at the same time," the little man remarked, hopping onto the seat. "I will sit just for a moment, until your friend comes back."

He spoke with an accent Yashim could not quite place.

"You may think of me, Yashim efendi, as a ferry," the stranger continued, swinging his short legs and staring imperturbably out to sea. "Like this one, I go back and forth, picking up and setting down. One friendly shore to the next, you see." The little man held up his cane and rested his chin on it, like a child peering over a railing. "Today it will be picking up. I am sure of it. I take something quite useless from where it is, and drop it off where it can do some good."

"And where would that be?"

The man's expression changed. "Just like the ferry, everyone must buy a ticket. Then there are no questions asked." He made a movement, quite slight: "Just give me what doesn't belong to you."

There was a gun in his right hand, intricate and tiny, like its owner. Its muzzle pointed at Yashim's stomach.

Yashim threw out his left hand. When the gun wavered he scooped up the little man's hand with his right, and held it pointing out to sea.

He felt the man's fingers relax. Yashim slid the gun from his hand. It was not cocked. He wondered if it was even loaded.

"Will you give me the little bit of skin?"

"The next time you try to fire this gun," Yashim said gently, peering into the chamber, "it will explode in your hand. The action is rusty and the bullet has rusted into the breach. But I suppose you do not mean to fire it."

"Will you give me the little bit of skin?"

Yashim snapped the gun into place and handed it back. "No, I'm sorry. You see, I, too, have a destination for it in mind." He glanced up. "Who are you working for?"

Palewski was advancing uncertainly along the deck, bearing two small coffee cups and swaying against the motion of the boat.

The little man caught his glance. He hopped off the seat and tipped his hat. "Goodbye. I wish you a pleasant crossing."

He walked away with pedantic dignity, tapping his cane along the deck.

"Who," Palewski said, "was that?"

"Exactly what I mean to find out," Yashim replied, getting up. "Come along."

The little man had crossed to the opposite rail, where he stood looking out over the sea. Yashim saw him raise an arm, as if he was loosening his sleeve.

Palewski leaned past Yashim and placed the cups on the bench. When he straightened up, Yashim could see the man moving briskly down the companionway toward the stern of the ferry.

"Go 'round the other way," he said to Palewski. "Or we'll be running in circles."

"Pincer movement? Jolly good."

Yashim crossed the deck.

The little man vaulted with surprising agility over the stern rail, and the last thing Yashim saw was his head and hat disappearing over the side.

Palewski had seen him, too. They both began to run.

But before Yashim reached the rail, a slender black caïque shot away from the boat's side and slipped into its wake. The gap between them was widening by the second.

In the caïque, with his back to the ferry, the little man raised a hand in a farewell salute.

"Good lord!" Palewski panted, as he joined Yashim. "The little rascal got away!"

Yashim slapped his hand on the rail. "I thought he'd jumped. I should have guessed he had an escape."

"What did he want?"

Yashim let out an exasperated sigh. "Do you still have your watercolor paints at the residency? He wanted that little piece of skin."

"I'LL clear a space," Palewski said.

They were in his drawing room on the first floor of the residency. The windows were open, but no breeze stirred the wisteria outside. The grate had been swept clean and piled with logs, ready for the distant season when fogs and snows would return to Istanbul, but the rest of the room was in its usual state of comfortable disorder. Books lay on the armchairs, on the floor, and piled up on the sideboard. The escritoire was covered in papers. It looked as if a regiment of scholars had been surprised only moments before and forced to flee.

"The translation," Palewski said, sweeping the sheets up and dropping them in an irregular pile on the seat of his armchair. "The watercolors must be somewhere . . ."

He found them in a shiny black tin box that had got lost under a large volume of maps.

"I'd rather you didn't use the sable brushes," he explained, handing Yashim a number 2 hog bristle.

"What's this made of?"

"Don't ask," Palewski said. He handed Yashim a small plate.

Yashim selected a tube of cadmium red, squeezed a pea-sized bulb of paint onto the plate, and mixed it with the brush.

He let the handkerchief drop onto Palewski's desk, and teased it open. The skin had dried slightly, and was curling and shrinking at the corners.

He took the skin between his thumb and forefinger and laid it on the desk, pressing it smooth. He dipped the brush in pigment, shook it, and began to stipple the ridged surface of the skin.

Palewski laid a sheet of paper on the blotter. Yashim picked up the skin and flipped it over onto the paper, taking care not to let it slip around. He took a second sheet of paper and laid it on top, then took a pile of books off the armchair and laid them on the paper.

He pressed down.

He and Palewski exchanged glances.

Yashim lifted the pile of books. Palewski lifted the paper.

And Marta came soundlessly into the room, bearing a tray.

Palewski looked up with a start.

"Ah, tea!" he enthused, letting the paper float back down. "Tea!"

Marta dimpled. "You need it when you've been to sea," she said, and approached the desk.

Yashim sprang forward and seized the tray.

"Just what I hoped for, Marta. I was afraid the ambassador might offer me something stronger."

Marta kept her grip on the tray. "When the kyrie has to work, Yashim efendi . . ."

She took Palewski's bookwork very seriously. Marta was always gravely courteous to Yashim, but he sensed that she sometimes considered him a distraction.

He relinquished the tray obediently, and she set it down on the desk as Palewski whisked the papers away.

"I'll pour," Palewski said.

Marta's lively black eyes darted from him to Yashim, and back. "As you wish," she said lightly. She turned and left the room, her skirts whispering against the rug.

"So," Palewski said.

Yashim carefully lifted the skin off the paper and they both craned over it.

"It's a face?"

Palewski straightened up. "Not a face," he murmured. "Rather the opposite, a *Totenkopf*. A death's-head."

Yashim looked baffled.

"It's a skull, branded on the man's arm."

"But what—what could that possibly mean?"

Palewski placed his forefingers to his lips and frowned. "The reality of death, Yashim. Worms, bones, the grinning skull. Death conquers all, in effect." The Islamic world had none of the imagery of faith or death that Catholics took for granted. No Madonnas, no cross. No *danse macabre*. "Here, I suspect, it's a regimental brand." He ran his fingers through his hair. "The soldier adopts the symbol because it represents what he wields. He deals in death, with all that implies. Also to demonstrate that he knows the worst that can happen to him. You conquer—and you heap up those skulls, the skulls of your enemies, as a warning and a recognition."

"Like Tamerlane," Yashim said.

"Tamerlane was a puritan. He stood against luxury and citified ease. To him, and to others like him, we are simply bones robed in flesh. In death, the reality is revealed. The soul, on the other hand, has nothing to do with all that. The skull reveals itself for what it is—an earthly prison. In Europe, the image became associated with the reformed church. Lutherans and Calvinists. Protestants in general. Most especially, among the Germans."

Yashim took a deep breath. "The Germans. He was a German?"

Palewski shook his head. "Yes and no. I think we're looking at a Russian brand. A Russian regimental badge."

Yashim looked puzzled.

"Medieval Germans," Palewski began. "*Drang nach Osten*—the eastward push. Teutonic knights settling the pagan lands of the Baltic, pushing into East Prussia, Estonia and Latvia, up the coast. Later on, the Russians moved in, and the Baltic Germans had no choice but to accept the tsar as their overlord. They gave up their independence for jobs in the Russian army. The Baltic Germans take to the military life."

Yashim nodded. "Like the Albanians, in our armies."

"Very like. In Russia, the foot soldiers are Russians, pig-thick and loyal.

The generals are Russians, too—loyal, but not necessarily so thick. But the officer corps is stuffed with *vons*—minor Baltic German aristocracy."

"I see. And the Baltic Germans—how loyal are they?"

"Good question, Yashim. Obviously not considered quite as loyal as the generals—nor quite as dumb as the foot soldiers."

"And the death's-head? This brand?"

"Belongs, as far as I know, to a regiment that doesn't officially exist."

"What is that supposed to mean?"

Palewski shrugged. "It isn't listed in the army book. You hear rumors. Stories about men with that insignia snatching a Tatar warlord, for instance. A platoon spotted in Afghanistan, to discomfit the British in India. It may be that the men who carry the death's-head badge belong to other regiments but take orders through another channel, which remains secret. That's what I think."

Yashim backed away from the desk and slumped into an armchair.

"A secret service?"

"A military secret service, yes. Not the same as the tsar's spies, quite— the ones I have to deal with," he added, a little grimly. "My position may offend the tsar—but it's a tactical detail. It doesn't affect Russian strategy."

Yashim blinked. The sun still shone, but the shadows had lengthened on the floor.

He glanced at the desk. The skin was curling up: as he watched, it gave a tiny start and rolled back and forth.

Yashim shuddered. "I think I need to take some advice."

Palewski nodded. "Don't forget to take the skin. I don't think Marta would like it at all."

In the far-off mountains, a shepherd prepared himself for death. He had lived many summers, but now he felt no warmth from the sun and he knew his time had come.

The shepherd explained everything to his son about the sheep, and the new lambs, and the standing corn.

He said nothing, however, about the feud. Of the dishonor that could only be cleansed with blood.

He blessed the boy, and turned his face to the wall.

"It seems we have two options." The grand vizier raised his heavy lids. "Instinctively I would prefer to do nothing."

Yashim coughed politely. "The Russians almost certainly know what happened."

The vizier blew through his nostrils. "Your little friend on the boat."

"If he was working for them—"

The vizier waved a hand. "Yes, yes. You know the situation with Russia is delicate. We have certain treaties, certain . . . obligations."

Yashim knew how heavily the Russians pressed upon the empire. For decades they had advanced steadily south, dislodging the Ottomans from the northern coast of the Black Sea. Tartary was theirs, and the Crimea, too. Their navy now cruised in what had been an Ottoman lake, the Black Sea. That was humiliation enough; but then the Egyptians had attacked.

In 1836 Mehmet Ali Pasha's well-trained Egyptian army swept up the Mediterranean coast. Sidon, Acre, Beirut, had all fallen to the overmighty vassal of the sultan, who had appealed in desperation to the only power capable of protecting Istanbul.

The tsar and his generals had been only too happy to assist. The Russians had moved closer to Istanbul—and politely withdrew when the danger was past.

"Meanwhile," the vizier added, "we have lost one sultan, and gained another."

He stared at Yashim as he might stare at a spot on the wall, thinking. The silence extended. One minute. Two minutes.

"You will inform the Russians," the vizier said finally. His eyes regained their focus and he gave Yashim a rare, and rueful, smile. "Perhaps that will be the last decision I make."

"I hope not, my pasha," Yashim replied.

THE day promised to be hot.

At the café Yashim folded his legs and sat on the divan, facing the street. The café owner nodded and slapped a brass jug on the coals.

Yashim watched the street slide by.

A few minutes later, the café boy brought Yashim his coffee, and a note. He drank the coffee.

The note was in French. *A cab is waiting at the end of the street. Take it.*

Yashim glanced up. His eyes met the eyes of the Sufi across the way. Close by, a man was sweeping the road with a long besom broom. A stout woman went past in the opposite direction, holding a huge turnip like a lantern in her outstretched arm. The houses opposite were shuttered, but one was merely latticed on the upper floor. An Armenian peddler with a mule sauntered down the street and stopped at the café as if uncertain whether to ply his trade here or move on. His glance fell on Yashim and rested there a moment.

Take it. No threat, no promise. No explanation, either.

Yashim gestured to the boy. "Who brought the note?"

"It was a ferenghi, efendi. We did not know him."

"A tiny man?"

The boy looked surprised. "Bigger than me, efendi. Not small."

Yashim got to his feet. Whoever had sent the note would have had time to set up. It lay to him to restore the balance and surprise them.

There would be a man on the street, maybe two. One to watch, one to follow. Keeping an eye on him—and on each other, too.

Yashim glanced left before turning right down the street. He picked out the stop man immediately: he was outside the Libyan bakery ten yards down the lane, eating a pastry—and eating it very slowly, Yashim imagined.

In Pera you could stand on the street for hours, window-shopping, watching the crowds, and no one would give you a second glance—but Kara Davut was a traditional *mahalle*. On Kara Davut, people tended to know one another by sight; strangers were uncommon. Strangers with nothing to do but watch the road were so rare as to be objects of curiosity.

The stop man had found something to do. Now he would be finishing his *corek* and tailing Yashim. He would be ten, maybe fifteen yards behind. Unworried as yet, because Yashim had responded to the note according to plan, and was moving in the right direction.

It was three hundred yards to the end of the road, where the cab was waiting. Like most streets in the district, Kara Davut was neither straight nor level: it rose toward the middle, then dropped steeply in a series of shallow steps that slanted around the hill. The steps were an impediment to wheeled traffic, but a boon to the porters, who plied their trade all over Istanbul.

There were bound to be two men to ensure that Yashim was in view at all times.

Yashim resisted the urge to glance around.

The second man did not, really, have to masquerade. Provided he stayed reasonably close to the cross street, on the steps, he would simply seem to be waiting for someone to come down. He need not try to be part of the *mahalle* at all, in which case he would not see Yashim until he was perhaps halfway down the stairs. Thirty yards.

Yashim glanced ahead: light traffic, no crowd.

He leaned into the rise in the street. Several people passed him in the opposite direction, tradesmen and apprentices on errands, two veiled women with sloshing pails of water from the pump, three schoolboys heading for the *medrese*, casting about for any diversion. Ahead, a *simit* seller with his tray balanced on his turban came over the rise.

Yashim let the man come close, then flinched.

"I don't owe you a penny!" he exclaimed, flinging up his arm. "You've got the wrong man!"

With his left hand he snatched out and grabbed the bewildered *simit* peddler's shirt.

The man put up his hands, instinctively.

Behind Yashim, the people strolling had stopped and turned. Not quite a crowd, but more than enough to make it hard for the stop man to see exactly what was going on.

Yashim grabbed the peddler's hand and dragged himself back. The peddler spun, off balance. The tray tilted.

Two dogs, apparently asleep in a doorway, rose with surprising agility and dashed forward.

The buns spun from the tray.

"My *simit*!" the peddler cried. A dog caught a *simit* in midair, while the schoolboys darted at the ground.

An old man stepped out of his shop and made to catch the tray.

Twelve yards back down the street, the stop man flung his *corek* to the ground with an exclamation of surprise, and broke into a run.

It was no time for caution.

His quarry had disappeared.

AT the back of the shop was a curtain, and behind the curtain a flight of wooden steps.

At the top Yashim flipped the catch on the back window, pushed the casement, and vaulted out.

It wasn't much of a drop, because the house was built into the slope. Dodging the laundry lines, he raced along the alley. It ended in a wall. There was a water butt against the wall, and Yashim was soon over the top.

He glanced back.

The elderly shopkeeper was leaning out of his window, shaking his fist, and someone—his pursuer—was trying to get past him. The shopkeeper turned and seemed to begin arguing.

Where Yashim's wall touched the backs of the houses on the higher street there was a latticed window, without glass. Yashim aimed a kick at the casement catch.

It broke, and as the window swung inward Yashim followed head-first.

The three women in the room were unveiled. Their sewing froze in their laps. They stared at Yashim openmouthed as he swept through, scattering apologies.

Downstairs he found the street door bolted from inside, and a moment later he was mingling with the morning crowd making its way toward the junction.

The cab was there, drawn up beneath the steps.

Yashim sprang onto the box and fished a coin from his belt.

"If you don't mind," he said, dropping the money into the driver's palm, "we can take the ferenghis home together."

20

AKUNIN, the stop man, sat slumped in the corner of the cab, chewing his nails. His companion sat on the bench opposite, humming tunelessly to himself and staring at the blind drawn across the window. Whenever the cab lurched he put out his hand and steadied himself against the dry leather seat.

At the Egyptian bazaar the driver hitched his reins and brought the cab rolling to a halt.

Yashim jumped off the box and made his way to the entrance of the bazaar, where he leaned back against a pillar amid a crowd of shoppers and porters and watched the two men descend from the cab. They paid the driver and made their way to the gate to the water stairs. Yashim followed, to see them settle in silence into a caïque, which shot off from the stage.

Yashim turned away to find a coffee shop where he could complete his breakfast; twenty minutes later he returned to the landing stage and took a caïque himself.

"To Therapia," he said. "The Russian residency."

21

PRINCE Alexander Petrovich Galytsin was called Alexander, after the tsar; Petrovich, after his father; and Galytsin, after the family estate outside Moscow. In Istanbul, where he served as military attaché to the Russian embassy, he was better known as the Fox.

He sat at his desk with his collar unbuttoned and stared unblinking at the two men who stood before him.

"You lost him," he said quietly.

The man who had hummed hung his head and mumbled something into his beard.

"Speak up, Shishkin."

"We—we didn't give ourselves away, your highness."

"Oh, wonderful." Galytsin picked up a stiletto letter opener and balanced it between his fingers. "Now you take me for an idiot, too. Stand up." Akunin had buckled at the knees. "I told you to take him by surprise, discreetly. You delivered the note. Three hundred yards on a dead-end street, and you lost him. And somehow you didn't give yourselves away? Which of you took the decision to abort the mission?"

The two men stared at their feet. At last Akunin said miserably: "It was me, your highness. It's—it's how we were trained."

Galytsin stared at the man. "At least you did that part right," he said. In affairs of this kind, the crucial thing was not to disclose yourself.

"He didn't see us, your highness. He couldn't know who we are."

Galytsin placed the point of the knife on his blotter and twisted it slowly. "You are dismissed, for now."

The men bowed, touching their forelocks, and backed out of the room. Prince Galytsin's eyes were fixed on the little hole he had bored in his blotter with the paper knife.

His secretary entered. "A Turkish gentleman, your highness. He says he is from the Porte, and wishes to speak to you."

"What's his name?"

"Yashim, your highness. He has no appointment."

An expression appeared on the prince's face that the secretary could not interpret. "Send him in."

"With no appointment?"

Galytsin raised his eyes. The secretary disappeared.

He laid the letter opener on its leather rack and took a fresh sheet of paper from the holder.

He wrote a few words across the top of the page, and laid down his pen.

"Yashim, your highness."

Yashim paused in the doorway. Galytsin was known to him by name, but they had never met.

"You expected me earlier, I believe."

Galytsin looked at him curiously. "The invitation was a little clumsy. My apologies. Please, do sit down."

Yashim settled on the hard chair.

Galytsin hesitated. "I am at your disposal, monsieur."

Yashim inclined his head. "I come from the grand vizier, your highness. Two days ago, at the monastery of Hristos on the island of Chalki, the monks discovered the body of a man. It is possible that he was a Russian. Fair-haired, big, early middle age, with a long scar on his face between the mouth and the ear. Someone disposed of him in the monastery well, where he was found. He may have been in the well for some weeks. His neck was broken, although the condition of the body makes it impossible to tell if he was dead before he was thrown into the well."

The prince's expression was impassive. "What makes you believe he was a Russian?"

"There were other signs, your highness."

"I should hope so." Galytsin waved a hand. "What you have told me is hardly conclusive. Fair hair? A scar? Why, it covers half the world."

Yashim reached into his waistcoat and brought out a silk handkerchief.

"This is perhaps more specific," he said. He dangled the handkerchief over the desk, and something dropped onto the prince's blotter.

Only Galytsin's eyes moved. "What is this?"

"The man had a brand, on his inner arm," Yashim explained. "Something you might recognize."

Galytsin touched the withered skin with the tip of his letter knife, and glanced up at Yashim.

"Well?"

"A . . . *Totenkopf*." Yashim frowned with the effort of remembering the unfamiliar word. He spoke many languages, but German was not among them. "A death's-head."

Galytsin skewered the flap of skin with his knife. "If, as you say, the man was a Russian," he began, lifting the blade, "the circumstances are peculiar."

The flap of skin trembled on the tip of the knife.

"I do not think that Greek monks make a habit of murdering Russians."

"That was my impression," Yashim agreed. "But you are in contact with the monastery?"

Galytsin smiled. "The tsar naturally feels sympathy for our co-religionists, the orthodox faithful, wherever they may be," he said drily.

He leaned aside and dropped the flap of skin into the wastepaper basket.

"Thank the grand vizier for advising me of the unfortunate occurrence. Perhaps you will do me the favor of keeping me informed?"

Yashim got to his feet, and bowed. "I am sure the grand vizier would wish it."

Galytsin flipped a hand carelessly. When Yashim had gone, he summoned his secretary.

"I want Yashim watched. If Akunin and Shishkin fail me again, I will have them cashiered and sent to Siberia. Make quite sure they understand."

He sat for a few moments longer, his pale hands folded neatly on the desk.

Galytsin was not a man given to endure disappointment for long. Smaller minds could be frustrated by little setbacks like these; but Galytsin took the longer view.

When you were playing for empires, even a setback could be an opportunity.

FOR Yashim, too, the interview provided an opportunity, for as his caïque returned him to Istanbul, it overhauled a fishing boat bringing in the morning's catch. Back at his apartment, Yashim laid two mackerel on the board. He liked all fish, but mackerel was best: he always liked a mackerel sandwich off the boats that drew up along the Golden Horn in the evening, grilling their fish on shallow braziers along the shore.

Today, he had more elaborate plans.

Taking the sharp kitchen knife an Armenian friend had given him, he made a tiny incision below the gills of each fish. Through the narrow opening he drew out the guts, taking care not to widen the little cuts any further, then he rinsed the fish and laid them back on the board.

He dropped a handful of currants into a bowl and covered them with warm water from the kettle.

With a rolling pin he rolled and bashed the mackerel from the gills to the tail. He snapped the backbones two or three times along their length, pinching the fish between his fingers until the skin was loose. Carefully he began to empty the skin, squeezing the flesh and the bones through the tiny openings.

He picked up the two skins, each still attached to its head and tail, and rinsed them out.

He dried his hands, and peeled and chopped a few shallots. While they softened in the pan, he crushed peeled almonds and walnuts with the rolling pin, chopped them fine with the knife, and stirred them into the shallots with a handful of pine nuts. As they colored he added the currants and a handful of chopped dried apricots. He put cinnamon, allspice berries, and a pinch of cloves into his grinder and ground them over the nuts, adding a dash of *kirmizi biber*, or black charred chili flakes.

He scraped the flesh from the fish bones and tossed it into the pan with a pinch of sugar.

He chopped parsley and dill, split a lemon, and squeezed it over the stuffing.

It smelled good already. He took a nibble, sprinkled the mix with a pinch of salt and black pepper, then stirred it and took it off the heat.

When it was cool, he stuffed the mixture back into the mackerel skins, squeezing and patting them to restore their shape.

He laid a wire grill over the coals, scattered the fish with flour and oil from his fingers, and laid them on the wire, turning them as they spat and sizzled.

Meanwhile, he sharpened his knife on a stone.

When the mackerel skin was bubbling and lightly browned, he took the fish from the heat and sliced them thickly on the board. Very carefully, he slid the fish onto a plate.

23

IN the palace Elif bowed her head and gently touched the strings of her violin, straining to hear their tiny hum. Her face was rapt; it was also very beautiful. All the orchestra girls were beautiful—it went without saying, for they played, and lived, for the pleasure and delight of God's felicity on earth, Sultan Abdülmecid.

They were dressed almost jauntily à la Franca, their shining hair drawn back and pinned beneath exquisite bejeweled shakos, in green tunics and black trousers. They carried European instruments to match their costume, as was the fashion, though at a word they could have reassembled with traditional tanburs, ouds, and neys, for each of the girls was an adept in either form.

Elif glanced up to where Melda was tuning her mandolin, her ear cocked to the belly of the instrument.

The two girls exchanged smiles.

Smiles were the baksheesh of the harem, of course, like frowns and enthusiasm, frostiness and barbed remarks. A smile or a stamped foot—the harem girls passed them back and forth as minor articles of trade. Behind every gesture lay the desire to be noticed. Behind the desire to be noticed lay the hope of preferment: up the ranks of the harem girls, closer and closer to the body of the man whose life, in a way, these girls were destined to curate.

But the smile that passed between Elif and Melda was a smile of sheer complicity.

Four hundred sequins in silver money, from the room they had sequestered. Two necklaces, one of onyx, one of jasper. A gilded coffeepot, three silk shawls, and a jade mouthpiece that Elif thought was more valuable than she let on.

She turned a peg a fraction and laid a finger to the string, watching the Kislar aga advance steady-paced into the great chamber. Behind him came a crocodile file of elderly women, visiting from Eski Saray—the Ceremony of the Birth was an outing they would relish. The lady Talfa, with her personal black slave, let the older women settle, then plumped down among the cushions.

The orchestra had been instructed to play only when the last guest was seated, so the musicians watched in silence as the harem cavalcade poured in. After Talfa came a stream of young girls, recently adopted into the imperial family—the whites purchased in Circassia, or in the market at Istanbul. They fluttered to the divan, or stole humbly into its shadow. Behind them came the other girls, Abdülmecid's girls—led by two matrons of honor, barely seventeen, who had borne him children in his days as prince—who all settled in order of precedence onto the low divan.

Elif suppressed a contemptuous little smile as she saw Bezmialem come in, at the tail of the younger women. She was pale, even for a Circassian, but still beautiful at thirty-two—she could easily pass for one of the girls, they all reckoned—with her blond curls and her small, white, oval face. Right now, she seemed to be just one of the girls, coming in without proper ceremony.

Elif's attention wandered to the Kislar aga, standing with his hands folded across his belly at the door to the private apartments of the imperial consorts. The aga was good at ceremony himself. She wondered if the young sultan would attend, and whether he would look the way she remembered; for Elif, like most women in the harem, glimpsed the padishah but rarely.

A squabble broke out among the women settling on the divan as Bezmialem sought out a place. They whispered angrily, hissing and fluttering their jeweled hands. The black eunuchs stepped forward, reminding the girls to put their jealousies away behind bland smiles and flashing eyes. The women whispered and rustled; the eunuchs piped and squeaked;

Bezmialem stood twisting her thin white fingers; and a cloud of little children—those of the late sultan and those of the present sultan, mingling with perfect familiarity with the children of slaves, for they were, after all, one family—fidgeted and giggled, or looked around with interest and hauteur as they sat at the edge of the divan, jeweled slippers sliding on the rich carpet.

Elif saw the Kislar aga raise his chin and beckon to someone she had not yet noticed in the crowd: a man in a brown cloak who stood quietly at the far corner. Later, had she been asked, she could have described in minute detail all the people in the room, their jewels, their positions, their choice of colors and fabrics; but she could not have recalled Yashim. For that was his special gift, to be invisible. Elif saw him—and her eye moved back to the Kislar aga.

The aga drew himself up and bowed minutely to the orchestra. Elif laid her bow on the strings and felt the scarcely perceptible tug of rosin on the hairs.

THE four kalfas held the cradle high. It was the cradle in which all babies of the imperial line were placed, tightly swaddled, for their first outing into the world.

For boys, it was the world of women, girls, and their neutered attendants that would move around them for seven years.

For girls born behind the lattice, raised in its fretted shadow, it was the only world they would ever know, and on their marriage they would exchange one shadow for another.

Yashim looked again at the cradle. The red tassel meant another girl: disappointment for some, but an opening for the others who shared the sultan's bed. The tassel swung out as the kalfas moved and for an instant it seemed to Yashim that they were out of step, that the cradle was not securely held. But then a hand went up; the women checked their step and began again to walk slowly around the room. Starting from the right, as tradition demanded.

The khadin, then, was delivered of a girl. She would not be joining the ranks of the most favored consorts of Sultan Abdülmecid. That chance might fall to others, also intimate with their young sovereign. Much would depend on how quickly the mother could recover from the birth; and on how much interest she could coax from the young sultan in his daughter. She was not his first; his third, if Yashim's memory served. But there: he was out of touch. The sultan was not the same sultan who had superintended his own beginnings in the palace service. This was not the harem he had known.

The tassel dropped back, to rest against the talisman of beaten gold, surrounded by blue glass beads that provided the newborn with protection. Still the kalfas held the cradle at the level of their shoulders. It was a heavy thing, ebony, inlaid with mother of pearl, with a slender rising prow: a tiny ship in which a frail new life embarked for a noble destiny, praise God.

The baby already had a secret umbilical name, whispered by a midwife or the mother at the moment of its birth. Yashim could not remember the mother's name. Ayesha? Was she the tall Circassian with ankles so fine that some of the other women had predicted they might break with the weight of her child? Always such solicitude for the welfare of their harem sisters! Voices trilling with concern—and spite, no doubt. Pembe, was it? He could not remember. She was not here among the family, nor did she follow the cradle. Perhaps she was not well. It was not a good sign.

He glanced at the divan. The valide was leaning back against cushions, one knee elegantly upraised and a slender wrist poised upon it. The younger women—Bezmialem, the sultan's mother, among them—sat at a distance; between them, many aunts. There was Talfa, the old sultan's younger sister, who had married a pasha and returned to the sultan's harem on his death; and her daughter, Necla; Yusel, her huge slave, on her knees beside her, her black face glistening with—what? Tears?

Yashim sighed. Of course he was not immune. A birth touched him, like a death: this lesser contact with the mysteries, when the curtain moved between this world and eternity; the ordinary miracle that the rich and imperial strove for, as much as the poor did, in fulfillment of their plans and dreams.

Perhaps, in the miracle of creation, they fulfilled themselves. Perhaps birth staved off a final encounter with the mystery. If so, that was a comfort Yashim could not share. He had been born, and he would die.

One of the women gave a sort of sob, and reached into a jeweled bag. As the kalfas with the cradle passed her, she flung her hand into the air—and over the music Yashim heard the tinkling of little silver coins as they scattered across the floor. A cloud of children darted forward to retrieve them. Across the bowed backs of the children milling on the floor, Yashim caught sight of the Kislar aga. His black face was stony.

Yashim blinked. The music—there was something wrong about the music. Even now, as he half turned his head, the violin seemed to whine; the flute sounded shrill and out of tempo. But as soon as he had noticed it, the music reassembled itself.

He saw Talfa, close to the elderly valide. She was scowling while her great black slave kneaded her arm and wept. To his surprise, Talfa dashed a knuckle to her eye, too. The valide's fingers clenched and unclenched, a sign of impatience. Uncertainly, Yashim allowed his gaze to travel around the divan again. Yes, people were actually crying.

He stiffened. There it was again. The violin was on edge, a little flat. The whole ensemble was slipping out of time. Yashim shifted his weight: only a few bars, murky and discordant, yet for a moment he had felt as though he were on a lurching ship.

The room righted itself. The music flowed on once more. The four kalfas moved gravely toward the aunts, sisters, and cousins of the old sultan. Talfa scattered her coins with a shaky hand. The old valide's mouth twitched.

It was a scene Yashim would not easily forget: the silent cradle, women crying, the band losing its way again, the children giggling and calling from the floor. Yashim shuddered, and muttered an involuntary blessing.

At last the kalfas turned to go back through the doorway. The Kislar aga stepped aside, and the cortege passed through. Nobody spoke. Some of the women looked afraid. Hands were held to lips. Apart from the gabbling of the children, the room was silent. Even the music had slowly petered out: in their neat little Frankish hats, instruments in their hands, the girls of the orchestra were looking about at one another, wide-eyed and bewildered.

From beyond the door came the sound of a woman's scream.

In the silence that fell before the scream came again, Yashim sensed a relaxation of the mood, like an escaping sigh.

"THE mother has discovered her infant," the valide said.

Yashim had to bow to catch her words. Around them women, eunuchs, and slaves were talking and weeping. An elderly eunuch patted his face with his bony fingers. Yashim noticed one mother snatch up her little boy and squeeze him, struggling, while the little boy opened his fist and tried to show her a collection of silver coins. Bezmialem, the young valide, had her head back and was squeezing the bridge of her nose between her fingers. Some of the younger women were shaking their heads, muttering to one another.

"You should not have come, hanum efendi," Yashim said. "A sad occasion."

The valide glanced at him sharply. "For the lady, *bien sûr*. At my age, Yashim, one is inured to grief. Perhaps one even seeks it out, a little. I have lived too long to pretend that my death will be a cause of it." She closed her fan. "The child was born without—the *orifice nécessaire*. I am sorry for the girl, of course. It will be a comfort to her to know that I was here."

The valide began to cough. Her hand went up and somebody pressed a handkerchief into it. She put the handkerchief to her lips and shut her eyes. "I wish to go home."

"Of course, hanum efendi." It was a girl from the orchestra, carrying a flute. She smiled at Yashim and gestured to a eunuch.

"Valide hanum!" Talfa, wet-faced, picked up the hem of the valide's shawl and pressed it to her lips and eyes. "Please do not go yet. Everyone is so sad. Won't you help me make her stay, Yashim?"

"I am tired, Talfa," the valide announced, crisply. "What was the mother's name?"

"Pembe, hanum efendi. A Circassian."

"You will please tell her, when it is appropriate, that I came tonight. And afterward, my child, I expect a visit."

"Nothing could please me more, valide hanum." Talfa tittered, wiping her tears away with jeweled fingers. "Shall I bring Necla also?"

The valide's brow furrowed. "Necla? She is very young."

"She is eleven, hanum efendi."

"Bring her by all means," the valide said, without obvious enthusiasm. "Next week, when I am recovered. Tülin?"

"I am here, valide."

At the band girl's signal, two slim black eunuchs bent forward to help the valide to her feet. She flinched impatiently, but at last she was upright between them.

"You, too, Yashim. I expect a visit, soon."

The harem ladies stood respectfully as the valide walked away, supported on either hand by eunuchs. Tülin, the flautist, hovered around them. Yashim found himself face-to-face with Sultan Mahmut's widowed sister.

"We miss you in the harem, Yashim."

Yashim blinked: the resemblance to Mahmut was strong. Poor Talfa. She should have borne a son before her husband died. With only Necla, she had returned to the imperial harem.

She took a lock of her hair and curled it on a pudgy finger.

"I've been thinking about the way you live . . . outside," she said, in the little high voice of the harem. "I often wonder why that is?"

"It was settled many years ago," Yashim replied cautiously. "By your noble brother's wish."

"Peace be on him," Talfa said, letting the curl of hair spring free. "Sultan Abdülmecid—I suppose he must have confirmed the arrangement."

Yashim hesitated. The new sultan had not revoked Yashim's permission to live outside the palace walls. Nor, on the other hand, had he confirmed it. Yashim guessed that Talfa knew as much.

"I am where I hope I can be most useful, hanum efendi," he replied. "And in the Abode of Bliss, are you not under the gaze of the all-powerful sultan?"

Talfa turned her head slightly and a dimple appeared on her cheek.

"The sultan has *so* many cares, Yashim efendi." She gave him a slanting gaze under her lashes. "It isn't fair that you should leave it all to him. And you were very good the other day. You could be so useful here, efendi."

She giggled lightly.

Yashim bowed, and felt his blood run cold.

As the caïque turned up against the sluggish current, Palewski leaned back on the hard cushions and stared at the footings of the new bridge.

For centuries, people had talked about throwing a bridge across the Golden Horn. On the Stamboul side lay the bazaars, the palaces, and the temples of faith; on the Pera side lived the foreign community, now a mixed bag of Italians and Levantines, who operated so many of the commercial enterprises of the empire. The great Byzantine emperor Justinian, who gave his city the incomparable Ayasofya, was supposed, by some, to have strung a chain of boats across the waterway. If he had done so, only the idea of the chain had survived: medieval Constantinople had protected itself from attack on the seaward side by hauling a massive chain, whose links weighed fifty pounds apiece, across the mouth of the Horn.

In 1453, when the city fell to the Ottoman Turks, Mehmet II had dragged his ships over land to get around it.

Fifty years later, the renaissance master Leonardo da Vinci had submitted a design for a bridge shaped like a curving bow, or a crescent; the sketch was put on file and forgotten. Three centuries passed. Then the late sultan—proponent of change everywhere in the empire—entrusted the project to his favorite, the Kapudan pasha Fevzi Ahmet, commander of the fleet. A man who had a reputation for getting things done.

Palewski sighed. Where the great plane tree that shaded the shoreline on the Pera side had stood, the ground looked dusty and hard-baked. The pasha's bridge would be as ugly and practical as any of the new buildings that had disfigured the old city in the past twenty years—the commercial houses of Pera, the blank barracks of the New Troop on Üsküdar, the sultan's hideous new palace at Besiktas. Worst of all, he thought, it would dissolve the ancient distinction between Stamboul, with its palaces and domes and bazaars, and modern, commercial Pera across the Horn.

It was growing dark when the caïque dropped him at the Balat stage. Palewski tipped the oarsman and made his way unhurriedly through the steep streets before stopping at a sunken doorway picked out in bands of red and white stone. The widow Matalya opened the door and Palewski removed his hat.

"Gone out, efendi," the old lady remarked. "Messengers back and forth, and I don't know what. Would you like to wait?"

Palewski agreed, and went on up to Yashim's apartment carrying his old portmanteau, stuffed with a shawl. Wrapped in the shawl was an excellent brandy—1821—which the French ambassador had once given him, though Palewski had forgotten why. He sat on the divan while the familiar outlines of the flat bled into darkness; just before it became too dark to see, he stood up and fumbled with the lamp. In Yashim's kitchen various plates and bowls were covered with muslins. The brazier was barely warm: he poked his finger into the coals, then wiped the soot off absently on his coattails. At last he found a piece of bread and a painted glass, and settled down to read Yashim's latest Balzac.

At the beginning of chapter three he eased off his shoes and drew his feet up onto the divan.

27

THE great *oda*, overlooking the Bosphorus, emptied out. The orchestra packed up their instruments. The ladies of the harem drifted away. The children were shepherded off by the black eunuchs, still sniffling. It had been a very remarkable day; not an auspicious one. There was lots to discuss later.

Only the lady Talfa remained, with her slave.

"Bring me coffee."

Yusel heaved herself to her feet and was about to waddle off when she raised her hands in surprise. "What have we here?"

On the carpet at the foot of the divan sat a little girl, fast asleep, with her head on her knees.

Yusel bent down and shook her gently. "Best run along now, little one."

The girl saw Yusel bending over her and scrambled to her feet, looking blankly from Yusel to the lady Talfa.

Yusel mimed a low *temmena*, a bow with the hand almost trailing the ground. The girl took the hint. She presented Talfa with a graceful bow.

She looked about five years old.

"Very pretty, very nice," Talfa murmured. The sad events of the afternoon had put her into a good mood. "And what, little one, is your name?"

"Roxelana, hanum."

"Charming! And tell me, Roxelana, who looks after you?"

Roxelana glanced down and traced a pattern in the carpet with her little slippered foot. "No one, hanum."

Talfa frowned. "No one? Where do you sleep?"

"I sleep—with the girls." She slid her foot against her leg. "Wherever I am, hanum."

"The Kislar aga knows about this? And Bezmialem?"

The little girl glanced up, biting her lip.

The princess let out an exasperated sigh. "It's a muddle, that's clear. Never mind, I'm glad we've had a little chat. I will see that something is done for you."

Roxelana looked down at her slippers and stirred her foot on the dark flags. "You won't send me away, hanum?"

"What a ridiculous notion!" Talfa giggled. "As long as you behave yourself, my dear, you'll stay in the harem forever and ever. Now run along. You can visit me this evening, after prayers, and we'll see what can be done."

The little girl bowed again, and walked with self-conscious solemnity to the door of the *oda*.

At the door she turned and flashed a timid smile. "Thank you, my princess."

Talfa waggled her fingers. A small smile hovered on her lips.

28

AFTER the funeral the young man sold his sheep and the standing corn.

He thought long and hard about his inheritance, knowing the pasha would have to die.

It was not a question of rank. It was a matter of retribution.

A matter of honor. He had already chosen his weapon: it would be a knife. A knife because it was easy to conceal, and very sure. He had slaughtered many animals with this knife.

Istanbul was a long way off, of course. But he knew the roads the camels took, as far as the boundary of his province. There would be people after that, to show him the way.

No one would notice the knife.

"BALZAC!" Palewski exclaimed, as Yashim came in. "Acceptable in small doses, with brandy. I thought you'd never come."

"It's Thursday," Yashim objected. "I always come."

"I know," Palewski said, tossing the book aside. "You have nobody else to cook for."

Yashim raised an eyebrow. "The Prophet, may he be praised, instructed the faithful to give charity," he replied, turning to the kitchen. "Especially to the friendless."

"Litwo! Ojczyzno moja! ty jesteś jak zdrowie," Palewski declaimed. "I am alone in a foreign land."

While Yashim set out the dishes, Palewski grumbled about the new bridge. "Ghastly. I had hoped, with the Kapudan pasha away with the fleet, that work would grind to a halt. No such thing—it's all modern methods now." He picked up a slice of stuffed mackerel and held it in midair. "You look tired, Yashim."

Yashim gave him a weary smile. "Husrev Pasha thought the Russians should know about their missing friend. The Fox was not very informative."

"And the *Totenkopf*?"

"He barely reacted. Picked up the skin and dropped it into the wastepaper basket."

"The Galytsins, Yashim, have lied for the tsar since the time of Ivan the Terrible. I once met a fellow who had been tutored in the Galytsin house. He said even their tutor told lies. Alexander Petrovich was a very good pupil, apparently." He ate the mackerel dolma. "Why did Husrev decide to let them know?"

Yashim shrugged. "In the interest of neighborly relations. Better it came from us than from the little man on the ferry."

"Hmm." Palewski reached for another dolma. "A Russian murdered on the islands. Russian ambassador demanding explanations. A useful little crisis for the grand vizier."

"Useful?"

"Dust in the sultan's eyes, Yashim. Something to frighten him a bit. Husrev wants to show his mettle. You'd almost think that if this crisis hadn't arisen, he'd have been tempted to invent it himself."

Yashim shook his head. "The man had been in the water for weeks. Husrev Pasha couldn't have known the sultan was about to die."

"We all knew, Yashim."

"Not to the day. Not to the week."

Palewski sighed. "I suppose you're right. Husrev's no shrinking violet, but getting a Russian agent killed on the off chance? It's too much." He reached for another dolma. "And in the middle of nowhere, too."

"Chalki?"

"It's an island, for goodness' sake. A place you go to escape the heat, or for Greek lovers to meet by prearranged chance."

Yashim nodded. "That's been bothering me. Chalki is only for monks and fishermen." He picked up a cabbage leaf stuffed with pine nuts and rice. "I'd understand if a Russian military agent ended up dead in a To-phane backstreet. But Chalki's a trap for the killer."

"True." Palewski pursed his lips. "Why not meet in the Belgrade woods—or in a quiet café up the Bosphorus?"

Yashim blinked. "Because Chalki was where they had to meet."

Palewski looked perplexed. "Had to meet, Yash?"

"Obviously, yes, if the Russian came to meet someone who was on Chalki already."

"One of the monks?"

Yashim wasn't thinking of the monks.

His mind roved back to that afternoon on the rocks, among the Greek fishermen.

"Tomatoes!" Yashim slumped back into the chair. "The pasha's mansion—that *konak*, among the trees."

"The garden of forbidden fruit? The fisherman said it was empty."

"That's not quite what he said. He said the pasha had gone away."

"He did, you're right. What pasha?"

"The Kapudan pasha," Yashim said slowly. "He took the fleet off, before the sultan died."

The admiral of the Ottoman fleet was always known as the Kapudan pasha: the term was from *capitano*, borrowed—like so many other Ottoman nautical words—from the seafarers of Italy.

"The Kapudan pasha? Fevzi Ahmet, of the ghastly bridge?"

Yashim sank his head into his hands. "Fevzi Ahmet Pasha," he murmured. "Commander of the fleet. I should have known."

"Known what, Yash?"

"That he could do a thing like this."

Palewski raised an eyebrow. "I had no idea you knew him."

"Oh, yes," Yashim replied softly. "I knew him—very well."

AT the palace at Besiktas, the lady Talfa turned her head slightly in the mirror, and caught a glimpse of Elif, frowning.

"That will do, Yusel," the lady Talfa said, waving her black slave away. She stared at Elif and Melda in the mirror for a few moments. "Your charge is a little girl. She is called Roxelana."

"I am afraid, hanum, that will not be possible."

Elif bowed her head as she spoke and kept her hands held humbly to her chest. Talfa couldn't see her look of sleepy satisfaction, but she heard it in the sweetness of her voice.

"Have you forgotten who I am?" Talfa, too, could make her voice sound sweet.

"No, hanum efendi. I know who you are."

"And you, Melda? It is Melda, isn't it? You think it will not be possible, either?"

Melda half glanced sideways; her head, like Elif's was bowed. "I— I don't know, hanum efendi."

"Well, isn't that strange? Elif thinks it quite impossible, and you don't know." Talfa picked up a tiny cup and sipped the coffee. She set the cup down again, and swiveled on her stool. "The last time we met, you seemed so very sure of everything. Now, I think, we are beginning to learn, aren't we?"

Elif cocked her chin. "We are orchestra girls, hanum efendi. Melda plays viola and the mandolin. I am first violin. Donizetti Pasha makes us practice for hours every day."

Talfa touched her hair. "Do try to lighten your voice, my dear. For the sake of the sultan and his other ladies, if not your own. There are plenty of girls who have the harem voice, so I suggest you pay them a little more attention. Now," she added, spreading her hands, "it's lovely that you can play, of course. But I fail to see what your music has to do with the little girl."

Elif compressed her lips, feeling the heat in her face. "We have our duties, Talfa hanum efendi," she said. "To the sultan's music."

Talfa tilted her head and gave a silvery giggle. "I think you'll find that playing an instrument is a privilege, my dear, not a duty. So it has always been considered in the harem. It passes the time, you see. Which leaves you, in effect, with no duties at all. You are a simple girl, but you must see that your sultan feeds and clothes you. Do you expect to give nothing in return?" She shook her head, smiling. "No, no. You will take charge of the little girl. You will teach her the ways of a harem lady, as best you can. It is by teaching that one learns oneself. She is a girl of rank, so you will behave very well with her." She dipped her finger. "You will keep your eye on her, at all times. And I," she added, "will keep an eye on you."

She clapped her pudgy hands together, twice, before Elif or Melda had a chance to reply.

Yusel stepped in at the door, and bowed.

"Our guests are leaving," Talfa said, waving a hand. "You may take the coffee away."

The two girls backed out of the room, their heads lowered.

Outside the door, in the court, Melda avoided Elif's eye.

"The bitch!" Elif hissed. "I'd like to kill her—and that little brat!"

She stamped her foot and balled her fists.

"Don't you look at me like that," she snarled, through gritted teeth. The tears stood in her eyes. "You'd best be my friend, Melda. Because I'll do it, someday. Just you watch!"

YASHIM awoke to a pounding in his head and squinted at the sunlight. He rubbed his temples, swung his legs off the divan, and groaned.

The pounding did not stop.

"*Evet*. I'm coming, I'm coming," he grumbled, picking his way past the empty dishes. A young soldier stood at the door.

The soldier saluted.

"Come in."

As he stepped in he whipped off his kepi and tucked it under his arm, standing stiffly amid the remains of last night's feast. The half-empty brandy bottle stood on a low table close to the soldier's knee, but the soldier was too rigid to notice it.

Also, Yashim realized, probably too young to recognize it.

"I have come from the palace school, efendi. The principal requests that you attend on him immediately."

The palace school—of course. In Yashim's day, the young men had worn turbans and pantaloons.

Yashim sighed. "Very well. If you would be so kind as to run down to the café on Kara Davut and order coffee for me? One for yourself, too, if you like."

The boy positively quivered with correctness. "We should not lose time, efendi."

"Which is why you could order coffee while I dress."

Half an hour later they arrived at the school gate, whose huge curling eaves projected over the street. Yashim turned to look back at the view, both novel and familiar: two sloping, crooked streets lined with low wooden houses, running down to a tiny open space. Not quite a square, nor even a piazza, it was simply a haphazard confluence of sloping lanes paved with huge, smooth cobbles. A thread of water spun from a brass spigot into a small ornamental fountain, fed from the aqueduct he could see in the distance, built by Emperor Trajan more than a thousand years ago.

Istanbul was a city that packed time like a spyglass in its case. It was a place where centuries passed in moments, and where a minute—like this one, standing on the school steps—could seem like an age. Yashim had not been back to the palace school, where the empire trained her best and brightest boys, for fifteen years.

"I lived here once," Yashim said.

The boy's eyes swiveled briefly toward him. "Yes, efendi."

Yashim sensed the boy's doubt and disappointment. "And you are—nineteen?" He smiled, a little sadly. "Almost ready to graduate, I suppose."

"Seventeen, efendi."

"You look older. Tell me, what talents do you have?"

The boy looked at him levelly. "Talents? Very few, efendi, from what I'm told."

They crossed the courtyard. At the foot of the stairs Yashim hesitated, inhaling the familiar smell of sweat and roses. "It's not Pirek *lala* still?"

The cadet looked blank. "Efendi?"

They came out onto a gallery overlooking an enclosed courtyard. For a moment Yashim was tempted to hang back: the man leaning over the rail was Pirek *lala*, the old eunuch with the iron-shod stick.

He blinked, and the old *lala* was gone.

"Bozu! I saw that! Keep your foot flat and try it again." The man at the rail was much younger, though his beard was gray. He was dressed in naval uniform. "The wrestling, Yashim efendi. I am the tutor."

Yashim salaamed. The hall was just as he remembered, with high rectangular windows on three walls and a floor of raked and watered sand. Below them a dozen or so youths grappled with one another, stripped to the waist, their bodies oiled and gleaming. Yashim watched them for a while, remembering another set of boys trying anxiously to perfect their moves, grunting with exertion as they shifted from hold to hold.

Yashim had been a good wrestler, agile and strong. He was out of practice now, but he'd never lost the technique. Twice, at least, it had saved his life.

"They look fit."

"They should be," the tutor replied, a little grimly. "I keep 'em busy, morning, noon, and night. I run a tight ship here, efendi. If they can't take the pace, out they go. Army can take 'em." He stroked his beard. "One I've had my eye on. Wrestles well. Not so much with the *gerit*—too young—but runs like a hare."

"Which one?"

"Name's Kadri," the tutor said. "Penmanship, rhetoric, wrestling, whatever—the best I've seen in fifteen years. He'll win his races every day for a week. He'll memorize twenty sutras in a couple of hours." He glared at Yashim.

"I see. Wonderful."

The tutor's beard quivered. "Half a dozen times I've been on the point of telling him to pack."

"You mean, to leave the school?"

"It's like this, Yashim efendi. Kadri just goes out, like a lamp in a draft. Finest student I've had, and then for a day, for a week: nothing. No results. Lights up again when he's ready, but it upsets the others, you see? Sense they're winning only because Kadri doesn't care."

Yashim nodded. The Ottomans had discovered esprit de corps long before the French gave it a name. It was the founding principle of the whole administration of the empire, and this school's purpose was to engender it in the ranks of those who would go on to rule.

Of course, the Ottoman elite was riven by cabals and cliques, whose shifting alliances interfered with the frictionless running of the empire. But esprit de corps remained the ideal.

The tutor was working his fingers together, one hand clasped above the other.

"He has no talent."

"You said he could run."

The tutor squinted at him. "Meant the talent of an Ottoman. If he has it, I can't find it. Excels at everything, but focuses on nothing."

Yashim bowed his head. "And you want me to talk to him?"

"Talk to him?" The tutor gave a shaky laugh. "No, Yashim efendi. I want you to find him."

To Yashim's surprise the tutor stuffed his beard into his mouth and chewed. "Forgive me, I did not make myself clear. Kadri himself is not the problem. The problem is that Kadri has disappeared."

THE lady Talfa waddled to the divan.

"Let me get comfortable," she said. She dropped her slippers and settled against the cushions. "There. You may begin."

She raised her chin and closed her eyes.

Her dresser knelt at the edge of the divan. She opened her leather bag and took out some little jars, a few pots, a sable brush, and a pair of silver tweezers, which she laid out on the carpet.

It was widely acknowledged within the harem that Talfa, the late sultan's sister, possessed less than flawless skin. One of the older women had suggested that Talfa resembled her late brother in a number of ways. "She has the same air of command. The same eyes. Only, the blessed sultan lacked such a fine mustache."

The dresser kept her face lowered as she opened the pot of wax and took up the spatula.

She frowned as she looked into the pot, and turned it slightly toward the light. Then she gave a little gasp.

Talfa opened her eyes.

"What's the matter now?"

The dresser let the pot slip from her fingers and brought her hand to her mouth.

Talfa's hand flew to her chin. "What is it?"

"I—I don't know, hanum efendi. There was something in the pot."

"In the pot?" A look of annoyance clouded the princess's face. "Well, pick it up."

The girl gingerly picked up the pot, and turned it so that Talfa could look inside.

She peered in, then dabbed at it with a finger.

Something black and long sprang out, and they both started. The dresser let the pot fall.

On the carpet between them lay the thick, ribbed tail of a rat.

Talfa's face slowly crumpled as she squeezed her eyes shut and opened her mouth. Then she screamed, and screamed, and screamed.

THE boys' dormitory in a long, narrow room high up under the eaves contained twelve cots and a table with a washbasin. On a stand lay a copy of the Koran, transcribed by gifted boys over the years; Yashim thought he recognized his own hand in the pages, but he could not be sure. It was a long time ago.

The fire in the grate was cold.

A barred window at the end of the room looked out over the many-domed roof of the refectory. Beyond it, across a narrow lane, he could see the leaded dome of a small mosque.

"Took him from Anatolia," the tutor said. "He'd been living wild."

"Wild?"

"In a cave, apparently. One of the clansmen found him. Sent him on."

Yashim nodded. It wasn't unusual for boys to be sponsored to the school. No doubt one of the clan chiefs of Anatolia had recognized Kadri's talents and sent him to Istanbul in the hope that one day he would be in a position to repay the favor.

The tutor shrugged. "Long time ago, Yashim efendi. For Kadri, I mean. He was only seven or eight—half a lifetime ago, in fact. Been in training ever since."

"He left from here?"

The tutor made a gesture of bewilderment. "Must be so. We do a roll call every night. Kadri was marked in."

Yashim squatted in the fireplace and looked up the chimney. "Maybe another boy answered for him?"

The tutor shook his head. "Kadri took the roll himself. I could show you the register. The boys agree that Kadri was there when they turned in."

"After the register, the doors are locked?" Yashim stood up, rubbing his hands. The chimney was narrow and capped with a cowl. "And in the morning, someone beats the gong."

The tutor nodded. "Older boys bring tapers to the dormitories. That's when they found Kadri missing."

"But he'd slept in his bed."

"Yes."

"And then?"

"The boys looked around, then came down to the mosque and told me what had happened. I came up and searched, too."

"Let's go downstairs," Yashim said.

It was a stone staircase, with a landing between the floors. Yashim stopped to contemplate the landing window, high in the wall. Then he moved on downstairs and into the courtyard, to study the dormitory block from the outside. It was just as he remembered, built in the spare classical Ottoman style, with deeply inset windows and dressed stone walls.

Beyond these walls so much had changed in the years since Yashim was there. Laws had been changed, the Janissaries suppressed. Egypt, the ancient grain store of the empire, had slipped from the sultan's grasp under its charismatic Albanian overlord, Mehmet Ali Pasha; Russia had moved closer.

"Fazil!"

One of the boys coming out of the gymnasium broke away from his companions and salaamed.

"Fazil shares the dormitory with Kadri. Tell the efendi what happened this morning."

Fazil gave his account. Kadri hadn't been in his bed when the gong went.

"Did you look under all the beds?" Yashim asked the boy again.

Fazil scratched one leg against the other and admitted that he couldn't be sure.

"How about your own bed?"

"I—I think so, efendi. Or one of the boys would have looked."

"And the chimney?"

"I can't remember, efendi. Later, I looked for sure. I am sorry."

"It doesn't matter," Yashim assured him. "Thank you for telling me." He was surprised how little seemed to have changed since his day. The boys, it was true, were dressed differently, in Frankish uniforms—but they were the same boys as before, lanky, handsome, darting from one classroom to the next holding their books.

He half smiled to himself as he caught sight of an imam in his white cap and long brown robes, treading solemnly along the cobbled path. That element of the curriculum, at least, was unchanged.

"Either Kadri is still here, tutor, or—" Yashim squinted up at the side of the building. "Is the catch on that landing window fastened?"

The tutor heaved a sigh of impatience. "Anyone who jumped from that window, Yashim efendi, would be dead at the foot of the wall."

Yashim nodded. "Let's find someone with a ladder."

DONIZETTI Pasha, the instructor general, cracked his white baton down on the lectern.

"Ladies, ladies, please." He leaned forward on his toes and blew out his cheeks so that his mustaches tickled his nose. "I hope you are not too stiff?"

He placed the baton down and laced his fingers together, arching them over his little bald head, leaning this way and that. "You must do the same. Stretch your fingers!"

The orchestra obeyed. There was the sound of instruments being laid aside, and a few suppressed giggles, because Donizetti Pasha was a man and his talk sounded intimate: stiff, fingers. To have these parts, these feelings, referred to by a strange man—well!

Elif, smiling, caught Donizetti's glance and blushed.

The maestro was no stranger to the palace himself. In his twelve years at the Porte he had written marches for the new army bands, airs for sultans, and innumerable studies and scherzos for the more musical members of the imperial family, including the rousing march unofficially considered the Ottoman imperial anthem, with its swelling brass and occasional daring swoops into a minor, Oriental key.

Donizetti Pasha nodded. "Good, good. Now, like this."

He waggled his fingers beside his cheeks. The ladies of the harem orchestra followed suit.

"*Ciao, ciao, ciao, ciao!*" Donizetti hunched his shoulders and his eyes twinkled.

"*Ciao, ciao, ciao, ciao!*" trilled the harem ladies. They looked about them and laughed.

"*Va bene!*" the maestro cried jovially. "Now your fingers are relaxed, and you can play like angels! Violins, especially."

He cast a meaningful glance toward the violins, and picked up the baton. "When you are ready. One, two, three. And—" He flicked the tip of his baton through the air, and the violins picked up the beat.

Giuseppe Donizetti smiled, and gave the violins a deep nod. Really, they were not too bad. Not bad at all! What a sensation they would make in Milan—the loveliest orchestra in the world, *belli di Bosforo!* Each a flower, plucked from the waysides of the Caucasus—*Ah, Giuseppe, Giuseppe! Lower your eyes, man! Concentrate on the score. For your own good health.*

He had tutored the young prince Abdülmecid, now the sultan, on pianoforte and violin—the youth lacked attack, perhaps, but he was competent and some of his compositions showed promise—but when the young sultan had first suggested that Donizetti Pasha should lead the ladies' orchestra every week, the Paduan maestro had found his heart beating like a drum.

"*No man other than the sultan has ever stepped into his harem,*" he had confided in a letter to his little brother. *"I am to make history! Not only shall I meet the sultan's ladies, but I am to direct them with my baton, every week!"*

To which his brother had replied with a dry warning. *"I advise you, my dear brother, to read the contract carefully before you commit yourself. As I understand the harem rules, your baton may be the first thing to go if you accept such a position."*

Donizetti Pasha had chuckled a little uneasily at the gibe. His brother, of course, took his own baton to the ladies of Paris and Naples without stint: it had been that way ever since his *Lucia di Lammermoor* had made him the darling of Italian opera. Giuseppe did not begrudge his younger brother his good fortune, either with the ladies or the stage: they had been born poor, and Giuseppe remained grateful for the attainments that had led him to a position of trust and honor within the Ottoman Empire. It was a snug billet, as a soldier might say; and he was a married man.

In the event, his anxiety—and his brother's warning—had proved unfounded. The sultan was as good as his word. Every Thursday, the girls of the orchestra assembled in the Grand Salon under the direction of the amiable Italian. They played minuets for him; they galloped into rondos; they beat the drum and scraped the string and blew the reed and fingered the stops for him; and if some of them believed themselves in love, why, Donizetti Pasha was far too short, and round, and twinkling on his toes to suspect such a thing.

He was the only man, beyond family, that many of them had ever seen before. Portly and innocent; but a man.

YASHIM took his leave of the tutor at the gate.

"Our best hope is that Kadri makes up his own mind to come back."

"I still don't think it's possible—"

Yashim held up a hand. "Nor do I. Not really. But the window was unlocked. There's a chance that he's still here, of course. We may simply have to wait for our young friend to make himself known. Eventually, at least, he has to get hungry."

The tutor snorted. "He disgraces himself, and us. Nobody runs away from the palace school. It has simply never happened before. Damn Kadri!" And he stuffed his beard into his mouth and chewed on it, angrily.

Yashim opened his mouth to speak, then shut it again.

ELIF and Melda burst into their room, giggling.

"*Ciao! Ciao! Ciao!*" Elif waggled her fingertips and Melda laughed again.

She reached up to remove the pin that fixed the shako to her glossy black hair and caught sight of the little girl crouched on the divan with her hands to her head, staring at them both with big, frightened eyes.

"Hey, princess!" Melda laughed. "It's only us."

Elif lunged forward, still waggling her fingers. "Boo!"

Roxelana scrambled backward, with a look of unfiltered horror. "No! Go away!"

"Oh, grow up, Roxelana," Elif said irritably.

Melda took off her hat and shook her head, and her long hair spilled down across her shoulders. She crossed to the divan and put her arms around the little girl, feeling her stiff bones.

"It's all right, princess. We're back. Did you get frightened while we were away?"

Roxelana blinked. She looked silently at Melda's braided collar, and at the buttons of her tunic.

Only later, when they were all lying together at night, did she say: "I don't like that funny hat, Melda. I don't like it when you wear those hats."

Melda gave her a squeeze. "It's just for the orchestra. To make us look smart for the sultan."

Roxelana was quiet for a while. "I think they make you look . . . bad."

"Why?"

"I don't know."

"Go to sleep," Elif murmured. "They're just hats. Shhh."

YASHIM picked his way through the marketplace, where a few street dogs scavenged among the litter of husks and hulls, rinds and squashed fruit.

George was still there, swinging baskets of summer vegetables onto a handbarrow.

"Why yous comes so late, eh? Yous buying cheap today, efendi? Like beggarmans?"

Yashim shrugged. "I'm looking for a boy. Run off from school."

"Maybe he finds himselfs a good job." George picked up an empty basket and began slinging eggplants, tomatoes, zucchini, and garlic into it. He dragged a handful of parsley from a bunch in a clay pot and stuffed it into the basket. "I am sorry that you loses this boy, Yashim efendi, but today"—he put his hand on his chest and smiled—"today, I finds a boy."

"A boy? Where?"

George laughed. "Eleuthra, my daughter, she gives me a big grandson this morning. A Hercules, Yashim efendi! Big like this." He measured out a giant baby between his huge hands, and spat to one side the way you did when you heaped praise upon one so young and defenseless.

Yashim smiled. "I'm glad for you, and for your daughter. May God bless the child."

George thrust the basket of vegetables at Yashim. "This is for yous. As my friend."

When Yashim got home, he put the vegetables on the table and went over to the divan. He knelt down and reached under the quilt until his hands closed on a small box, which he took to the window.

George was forever giving Yashim his vegetables for nothing because Yashim had saved his life; but the weight of his obligation was becoming so burdensome that Yashim was almost tempted to buy elsewhere, on the sly. The trouble was that George always brought the youngest and freshest produce to market. Some people sold vegetables, and some grew them: George did both.

Yashim picked through the coins in the box. They turned up in the bazaar from time to time: Byzantine bezants from the days of Greek dominion, Persian silver from the reign of Shah Abbas, crude rubles from the early Russian tsars. Sometimes a gypsy, sitting over his tiny lamp with his tweezers and pliers, would open his little sack of metalware and pull out a coin from a distant era or a faraway place.

His fingers closed around a sliver of pure gold, a Persian daric from the age of Darius, found by a caïquejee in shallow water. It had come out of the water as bright and clear as it had gone in, two thousand years before—or so the goldsmith who had weighed and priced it had said.

Now he put it on the shelf. He would give it to George's grandson. It was, he hoped, a lucky coin. He would have a little box made for it, to stop them from punching a hole in it and having the boy wear it around his head.

He went back to the kitchen and began sorting the vegetables from the basket. He did it slowly, turning each one in his hand as though looking for blemishes, letting his thoughts settle.

A boy was loose in Istanbul. It was not a disaster. For a quick-witted young man, Istanbul was a very interesting place; a hospitable place, even, Yashim reflected.

When the tutor said no one had ever run away from the palace school, Yashim had not tried to contradict him. But one hot afternoon, near the end of his last year in the school, Yashim had walked out of the gates and down the hill to the Grand Bazaar.

Yashim's father had sent him to the palace school because he could think of nothing else that might assuage the agony of his condition. So Yashim had been older than the other boys: already, in most respects, a man. Loose in the city, he had walked at random all that day, and spent the night curled beneath a caïque upturned on the shore. In the morning the caïquejee had found him there, fast asleep, and given him breakfast. A day later Yashim returned to the school. The old *lala*, his tutor, made no comment—he seemed to think he'd gone to Eyüp, to the tomb of the Companion of the Prophet.

But a few days later he had been introduced to Fevzi Ahmet.

Yashim took two eggplants, topped and tailed them with his paring knife, and sliced them lengthwise. He laid the slices on a plate and sprinkled them with salt.

Three weeks ago, in the dying days of Sultan Mahmut's reign, a Russian agent had visited Chalki. Evidently not for the good of his health. Not for the good of his immortal soul. He came because Fevzi Ahmet, the Kapudan pasha, lived on the island.

Perhaps he came to spy on the Kapudan pasha. Perhaps Fevzi Ahmet found him in his garden, or rifling his papers. Time was short; the fleet about to sail. He killed the Russian with his bare hands, disposed of the corpse in the monastery well, and left.

But if Fevzi Pasha had caught a spy—why would he try to conceal the body? Why, above all, would he not try to inform the grand vizier?

If Fevzi Pasha wanted the death to remain secret, the dead man must mean more to him than he wanted anyone to know.

IT took Yashim less than two hours to reach Chalki. He crossed in a hired felucca because he did not want to be observed, landing at a small fishermen's jetty about half a mile from the main quay.

The fishermen he found mending their nets told him that Fevzi Pasha had bought the *konak* about three years before. He had made himself unpopular with the islanders by forbidding them to use the rocks down by the shore below the house; he claimed that he and his household—his women, the fishermen assumed—required absolute privacy. This in spite of the high walls that surrounded the *konak* and its gardens.

"You'd have to pile those rocks one on top of another to look over that wall," one fisherman remarked. "Perhaps he's afraid someone wants his money."

"I wouldn't mind seeing it," another added. "He doesn't spend it around here, leastways."

"Too right. What, a couple of fellows to do his garden?"

"Never sends to the market, either."

"That's right. Only a little market, kyrie, not like what you'd see in the city. But it's money for the islanders. Muslims here, as well as Christians, but he won't use them. Everything from stores, I'm told."

Yashim took a good look at the pasha's house and grounds. The estate stretched to about three acres, enclosed by an eight-foot wall topped with overhanging tiles, built to take advantage of every natural slope; even from the hillside it was impossible to see over it. There were two gates, the lesser one approached by a narrow mule track.

Yashim could hear dogs barking within the walls.

Later in the afternoon, while he was drinking tea in a small café along the shore, he again met the fisherman who cooked with tomatoes, and he took advantage of the license of the islands to invite him for a drink.

For a Muslim to sit with a Christian, openly drinking ouzo—even if the Muslim gentleman stuck to his tea—would have been unthinkable in most parts of Istanbul itself. Perhaps, in a dark Tophane tavern where foreign sailors regularly loitered for their billets, such a meeting would just have been possible; but here on the island—that place for romantic assignations, as Palewski had said—the rules seemed to be more relaxed. Yashim sipped his tea while his new friend watered his raki and drank it, flushed and happy, at Yashim's expense.

Within an hour, Yashim had found out how to get into the pasha's garden.

"But not dressed like that, if you'll forgive me, kyrie," the young man ventured, with a charming smile. Then some of his confidence seemed to evaporate, because he added, "You'll have to wear some of Dmitri's things," and scowled, as if the reality of what he had agreed to do had just struck him.

"Let's talk to Dmitri, then, my friend." Yashim stood up. The young fisherman got slowly to his feet, punching his fist into his palm.

"My trouble, kyrie, is that I talk too much."

As Dmitri predicted, the gate opened as the distant bells of the monastery rang for vespers.

"I've brought my mate again," Dmitri said, jerking his thumb.

Yashim put a finger to the brim of his hat. The doorkeeper let them through the gate and closed it after them, shooting two bolts before he walked away.

"I'll be back in an hour," he said gruffly, over his shoulder.

Dmitri picked up a watering can from beside the gate. "You can take the mattock," he said.

Yashim swung the mattock over his shoulder and followed the gardener to the well, set back behind a hedge of prickly pears and a drooping willow tree. He laid the mattock down, and glanced over the prickly pears.

Across a courtyard, neatly paved in a geometric pattern of small stone blocks, a tilted apple tree was laden with small fruit. Just beyond it stood a fine *konak*, with spreading eaves and whitewashed walls.

The shutters on the ground floor were closed.

Beyond the *konak* was another door, which belonged to a small lodge, or guardhouse, built up against the wall.

A dozy blackbird sang in the apple tree. Otherwise the courtyard was perfectly still. A huge fig drooped its man hands from the southern wall, and from it arose the hum of drowsy bees; the cobbles below were stained and spotted by dropped fruit.

A pair of swallows worked the intervening air.

As if to dispel a dream, Yashim brushed a hand through the air above his head, and approached the *konak* across the dry cobbles.

40

A T this hour of the day when the sun slanted almost horizontally across the landscape, you could sometimes make out dark forms behind the latticework that protected the upper windows of every Ottoman house. Men spoke of glimpses of a pretty hand, or a pair of liquid eyes, to which imagination attached the figure of a houri from Paradise. Yashim ducked under the pears and walked quickly across the courtyard to the back door.

My name is Yashim: I am a lala *from the palace,* he could say. *We have been concerned for your safety while the pasha is away.*

Nobody answered his knock. He listened. No footsteps; no whispers.

Yashim tried the shutters. They were fastened from the inside, but overhead was a balcony facing away from the church and toward the hills. With a swift glance around, he shinned up from the shutter to the balustrade.

A lattice door pierced by a thousand little openings was shut fast by an inside hook. Yashim slipped a knife from his belt and slid the blade into the jamb. It clicked against the hook and the door swung free.

He stood, breathing heavily in the doorway.

Once before he had entered a harem like this, by stealth. He'd been looking for a man hiding among the petticoats—and Fevzi Ahmet had been waiting for him downstairs.

Now it was Fevzi's house. Fevzi's harem.

He stepped through the doorway.

"Ladies! Ladies! I am Yashim, a *lala* from the palace! Come out, and do not be afraid!"

FEVZI *Ahmet, coming into the guardroom. Pulling off a pair of gloves.*
He spits.

"Nothing. A time waster."

"Perhaps I could talk to him? I've been wondering—perhaps he doesn't realize what he knows?"

Fevzi pours himself a glass of tea. "No. There's no point, Yashim."

"Never give up—you say that yourself, Fevzi efendi."

The bloodshot eyes. "There's no point. He's already dead."

42

THERE was no reply to Yashim's call; he knew he had not expected one. He slipped off his shoes and stood at the head of the stairs, gazing at the doors that led off the upper landing and wondering where to begin. There was a faint smell of starch and roses.

The house was an old country villa built by some Greek merchant, with wide, scrubbed oak boards, walls of planked and polished cedar, and a plaster ceiling decorated a long time ago with a painted motif of flowers. Here and there the ceiling needed repair.

Gingerly he tried a door. It swung back onto what might have been an apartment for one of Fevzi's ladies, but when Yashim stepped cautiously inside he was reminded of a linen merchant's warehouse. Even in the Grand Bazaar in Istanbul, the greatest emporium on earth, with its fourteen miles of covered alleys, its workshops and restaurants and cafés and hammams, Yashim would have been surprised to find such a collection of printed cotton quilts, hammam towels and sheets. In teetering piles on the divan, spilling onto the rugs on the floor, stacked against the walls, were pantaloons, with frills, and pretty striped chemises; handkerchiefs and pattens with cotton sides; yards of muslin of a fine grade, and bolts of cloth—blue, green, a deep indigo, patterned cotton, figured silks.

Out on the landing he stopped to listen. The silence rushed in his ears.

He pushed the door to the room that overlooked the entrance.

In the corner, a narrow pallet lay rolled up on the floor. Otherwise the room looked empty. The shutters were closed in the room beyond, and Yashim stood for a while on the threshold to let his eyes adjust to the slatted shade.

Two blue eyes were staring at him across the room.

He stumbled back, shocked: it was a child. He looked again. Its eyes were fixed on him, under a cascade of light brown hair.

His heart was thumping as he crossed the room. It was only a doll, a ferenghi doll nestling in shavings packed into a cardboard box. The lid of the box lay beside it, as if someone had lifted it to take a peek; on the lid were the words A. DAUMIER—JOUETS—COSTUMES—POUPÉES and beneath, in smaller type, an address in Paris.

Around the box, heaped on the lid of a trunk pushed up against the wall, lay an array of children's toys: a mechanical monkey beating a drum, with the key on the drum; a miniature dressing case; a hoop; a collection of little wooden animals. In spite of himself he reached into the box and picked up the doll. It was stiff, dressed in the French style, with a head and hands made of painted china.

Yashim touched his nose to the light brown hair. It felt real. He did not think he had ever seen such a horrible thing. Its dreadful blue eyes bored into him expressionlessly: Yashim was not overly superstitious, but blue eyes were always a sign of bad luck . . . the little painted smile, the tiny cold china hands raised in perpetual supplication, the mockery of fashion. Worst of all, perhaps, the hair, grown from a real woman's scalp. Repelled, he put it gingerly back into the box.

As he did so something inside the doll made a muffled clunk. "Mamaaa . . ." the doll sighed, as a little bellows inside subsided.

Yashim jumped. "By Allah!"

He picked up the doll again, and tilted it back.

"Mamaaa . . ." it wheezed.

He put it back with a tremor, and turned, nudging something with his foot. He bent down and picked up a wooden duck. It had a stick coming out of its back, and wheels. As you pushed the duck along its leather webs went *flip-flap* along the floor. Much better than that horrid doll.

He put it on the chest, then he went into the other room and unrolled the pallet bed.

It had been slept in, often enough: Yashim could see the faint impress of a man's form where the wadding had settled. He stood staring down at it for some time.

"I *suppose you want me to be grateful. You'd like that, wouldn't you? Yashim, the little* lala *everyone loves. Even Fevzi Ahmet.*"

Yashim shakes his head. "I wouldn't expect it."

"I know what's wrong, don't I?" Fevzi Ahmet inclines his head. "What makes you think too much. What makes you soft."

He leers. Yashim does not react.

"And you can't change, can you? I can teach craft, but there are some things that even I can never give."

And he makes a little bow, of pure contempt.

Yashim thinks: I'm not like you. Out of all this bloody mess, this ruin of hopes, I have this small satisfaction. I know now, and forever, that I could never wish to be like you.

44

DOWNSTAIRS a door opened into a salon paneled in polished walnut, furnished on two sides with a low divan. On one side stood a tall, narrow fireplace with a scalloped lintel of stone; on the other the paneling was fretted and carved into a series of elegant cupboards and shelved alcoves.

Yashim knelt in front of the fireplace. A little white ash, mixed with fragments of charred wood. He stirred it with a poker.

He leaned the poker against the wall and stood up, brushing the ash from his thighs.

Everything seemed laced with expectancy. New toys, still in their boxes of shavings. Bolts of cloth, awaiting a woman's shears. Towels, slippers, quilts, and divans, unused.

Not a house that had been abandoned by its women and its children.

A house that was waiting for them, instead.

He turned his head suddenly, as if someone had entered the room. There was nobody there.

He crossed the hall. The room beyond was the mirror image of the one he had just left, but it, too, contained no paperwork.

He returned to the hall and followed it to the kitchens at the back, poking his head into the understairs cupboard. He was about to close the door when he noticed something sparkling—a bright copper nail, driven up into one of the treads. He looked more closely. There was a small piece of stained linen fixed to the nail, which was wound with colored threads. He reached out; the nail came away easily in his hand.

In the kitchen a thick mortar, like his own, was mounted in a cradle.

Against a wall stood a narrow table, heaped with jars and bowls—spices, saffron, dried mint, sumac, salt. He tried the jars, stirring their contents with his finger.

He touched the ashes in the stove: they were brittle under his fingers. Damped, perhaps, by summer rain. Then in the heat, they'd dried again. They had not been warmed for many weeks.

He looked at the copper pans that hung on the wall above the stove, twelve of them—but only two were blackened on the base.

For coffee, he thought. A pan for coffee and a pan for rice.

He ran his fingers along the rough oak boards. A kitchen furnished an account, like the impress of a man on a pallet bed.

When he imagined his own kitchen, he saw the jars and the mortar, the pans and the little stove. The kitchen of a man who lived alone, like this.

He pursed his lips, and reached into the crock of rice. The rice slithered between his fingers.

At the bottom he felt something else.

He gripped the packet and drew it out carefully, spilling rice across the board.

"TAKE this!" Dmitri shoved the mattock into his hands. "You never said— Shhh! Here he comes."

Yashim swung the mattock over his shoulder again and stooped slightly, shielding his face.

"All done?"

"Well enough."

The gatekeeper shot the bolts and drew the door open. "Leave the tools," he said shortly.

Yashim laid the mattock against the wall.

"I don't know you," the gatekeeper said.

"Petros couldn't come this evening. His wife's sick."

"Oh? What with?"

Dmitri shrugged, and made a gesture. "Women's things," he said vaguely.

The gatekeeper gave a vulgar laugh. "Only one reason a man marries, I can think of. You married?"

He peered at Yashim, who shook his head and grinned stupidly.

"Simple, is he?" The gatekeeper, who had been so taciturn and uninterested, seemed to be in a mood to talk.

"It's past his bedtime." Dmitri took Yashim's arm. "We'd best be off. He doesn't like the dark."

The gatekeeper scratched his head, disappointed. They heard him scrape the bolts behind them.

"You were good," Yashim said. "For a moment I thought—"

Dmitri hissed angrily: "You never said you'd go inside."

They walked on in silence until they reached the track.

"I'm going this way." Dmitri held out a handful of tomatoes. "If you like . . . ?"

Yashim shook his head. He watched Dmitri walk away, until he was lost in the dusk that gathered beneath the trees. Then he turned and walked in the direction of the quay.

He didn't hear the sound of running feet until it was too late. A man, running barefoot toward him. The man was a shadow between the trees, and the last light had begun to fade.

Yashim stopped where he was: the man approaching flung back his head to look behind. Yashim heard his panting breath, and at the last moment he swiveled to one side.

He might have got clear had he jumped from one rut in the track to the other. Instead, the runner crashed blindly into Yashim, whose legs gave way: the runner pitched forward over him, hands outstretched, and the two of them rolled on the ground.

Yashim was winded. He threw up a hand to grab the man's wrist but his fingers closed instead on something round and hard. The runner was already somersaulting over him, and he broke free with a tug that seemed to drag Yashim's fingers out of their sockets. Before Yashim could stagger to his feet the man was up and off, pelting down the track.

"Hey! Hey!"

Someone else was lumbering heavily up the track. Yashim held his side: the collision had bruised him, and he needed to suck the air into his lungs. His hand hurt.

"You there! Hey! Stop, thief!"

Yashim shook his head and straightened up.

"Not your thief," he gasped. And then it struck him: the word was *kleftis*. The man lumbering up the track had shouted "*klepta,*" which was Greek, but ancient Greek.

"What the devil—?"

The last remark was made, not in ancient Greek, but in a language Yashim, who had every language he was likely to meet on the islands, and four more, knew most imperfectly. The tone, and the voice, seemed unmistakable.

"Compston!"

The dark bulk of George Compston, second secretary at the British embassy to the Sublime Porte, coalesced at Yashim's elbow.

"The deuce! *Jer voo connais, monsieur. Ce klepta*—I mean, *ce voleur, monsieur*—" He panted, and wiped his brow: "My God! Yashim efendi! I mean to say!"

"*Mais oui—c'est moi,*" Yashim replied, half smiling in the dark. He took the Englishman's arm and felt for his hand. "Your watch, I think."

He pressed the watch into Compston's hand. The young man gurgled with surprise.

"B-by all that's holy, Yashim efendi! Pater's Hunter! Well, well . . . The blighter had it off me by the quayside, when I was taking a walk with a girl . . . snatched it out of my weskit. I've been running ever since. And a pretty girl, too."

He held the watch up to his ear. "Still ticks! We can iron out the creases, Yashim efendi. Good work! Chain's gone, though." He paused. "You didn't happen to get the chain?"

"I'm afraid the chain broke off," Yashim replied drily.

"Too bad. Little cutpurse, good day's haul. But not the Hunter, eh?"

"It was only chance—"

"Bloody miracle. Pater's Hunter," Compston murmured. "Can't thank you enough, Yashim efendi. Pretty much the old man's parting shot. Go forth, young man, and all that. Solid gold. Not that it's what matters. I mean to say."

"It was nothing."

"Look, if you're heading for the city I could send you on." He linked his arm in Yashim's, and they strolled down the track together. "I brought the embassy yawl."

They reached the quayside a few minutes later, Compston still extolling the virtues of his father's watch, eager to examine it under the light.

"No, not a scratch I can see. Tick-tock, good as new. Pity about the chain, but it's the watch that matters. Hi! Caïquejee!"

He gestured cheerfully to the boatman. "New passenger! Alexander the Great. Hop in, Yashim efendi. Stavros gets you back to Istanbul in under an hour, or I'm a Dutchman."

"You aren't coming?"

"Back to strolling, efendi." Compston raised a hand. "Take the yawl. Least I can do for you." He glanced about the quay. "Now, where's that dashed girl?"

ONE by one, along the edge of the Golden Horn, the fishing boats drawn up on the strand lit their lamps as dusk descended over the Bosphorus. Dark figures crouched beneath their prows, tending the braziers where they cooked their fish: mackerel, mostly, headed, gutted, and then split apart to sizzle for a few minutes over the glowing charcoal. The warm air reeked of fish oil dripping into the fires.

A Nubian sailor slapped his hams and squatted down by one of the braziers. The fisherman took his coin, and tipped a hot mackerel fillet into a flat roll.

Overhead, in the branches of a plane tree, Kadri licked his lips, and waited.

THE embassy caïque swept over a glassy sea. Yashim lay back, reveling in the wind, pondering his discovery.

At length he saw the dim outline of the Topkapi Palace, lights in the tower of the Third Court, and the curve of the dome of Ayasofya. As the ferry wheeled into the Golden Horn, the great mosques of Bayezid and Süleyman seemed like curious configurations of the hilltops; beneath them, all along the Stamboul shore, a parade of tiny lights winked in the gathering darkness where the fishermen had set up their braziers. The quayside was empty. The fishermen had already gone, leaving their nets. The men who hung around the quays had retreated—some to the Greek bars that thronged the lower streets around the port, others to their wives and children.

A whiff of grilled fish wafted across the water.

The fishing boats drawn up on the strand were all alike, all selling mackerel fresh from the sea, and Yashim found it hard to choose one over another. He saw a sailor sitting on his hams and munching a sandwich with evident enjoyment: the firelight flickered on his black skin, and his teeth were very white in the darkness.

Yashim approached the boat and pointed to the flaming grill. "I'd like one nicely done," he said.

The fisherman nodded, dropped a split mackerel into a round of bread, and held it up. And at that moment something odd happened.

The sandwich disappeared.

Yashim's hand met the empty hand of the fisherman, and they both startled.

Overhead a branch creaked in the darkness.

48

YASHIM took a step back and looked up. He saw the silhouette of the tree stark against the stars, and with it an impression of something moving along the branch above. He stepped back on his heels for a clearer view, and then darted under the tree. The lower branches were too high to reach, but they swooped out to almost touch the roof of a single-story godown.

He heard a twig snap. Yashim ran toward the godown, put one foot on the sill of its great barred window, and grabbed at the lowest branch.

Aware that his retreat was in danger of being blocked off, Kadri began to run along the branch, balancing with open arms and still holding the stolen sandwich. As he reached the end his body sank; he bunched his muscles and prepared to jump.

Under Yashim's weight the branch dipped and swayed.

Kadri sprang. The angle was steeper than he had expected: the ground had moved beneath his toes.

He hit the parapet with his belly, and gasped as the wind was knocked out of him. A sharp pain shot up his knee.

Yashim sprang to the sill. The boy thrashed his legs; Yashim reached up with both hands, took hold of an ankle, and leaped back.

He landed hard on the ground. The boy was beside him on his hands and knees, head hanging, still gasping for breath.

Kadri turned to the stranger who had brought him down.

To his bewilderment, the stranger began to laugh.

"You're Kadri," he said, nudging something with his foot. "And that, I'm afraid, was my mackerel sandwich."

COMPSTON turned from the landing stage, casting about for the girl.

Unable to see her beneath the trees, he retraced his steps along the path, stooping to pick something off the ground. Such was popular reverence for the Koran that it was unusual to find scrap paper in the street—people tended to rescue it, in case it contained the Holy Word.

But here was a bundle of papers, riffling in the evening breeze. Compston grunted in surprise. It was too dark to see what was written on the paper, so he thrust the packet under his waistcoat and went on, thinking about the fair Armenian and wondering where the deuce she had got to.

HIGH above the Golden Horn, on the first hill of the city of seven hills, small lights burned in the near-deserted harem of the Topkapi Palace.

The visit to Besiktas for the unfruitful Ceremony of the Birth had left the valide feeling fretful and tired. Returning to the Topkapi Palace, she had heard her own shuffling footsteps echoing on the cobbled passageway.

Now she lay on her divan, and sank her cheek onto her hand.

"I am bored, Tülin. For the first time in my life I am bored, and quite alone. I used to enjoy teasing my son, but now he is gone, and Abdülmecid is not the same. I think it is your fault."

"My fault, hanum?" Tülin's eyes filled with tears.

"Your fault. I'm sure of it." The valide gave a nod. "Yes, before you came I was more content. I used to read my books. I even liked to watch the birds. And now? Now I feel I have been a widow for a long, long time."

"If I make you feel like this, then you must send me away, valide." Tülin's lower lip trembled.

"And where would you go, *ma chérie*? What would become of you? Answer me that."

Tülin could not find an answer. She touched her forehead to her mistress's slippered foot. "I am your slave, valide hanum."

"Hmmph. Don't worry, little one, I will not let you down. You have been good to me, and you are patient."

"But I make you unhappy? Oh, please say it isn't true!"

"*Tiens*, you are a lively girl, and you make me feel that I have wasted my life."

A look of horror passed across the girl's face. "You are the principal valide. You have brought a son and a grandson to the imperial throne. Is that not enough?"

The valide's face lit up with a mischievous smile. "Little Rose should have wished for so much."

"Rose?" Tülin echoed.

"Rose Tascher de La Pagerie." The valide lifted her chin.

"A ferenghi? Like you, valide?"

"Like me? Not at all. She was always dreadfully unlucky." She pursed her lips, and added: "Bismallah."

"Will you tell me about Rose?"

"I am sure I have told you all this before, but why not?" And so the valide sultan, mother and grandmother of sultans, began to explain how two French girls, born and raised on the same remote Caribbean island, each became consort to two great emperors.

Aimée, the daughter of Monsieur Dubucq de Rivery, planter of Martinique, was sent first across the Atlantic, to complete her education in Paris—and find a husband. But when her ship was taken by pirates off the coast of Spain, Aimée found herself not in Paris, but in Algiers.

From where the dey, admiring her white skin, had her sent to his overlord, the sultan, in Istanbul.

"The rest you know—or may imagine," the valide concluded.

"But I know—it was you!" Tülin's eyes were shining. "You were under the protection of God, hanum efendi."

"Hmmph." The valide sounded unconvinced. "It felt somewhat different, at the time."

"And Rose? You were going to tell me about her, too."

The valide gave a little shrug. "Rose? She crossed to France the following year, but not—it would seem—under the protection of God. She reached Paris. Some time later, she married a Beauharnais. Rather minor nobility, Tülin, but I have no doubt her father was delighted. He was a great drunkard, and practically a bankrupt."

"I understand."

The valide went on to sketch the principal events in Rose's life, including her meeting with Napoléon. The great French commander renamed her Joséphine, and had her crowned as empress in Notre Dame.

"Eventually, my dear, he cast her off in favor of a stout Austrian princess. Quite a humiliation. Which goes to show, I believe, that we Ottomans manage these affairs with greater tact. More discreetly, at least, within the harem. Poor Rose."

"Did she never see the emperor again?"

"Never, I believe. She was pretty, in a rather common way. But she lacked something, I suppose."

"What did she lack?"

"Rose lacked—address." The valide took Tülin's chin in her hand, and smiled. "You are very sweet, Tülin. You listen very well, and it's not everyone who knows how to listen. But sometimes, do you know? I think there's more going on in that head of yours than meets the eye. I don't think you entirely lack address yourself."

Tülin dimpled, and bowed her head. "The valide thinks too much of my modest abilities. I wish only to amuse you, and keep you from feeling . . . bored."

"Well, Tülin, that is an excellent ambition." The valide's eyes narrowed. "And what, my dear, do you propose?"

"NEVER mind about the sandwich," Yashim said. "I'll buy another."

He smiled as the boy got warily to his feet.

Yashim smiled. "You won't run away when my back's turned, will you?"

The fisherman eyed them both suspiciously as they returned to his boat.

"You owe me for the mackerel," he said accusingly, as though it had been Yashim who had made it vanish.

"Here I am again; and we'll have two more, if you please."

Yashim paid for the sandwiches and led the way along the shore. After a hundred yards or so they found a small jetty and he invited Kadri to sit down.

"As good as any kiosk in the palace," Yashim remarked comfortably, swinging his legs over the water. He liked the view over Pera, especially at night, when the streets were lit and the lights from the new apartment buildings sought their reflection in the still water. The outline of the old Genoese fire tower was distinct against the stars.

Yashim watched from the corner of his eye as Kadri tore into the mackerel with the appetite of a boy who hadn't eaten all day. He was small but well proportioned, dark-skinned, with clear dark eyes and a shock of black hair that stuck out in comical tufts around his face.

"Have the other one," Yashim suggested, holding out the untouched sandwich.

He could see the pale disk of Kadri's face in the dark, but not his expression.

"Thank you," the boy said. "I have eaten." And then he added, "Thank you for the sandwich, efendi."

"Take it, I'm not hungry," Yashim said.

After a decent pause, Kadri's hand came out and took the sandwich.

"I expect you're wondering who I am," Yashim said. "My name's Yashim. Your tutor called me in to find you. It's the kind of thing I do."

"You find people?" There was a tone of disbelief in Kadri's voice. "I didn't know there was such a job."

"No, well. I don't live entirely on that kind of work, to tell the truth."

"Because people don't disappear often enough?"

"That, or I can't find them often enough."

The boy's laugh was pleasant and unforced. "You found me, though, efendi."

"I knew where you'd go."

"In the whole of Istanbul? How?"

"Because it's the same place I went when I ran away from the palace school myself."

The boy was quiet for a moment. "You, efendi? You ran away?"

Yashim smiled ruefully in the dark. Kadri had been about to say something else—surprise that he'd been to the same school. Like the cadet at the gatehouse.

"Do you want to go back?"

"I—I don't know, Yashim efendi. When I was hungry, I thought about it. But really I just wanted to get away. Or . . ."

Yashim imagined his face, screwed up with the effort to express what he felt.

"Or to be somewhere else, for a change?"

"That's it, efendi. I just wanted to go into the streets. The ordinary streets."

"And the ordinary rooftops, I imagine."

"You know?" Kadri almost gasped.

"I think so," Yashim said. "I guessed, when I saw the window on the landing."

The boy leaned forward and put his chin in his hands.

"I think, Yashim efendi, that you find your people every time."

Yashim laughed. "I try, Kadri. In the meantime, it's getting late. If you aren't going back immediately, we're in danger of running out of options for the night."

"Where will we go?"

Yashim was getting up. "I have an idea. Come."

A single lamp burned low on an inlaid table, and above it a lozenge of incense drifted its heavy scent into the air.

Pembe lay against the pillows quite still, her eyes motionless, her hands folded placidly on her breast.

The girl neither saw the lamplight nor smelled the perfume in her nostrils. Her thoughts wandered down the cramped, dark corridors of her own small past, and into the ruins of her future.

In the past she could see a man in a sheepskin hat. Her father greases his carbine with mutton fat. A woman stoops to drag the stones from a patch of ground: when she straightens she is beautiful; she turns a wisp of her hair in her fingers and tucks it back beneath her kerchief and the hair is streaked with gray.

The girl remembered the first time she saw the sea. A ship. She thought they were both beautiful. The sun glittered on the water as it rose, lighting her path: a road strewn with flashing jewels.

Jewels around her neck; perfume between her breasts, and the tinkling of the bangles that she wore around her ankles. The path had glittered and she had smiled, knowing she was beautiful like the sea. Of course she had been chosen. Unafraid, warming the prince with that smile and the unblemished beauty of her white limbs.

There was to be a boy. His first. Her precious charge. For him she would be the man who oiled a gun, the woman who picked stones: unremitting, watchful, no fool. But she would be the khadin, too, first of them all, with honor and wealth and a world at her command. One day, at the end of the glittering road, valide.

Instead of which, an evil day brought her a girl. Nothing—and worse than nothing. A monster. Freak. A cursed thing, which had lived only a few days.

The door opened slowly and she saw the aga come in.

He tiptoed to the divan. She swayed as his weight settled, but she did not blink or move her hands.

Her mind picked among the pathways: something that stood between her and the light. A dark form. Not a man. Not a beast.

It was a woman, and Pembe's heart burned with a desire for revenge.

When she spoke, the aga did not recognize her voice. "I know who did this to me."

Ibou glanced nervously around the room. "It is the will of God, Pembe. It should strengthen you."

The girl turned her head and spat.

"It happened after she came," she went on. "When she beheld me with her eye. I felt it on me, but then I was not afraid."

"Nonsense," Ibou replied. He patted her hand.

The girl's lips peeled back. "Talfa." She spat the name through bared teeth. "She was jealous. Because I was young and beautiful, and was growing with a child. She wished to kill me in her heart."

"The lady Talfa?" The aga glanced uneasily at the door. "You are alive, by the will of God."

Her head sank back onto the pillow. "No, aga. No. I am dead already."

53

THE Polish ambassador to the Sublime Porte sat at his drawing room window and willed a breeze to rustle the wisteria. It was infernally hot, as hot as any summer Palewski had known in Istanbul.

He reached out for the slender green bottle at his elbow and rolled it gratefully around his forehead. The residency cellars were very deep, and very old, and impervious to the temperatures outside. He sighed and put the bottle down again.

A flying beetle whizzed past his nose and flung itself with a *ping!* at the glass mantle of the oil lamp. Palewski reached forward and in one swift motion caught the insect in his hand. He moved the book from his lap, leaned out the window, and hurled the beetle into the night air.

As he did so, he noticed two figures slip between the iron gates below and approach the front door.

"We aren't buying anything tonight, thank you!" he shouted down to them.

"It's me, Yashim! May we come in?"

"You? Well then, yes. Come in! I mean—wait. I'll have to unlock the doors first," he added, a little more loudly.

Yashim grinned in the dark. He knew perfectly well that the Polish residency was scarcely ever locked; there was no point, as Palewski often remarked. The old-fashioned mansion had declined over the years, so that a child might have climbed in through the slipping sashes, or popped the bolts on the garden door. But it was sensible to keep up appearances.

Palewski shot the bolts on the front door, and in the lamplight Kadri saw a man of about fifty-five, with curling gray hair and a loose cravat. Very tall, he was wearing a plum-colored waistcoat with unmatched buttons, long trousers, and a pair of worn velvet slippers.

"Come in, by all means," he said, "and bring your friend. Is it late? I rather think Marta must have gone to bed."

Yashim stepped into the hall, and Kadri closed the door behind them. Yashim made introductions.

"Capital! Splendid! Are you hungry? Well, never mind. It wouldn't do to go hungry." He glanced at Kadri. "I was always hungry at that age. There'll be cheese and things in the pantry. You go on upstairs, Yash, and take your young friend with you."

With that he turned and went off down a corridor, leaving his visitors in total darkness.

Yashim chuckled. "I know the way. Mind the stairs—best keep to the side, the carpet can be a bit loose."

They groped their way up the stairs and reached the drawing room, where their eyes grew sufficiently accustomed to make out the low shapes of the armchairs and the fainter oblongs of the open windows.

Kadri sniffed the air. "It smells different," he said. "I like it, though."

It smelled, Yashim thought, of beeswax and old books. "I like it, too," he announced to the dark.

They heard Palewski coming upstairs, and finally the lamp came into the room.

"Sorry to leave you in the dark. I forgot." He put the lamp on a sideboard and lowered a tray down beside it, laden with a wedge of white cheese and a bowl of olives.

"Best I could do," he added, waving Kadri toward the tray. "Someone must be raiding the pantry in the night." He paused. "Me, I suppose. Help yourselves."

He picked up a spill from the mantelpiece and lit it at the oil lamp. Soon the room glowed in the light of several lamps and a few candles strategically placed in front of the mottled pier glasses that stood between the windows.

Kadri's eyes were round with interest as the unfamiliar room sprang into view, moving from the violin on the sideboard to the fireplace armchairs and the shelves that lined the farther wall.

"I'm afraid the books are a bit of a muddle," Palewski explained. "Trying out a new arrangement. Found a curious treatise on Roman law, never seen it before. Moldy stuff, well past its best. Turns out my father wrote it. Do sit down."

He gestured to the armchairs. Yashim took the one he liked, with the stuffing coming out of the seat; Kadri, slightly bemused, settled for the arm of the other.

"I didn't know the palace boys were allowed out," Palewski remarked cheerfully.

Kadri's head sank. "No. It is forbidden."

Palewski glanced over at Yashim, who gave an almost imperceptible shrug.

"Kadri has just run away, for a while," he said.

Palewski nodded, as if it were the most natural thing in the world. "Do have some more cheese, Kadri. As for you, Yashim, let me find you a glass."

"What is that?" Kadri pointed to the green bottle that Palewski had just picked up.

"Glad you asked. Late vintage Riesling." He poured some into a stemmed glass and handed it to Yashim. "Not the usual stuff, Yashim. Piesporter—southern bank of the Moselle," he added, leaning an elbow on the mantelpiece and holding his own glass up to the light. "Spätlese—noble rot, Kadri. Bishop of Fulda, I recall. Von Bibra. Heinrich? Helmuth? Plums, figs, late summer, all that sort of thing. I ran into a whole case of the stuff at Macarios's, God knows how. He thought it was some sort of German beer."

Kadri looked surprised. "It is alcohol?"

Palewski raised an eyebrow. "Slate and sunshine, Kadri. It's late summer in the mountains—green mountains, where it rains early in the year." He drew Kadri's attention to a colorless bottle standing on the sideboard. "That, young man, is alcohol."

"It is forbidden," the boy said, primly.

"It is certainly forbidden to boys," Palewski agreed. "Like running away from school."

Kadri smiled shyly, and lowered his eyes.

"Kadri didn't exactly run," Yashim pointed out. "He jumped."

Kadri's eyes flickered toward Yashim.

"He got out through a window. The window," Yashim added, "was thirty feet above the ground."

"Ah. The old knotted sheet routine," Palewski murmured, approvingly.

"No sheets were missing."

"A ledge."

"No ledge."

Palewski cast his eyes at the ceiling. "Wings?"

Yashim shrugged. "Sometimes the impossible is the only possibility."

Kadri looked away and bit his lip; he lifted his chin slightly, instincts of pride and reserve warring in his expression.

"I couldn't work it out," Yashim said, "until I caught you, in the tree."

The boy looked around and smiled.

"Your tutor said you could run. He didn't tell me you can jump as well. It's a talent, Kadri."

"But not one recognized by the school, perhaps," Palewski interjected.

Kadri scratched his burred head. "Before Hamdi Bey took me I lived in the mountains, efendim. On my own, I mean. There was an earthquake when I was in the fields. My family was at home. My uncle wanted to take me in, but he—that is, we—" He swallowed. "He was a hard man. I survived in the mountains. I didn't want to be caught."

"Good for you," Palewski said.

"There were stones, and columns, and rocks." Kadri shrugged. "I lived like a goat."

"But thirty feet . . ."

Kadri grinned. "It's not so far across the gap to the other side."

"But still ten feet, at least. And the lane between the refectory and the mosque is even wider, I imagine."

"I can run and jump," the boy repeated. "It's mostly about knowing how to land, I think."

"And from the mosque?"

"I used the minaret, Yashim efendi. It's small, like a tree. I swung around it, onto the wall, and off the wall onto the rooftop beyond. I didn't even break a tile."

"Scuttling across the rooftops? What fun!" Palewski raised his glass in salute. "And how, if I may ask, did you two find each other?"

Yashim laughed. "Kadri found my sandwich."

Palewski raised an eyebrow, and Yashim explained.

"I just put myself in the right place," he added finally. "The palace school takes you up and up, and away from the world. It's like climbing beyond the tree line."

"With better views, in the end," Palewski said.

"Oh, certainly. That's what they tell you, in so many words: work hard, and one day you'll get to turn around and have your view. Maybe it's over a province you govern, or an army at your command. It could be the empire, when you get made grand vizier." He glanced at Kadri. "But sometimes you want to stop climbing, and straining, and getting above everyone."

Kadri pursed his lips thoughtfully.

"You make up your mind to come off the mountainside for a while," Yashim continued. "And you run down—like a stream."

"Yes, Yashim efendi! You go down, you're right. In the valley there's life, there's people . . ."

"Funny, isn't it?" Palewski said. "I always wanted to run away *to* school. Any school. Jolly boys, ghastly masters with pretty daughters, pranks in the dormitories. Instead I had tutors at home, and my father's thoughts on Roman law and the Czartoryskis, who thumbed out their daughters like playing cards." He looked thoughtful. "But I'd rather have been a mountain goat, like Kadri."

Yashim looked into his wine. "I was wondering," he began, "whether you could put Kadri up here, for a while. If Kadri agrees."

"Here? Why not? Be delighted. I'll tell Marta right away." He made for the door, then stopped. "Bit late. Tell her in the morning. I'm afraid you might have to bunk down somewhere . . ." He waved a hand vaguely toward the ceiling.

Kadri's swarthy face had reddened. "I would not wish to be a burden," he said.

"No burden at all. We can discuss Roman law and drink up this case of Riesling," Palewski said amiably. He peered at the boy. "Or rather, not, of course."

Kadri lowered his eyes.

"When you ran away from the school, Yashim efendi—I mean, tonight I met you and Palewski efendi. You have both been so—so kind, and generous. But . . ."

Yashim nodded. "When I ran away I met a caïquejee, who gave me breakfast. Some kind people. A big Greek, who threw me a melon."

Kadri looked dubious. "A mackerel sandwich is better."

Yashim smiled. "He sold fruit and vegetables, not fish."

"And then you went back to school again?"

"I went back to the school," Yashim agreed. "After that, they found me a job."

Yashim meant to say something else: that he met Fevzi Ahmet, and the direction of his life was changed.

Absently, he put a hand to his pocket.

Palewski cocked his head. "That old Greek at the market? Whatsisname, George?" He turned to Kadri. "He did better than that, my young friend. Yashim saved his life."

"How was that, Yashim efendi?"

Yashim did not reply.

"George got attacked," Palewski answered for him, settling back into his chair. But Yashim was not listening anymore.

The packet he had discovered in the crock of rice was gone.

54

"You *think your conscience feeds you? You think the sultan commands you to avoid blood?"*

The walls of the prison run with damp, like the sweat on a man's back. Black mold mottles the stones, and the straw underfoot is wet. The air is clammy, and it stinks.

Yashim and the turnkey hurry after Fevzi Ahmet, who strides down the tunnel breathing heavily through his nostrils. At each gate the turnkey stoops almost apologetically, fumbling with the lock, and they wait for the lock to be turned behind them.

Under a torch, two guards are playing dice.

They straighten up immediately, flinging the dice against the wall.

When the man is brought in, chained by his neck and his wrists, he turns his head from the light.

The guards shackle him to the wall, hands above his head, his back to Fevzi Ahmet.

His hands have no fingernails.

Yashim keeps his mouth shut, but he can hardly breathe.

Fevzi Ahmet produces a knife. He gathers the man's long matted hair in his fist and saws at it with the knife.

He drops the hank of hair to the floor. He takes hold of the man's ear.

The muscles along the man's back begin to move.

"Your brother, the bishop."

"I don't understand," the man whimpers in Greek. "My brother? I have not seen him."

"I can't understand," Fevzi Ahmet says.

Yashim says: "He says he hasn't seen his brother."

Fevzi Ahmet frowns and jerks his head.

"I don't understand Greek."

Yashim sees Fevzi Ahmet's arm rise. Hears the man scream.

"Your brother, the bishop," Fevzi Ahmet repeats, through gritted teeth.

Later, when the man is dragged away, Fevzi Ahmet wipes the knife on the warden's sleeve.

55

FAR up the Bosphorus, the pages who watched the tapers in the sultan's chamber nodded drowsily. The young sultan, almost stifled by the weight of the great brocade across his bed, dreamed about women and ships.

On the floors above, some seventy women lay asleep. Talfa sprawled hugely across a divan, her black slave flat on her back on the floor at her feet, snoring. Overhead, Bezmialem's pretty eyelids flickered as she dreamed, not for the first time, of the moment she had turned back the quilt and started creeping up between the old sultan's mottled thighs. On divans in other rooms, girls slept in a tangle of beautiful limbs, like puppies; lips parted, fingers unfurled, unguarded. What were their dreams, as they stirred and whimpered in the dark? They dreamed of the Circassian hills, no doubt; and of sheep bells and gunshots in the ravines; they dreamed of jewels and soap; of jealousies and love: galleries of dreamers, every one of them following the moving images that flitted innocently behind their eyelids.

Not quite everyone, perhaps. Here and there, a sigh, a moving hand, a caress: for love, too, has its place in the gallery, in the darkness. And what of fear? Of eyes that stare in the dark, of rigid limbs, cold hands, and the icy clutch on the heart among those unfortunates who hardly dare to sleep? They must be counted among the seventy.

Ibou, the chief black eunuch, tries to lift that obscurity with a burning lamp: he, too, is not asleep. He wakes, rises, and lights the lamp to sit with his head bowed, wearily padding in his mind from floor to floor, from room to room, trying to remember everything he has seen, trying to forecast everything that may occur. Now and then his hand drops to the little plate beside him, and he pops another sweetmeat into his mouth, and chews.

56

"You will have coffee?"

"As you wish, my pasha."

The grand vizier clapped his fingers together. "Bring coffee, Jehan." He leaned back against the cushions and passed his hand over his eyes. "You have something you wish to report?"

"Yes, my pasha. The Russian who died—"

"Look, Yashim. Accounts." Husrev lifted a hand and patted a heap of papers at his side. "Petitions. New appointments." He leafed through the heap. "A report from Syria. News about the Russians. Some news *from* the Russians, too—they wish to complain. Here—an ambassador presents his credentials. Sometimes I think we love reports too much," he added, letting the pile fall.

The servant entered with a tray suspended on three chains, and presented Yashim with a little cup.

"It is strange, Yashim. People believe this empire grew great because we Ottomans knew how to fight. Our *gazi* warriors, burning with zeal to subjugate the infidels. The horizons boundless under the hoofs of our steeds. Bright steel. Janissaries in formation."

His lids drooped, his finger tapped the pile of papers. "But what made the empire work was this. And this," he added, touching his forehead.

"We were a shepherd race, Yashim. Nomads. Planning a route. Sorting the flocks. Pitching and striking camp, never forgetting a single cord or a scrap of news. We made an empire because we were fast, and fought well: but we held it because we were organizers, Yashim. Because of this."

He hefted the pile again. "I observe the arrival of some paper or another. Then I pass it on. I am a shepherd of infinite documents."

He looked sadly at Yashim. "You have been back to Chalki."

"Yes, my pasha. I have been back."

"To the monastery?"

"Not the monastery. Neither the abbot nor his monks appear to have been involved in the man's death. The impure water made them ill, and they readily told us what they had found. The tattoo, the brand, frightened them, that's all. If they had killed him, they would have concealed his body somewhere else."

"And we would never have known?"

"Possibly. Probably. There isn't much else on Chalki. A small brigade of guards, the governor, Greek fishermen." Yashim paused, half hoping the vizier might interject. "The Russian had been dead for several weeks," he added.

Husrev Pasha shook his head. "So?"

"Three weeks ago," Yashim said slowly, "the fleet set out to patrol the Cyclades."

Husrev grunted. "The Cyclades was a blind, as it happens. The Kapudan pasha was given secret orders to cruise off Alexandria. The sultan decided this before he died."

"A show of force?"

"My predecessor believed it could be useful." He shifted his weight on the divan. "However—the fleet sailed. And Chalki? I fail to see the connection, Yashim."

"There is nothing on the island for a Russian agent, except—" Yashim swallowed. "The Kapudan pasha left with the fleet. Fevzi Ahmet Pasha lives on Chalki."

The grand vizier did not blink. "The Kapudan pasha," he repeated.

Yashim bit his lip. "This afternoon, Husrev Pasha, I went back to speak to his people."

"His women? About the Russian?" Husrev's tone was a mixture of disapproval and surprise.

"Women notice everything, Husrev Pasha."

"That was not my point."

Yashim understood what Husrev meant: a man's harem was sacrosanct. "I can talk to women," he said softly.

Husrev flicked his fingers in a gesture of disdain. He would believe that a woman's testimony was worth half that of a man, as sharia law dictated; but Yashim had dealt too often with women to think like the grand vizier.

"In the end, it was not necessary. His harem was empty. Fevzi Pasha has no women."

Husrev Pasha's eyebrows rose. "His household?"

Yashim had considered this. "Apart from a couple of gardeners, who are paid for their time, he seems to maintain no household. He eats from naval stores. I imagine he gets his people from the same place—the navy."

Husrev Pasha thrust out his jaw. It was almost unthinkable for a man of rank, with all his largesse, not to seek to bestow it upon the women and the menials who formed his household; maintaining a large retinue was itself a sign of rank. It was, in a more subtle sense, a moral expectation.

The Ottomans were not a nation. Turkish, Greek, Bosnian, Serb—they formed a caste; almost a family. Just as the sultan, as head of the family, maintained his pashas and his odalisques, so the Ottomans maintained their retinues in turn. It was the weave that held the fabric of Ottoman society together, and it was observed to the letter—even when a great man found himself displaced, out of favor, unemployed, his largesse flowed; perhaps all the more so, then.

Husrev Pasha laid his fingertips on the pile of papers and peered at them, tapping them slowly.

"A shepherd of documents," he muttered.

"My pasha?"

"When I was a boy, Yashim," he growled in his deep, slow voice, "I tended sheep. Now I watch the reports come in. I worry about the reports, sometimes, but there is so little that I can do. Revenues down? Trouble between peoples?" He pulled a face. "What of it? Every year the same thing. Like sheep into the fold." He raised a finger. "Only the missing one makes all the trouble."

He cast a thoughtful glance at Yashim.

"The Kapudan pasha has missed a report."

Yashim said nothing. He sensed that the old vizier was really thinking aloud. His lips barely moved above the low, disarming rumble of his voice.

"What of that? Eh?" Husrev turned his thumbs outward. "What do I know of winds, and storms, and the sea? I am an old Bosniac, Yashim."

The papers, Yashim thought. I must tell him about the packet that was lost.

The grand vizier pulled at his lip and considered Yashim.

"You knew Fevzi Pasha well?"

"I knew Fevzi Ahmet Pasha before he became a commander. Before he received horsetails."

"Three horsetails." Horsetails, carried on a lance, were the mark of rank in the Ottoman Empire, and it was a sign of the old Ottoman respect for the sea that the Kapudan pasha had as many horsetails as the grand vizier. Land commanders had only two. "He receives many honors. The late sultan, God's mercy on his soul, was pleased to advance him very high."

"He is the Kapudan pasha," Yashim said, more evenly. "I have not seen him for . . . ten years."

There was so much more he could say. But it was too late: the time to speak had long since passed, and he had made a promise, to himself.

Out of loyalty? Or shame.

"We didn't part as friends," he said at last.

Husrev Pasha leaned back against the cushions. "I wonder, Yashim efendi. There is something dark in this. You tell me strange things. I wonder what I should believe."

Yashim felt the flush rising to his cheeks.

"Let us not forget, we start with a dead man," the vizier continued. "A Russian. Perhaps he came to meet the Kapudan pasha on Chalki." Husrev held up a heavy hand. "A man in Fevzi Pasha's position makes many contacts. He draws from many sources."

"Of course."

The vizier let his eyelids droop. "We wait." He made a little gesture of dismissal. "Sometimes, Yashim efendi, all we can do is wait."

AT night distant thunder rolled over the city, and lightning flickered behind the mountains of Asia; but the weather did not break. Beyond the city walls the crops had to be watered by hand, the more tender leaves protected by rattan screens. Tempers frayed in the bazaar.

At the sultan's palace, Ibou, the chief black eunuch, laid his hand on the balustrade and squinted up the staircase. Two dozen shallow stone steps; a landing; another twenty steps. He must have climbed them twenty times a day, up and down, up and down, for these past three years; his hand fluttered to his heart. It was no doubt they that induced the strain.

These steps, and the girls, of course. They were young and impudent.

He began to climb: Besiktas seemed all stairs. At the old palace at Topkapi, one pavilion opened into the next, a stone encampment tumbling magnificently over acres of Seraglio Point. Now, in this great box of a palace at Besiktas, people were forever tramping up and down, peering out at windows, running into each other at awkward moments, and arguing over precedence. How could you tell which room was the greater, which apartment the more covetable? The girls talked of views these days, peeping and gazing out quite shamelessly, as if a little patch of sky was not enough!

"Ibou! I've been looking for you."

The eunuch bowed. "I am at your service, Talfa hanum efendi."

Talfa sniffed. "Why have you not listened to what I have told you? The dormitories are not clean. Yesterday I found Amalya and Perin wearing linen that would have disgraced a street gypsy. I go into their room and find clothing all over the floor. They tread upon it with their slippers."

"It is a disgrace, hanum. I have made them pick everything up. They are much better today."

"Are they in the laundry, then?"

Ibou's eyes flickered. "Today, not. They say they are tired, Talfa hanum.'

"Tired, aga? How should they be tired, when they do so little?" She looked at him sharply. "You know how it is said, that a fish stinks from the head."

Ibou's eyes drooped. "I understand, hanum." He gestured weakly to the stairs, the corridors. Of course he felt tired. In Topkapi, the harem apartments had been swept and scrubbed by the girls themselves. They shook out rugs in the courtyards; they polished the tiled floors until they glittered; they took brooms and swept out the cobwebs from the corners. When they opened a door they stepped out into the open air, and kept themselves as clean as cats.

At Besiktas the girls could barely go outside, unchaperoned; they could not open the windows, for fear of being seen. They swept the dirt into the corridors, where it blew back in again; and half the carpets were nailed down. It all looked very grand from the outside, no doubt, but Ibou knew better. Just the other day, he had reprimanded a girl for wearing a shift so grubby that she looked like a beggar—and she had the cheek to answer him back!

Sometimes he yearned for the old days in the library, where everything was still and in its place. Books were cleaner than women.

"I have been to the laundry, also," Talfa continued. "Two of the other girls are washing in there. My girls."

The chief black eunuch bit his lip. Talfa was royal by blood; she could take care of herself. It was these other girls who fell into slovenly ways. It all came of living in this box.

"Explain to these girls, Ibou aga, that you will inspect their rooms yourself every week from now on. They are not *gözde*. They are not favored by the sultan's attention—nor ever will be, unless they learn to take their responsibilities seriously." She bent forward. "Amalya is the worst. Let us see how she feels about slopping out for a month. Tell her this."

"Yes, hanum. She will be very unhappy."

"That is the point, Ibou. We cannot have these girls making the rules."

"No, hanum. I shall tell her that this is your decision."

She eyed the eunuch narrowly. "Your decision, aga. I may advise—but the girls are your responsibility. And Bezmialem's, of course," she added. "But the young valide seems to have a headache. Poor thing."

The lady Talfa waddled off along the corridor.

Ibou put a hand to the lattice and peered out. He could see ships on the Bosphorus, and he sighed. Lately he had felt so tired. Wondering about the girls. Sleepless nights. Climbing these stairs.

He knew that he was afraid of Amalya. Of what she might do to him, in revenge.

He needed advice. But Ibou, the Kislar aga, did not know who to ask. He did not know who he could really trust.

HIGH summer vegetables glutted the market. Every stall was piled with pyramids of glossy eggplants, both the purple and the white; sacks of spinach, green onions, fresh beans of every shape and color, popped from their skins. Everyone sold tomatoes, even George—who made a pyramid of fruit that resembled purplish turbans.

"So sweet, Yashim efendi!" He kissed his fingertips. "Truly, these tomatoes are a gift to us all—and the poors, especially."

Yashim met Kadri in the market, where he had gone to buy the ingredients for the pickles he always made at this time of the year. The boy helped him carry the baskets home.

Yashim tipped a basket of peppers onto the bench where he worked, the long peppers shaped like slippers, pale green and subtly aromatic.

"If your hands are clean, Kadri, you might wash the peppers," he suggested. He set the kettle to boil, and poured a pint of white wine vinegar into a bowl, in which he dissolved a couple of spoonfuls of salt, and let it stand.

He sliced a few carrots and broke out the cloves from two heads of garlic, brushing away the dry skin but leaving the cloves intact. In deference to George's unexpected enthusiasm, he had bought tomatoes; they had discussed the question, and George had agreed to supply him the tomatoes green and still hard, as unripe as the apricots he always used. Ripe tomatoes, Yashim insisted, would spoil the crunchiness of the pickle. Finally, he took a pointed cabbage and tore it into pale shards.

On the bench he lined up his jars, all French, with tight-fitting lids, imported by English merchants and sold in the Egyptian bazaar; Yashim used earthenware crocks, too, which were cheaper—but pickles winking behind glass were irresistible, like a warm fire on a cold night.

He sluiced the jars with boiling water and began to pack them, laying the peppers and the other vegetables on a carpet of cabbage leaves, alternating the layers as he filled the jars. When they were full, he used a wooden spoon to press the layers down, satisfied by the sound of crisp vegetables creaking and snapping.

"Now, Kadri, the vinegar."

Kadri poured carefully, his tongue between his teeth, until the vegetables in each jar were completely submerged. To make sure, Yashim dropped a small ceramic disc on top, to weight everything down; then he screwed on the lids.

"It'll be good," he said. "But not for a few weeks yet. We'll make something quicker, too. Can you shell those peas?"

Yashim laid a colander on a cloth and began to chop vegetables—a cauliflower broken into florets, some carrots. He tossed in a bunch of tiny green beans topped and tailed, and sprinkled each layer with a handful of rough salt.

"Drop the peas straight in," he said. "We'll leave it to sweat while we go to eat."

Yashim took Kadri to the Kara Davut, where the air was tinged with the scent of hot charcoal and roasting meat. They sat on tiny wicker stools outside a kebab shop that the porters used, opposite the bakery, and within minutes their kebabs were spitting over coals while the baker made up *pide* by ripping a chunk of dough from a bowl, working it on a marble slab, then shaping it and slapping it onto the side of his oven.

"*Ayran*, efendim? It's iced, very cool."

Ayran was a drink of yogurt, whipped with water and a pinch of salt, and they accepted it gratefully, smiling at each other over the rims of their glasses. "I see you're growing a mustache at last," Yashim said. Kadri grinned, and wiped his upper lip.

"You know, Kadri, it's at times like this that I pity sultans in palaces."

It could have been him, of course. If Talfa had her way, the luxury of eating on the street would be all but lost to him.

Kadri nodded. "I don't want to go back to school," he said. "Not yet."

"That's what I was afraid you'd say." Yashim sighed. "They may not have you back if you leave it too long. If that matters," he added, after a pause.

He glanced at his new young friend. Kadri looked better than he had looked just a few days before: the pimples on his forehead had cleared up and his eyes were brighter than ever.

"What do you think, Yashim efendi?"

"About the school?" Yashim looked up at the sky. "I'm not sure I can advise you, Kadri. The school exists to produce a special caste of men, who go on to run this empire. You can become one of them."

"You didn't," Kadri said.

"Efendim!" The waiter set a tray before them, with the little cubes of roasted lamb, bread, and a gypsy salad of cheese with red onion and peppers.

Yashim laughed. "I like to believe I have my uses, Kadri. The school also, perhaps incidentally, gives you training. Persian, Arabic, the classics. Things that a man should know. Rhetoric and logic. You study ethics, and the wisdom and poetry of the holy Koran. Those are things that can give you happiness; a consolation, at least."

"It sounds—gloomy."

"Not at all." Yashim smiled. "It's learning how to live. But it's not the only way," he added. He popped a morsel of tender lamb into his mouth and glanced at his young friend. "The *medrese*s will teach you a great deal, if you prefer that route. Or books. Books teach you a number of things, including how to distinguish truth from fiction; and how to govern yourself."

Kadri nodded. "I can't decide."

"No matter. I'll have coffee, and then we must finish our work."

Back in his kitchen, Yashim inspected the vegetables: the cloth under the colander was soaked. He squeezed four lemons into a bowl and beat them into a pint of olive oil.

"We'll pot this up," he said, "and then—I have an idea."

Yashim tossed the vegetables in the colander, and then raked them into two glass jars, finishing with the dressing.

"This is for me—and this is for a friend," he added, screwing down the lids. "I think, Kadri, you should stay with the ambassador—you seem to get along well. But in the mornings you could do something else."

Kadri looked doubtful. "What could I do, Yashim efendi?"

"Come with me. And bring the pickle, too."

At the Balat stage they took a caïque to Pera, from where they made their way uphill, toward the Galata Tower, and then higher, to the fringes of the Frankish town that was constantly growing and rebuilding itself across the hill.

Yashim crossed into a side street and stopped at a shabby-looking door.

"Ready?"

Kadri looked anxious, but he forced a smile. "Ready, Yashim. What is this place?"

Yashim rapped on the door. "A den of iniquity. Riffraff. Dancers and actors. It's run by an old friend of mine, who used to be a *köçek* dancer. It's a theater."

Kadri giggled. "It's not something they teach us about at school."

"That, Kadri, is the whole point."

The door opened a crack. A pair of dark eyes examined them for a moment, and then the door opened wide.

"Preen's upstairs, Yashim." It was Mina, who attended to the accounts. "Come in—and bring those pickles. And your little friend, of course."

59

"CAN you sing? Dance?"

Kadri shook his head. "I can run—and jump."

"All right, darling." Preen pursed her lips. "Let's work with that. For the time being, I'll get you to help Mustafa with the props and scenery. Learn some of the ropes."

"I'll pay for his board," Yashim said, fishing out his purse. He shook the money into his hand.

"Don't worry about that," Preen said, with a wave. "Another mouth makes no difference." She frowned, and pointed at something glinting in Yashim's palm. "What's that?"

"Oh, something . . . a nail," he said carelessly. "I found it—in someone's house."

Preen peered at it for a moment, then her head snapped back. "Get rid of it, Yashim. Throw it out." She gestured toward the window, but then her expression changed. "No, don't throw it. You shouldn't have touched it."

Yashim picked up the nail and spun it between his fingers.

Preen winced. "Stop! You don't know what it does!"

"I'll throw it away," Yashim said reluctantly.

"No, no." She bit at her finger. "I know a woman, not far away. It's better that we go to see her. Believe me, Yashim, don't be stupid."

Yashim shrugged and put the nail in his pocket.

"We can go there now," Preen continued. "Kadri, come and meet Erkan, the Strongest Man in the World."

The Grande Rue was lined with European shops, behind whose bright windows people came with money and left with packages wrapped in paper. Preen led Yashim across, and plunged into the network of alleys that lay in a tangled skein above the Bosphorus. Here, by a dimmer light, matters were decided by superstitious gestures, by almanacs and eggs broken into a bowl of oil, by imprecations and talismans. Here people sought out propitious days, avoided dark corners, waggled their fingers behind their backs, resorted to nostrums, prayers, and the prognostications of wise women. These were the ordinary calculations of the everyday world, in which every moment held its weight, every movement was a portent, each word and gesture held a meaning.

Yashim put a hand to his pocket and felt the nail, with its little ridge of thread, and hastily withdrew it again.

Preen knocked at a door.

"Who is it?"

"Preen, Mrs. Satzos. With a friend."

"Please come in. The door is not locked."

The light seemed to bend and flutter toward them. The whole room was lit by dozens of tiny candles, burning and flickering in glass jars all around the walls.

A little table held a jug and a bowl, and several plain glasses. The walls were lined with shelves. On the shelves stood the flickering lights, and over each of them loomed an indistinct shape. Some were crosses, of tin or bronze, occasionally inset with small beads of colored glass that twinkled in the candlelight, but there were also books, set flat against the wall, and on one shelf—a more disagreeable surprise—a row of stuffed dolls with beady eyes and silk faces, their arms fixed in a gesture of benediction. Behind one candle he noticed a hand of Fatima, made of punched tin. Several small icons, almost black with age or soot, defied analysis.

"I brought him straight to you, Mrs. Satzos," Preen was saying. "He wanted to throw it out the window. Yashim?"

Yashim laid the nail on the cover of a brassbound book he supposed to be a Bible.

Mrs. Satzos leaned forward. She was a small, birdlike woman with ice-white hair braided into a bun and dark patches around her eyes.

"You did right to bring it to me. You found this in your house? Your room?"

"In the house of—a friend. He's away."

Mrs. Satzos frowned.

"Away—gone to sea," Yashim explained.

The old lady cocked her head, as if she found something puzzling. "And the women in the house . . . ?"

"There were none."

Mrs. Satzos looked at him kindly. "As you wish. The little threads—what do they suggest to you, efendi?"

"I don't know. I thought there was something deliberate."

"Whoever twisted this thread around the nail was thinking of the past." She peered more closely at the nail. "The knot tied here, you see? I think it represents an event. Perhaps a decision. Whoever tied it wanted your friend to remember something."

Yashim glanced at Preen. "So it is not a curse?"

The old lady clicked her teeth impatiently. "Curses. Charms. Kismet!" She dismissed the thought with a wave of her hand. "That is for the bazaar, where people go like children to Sufis and gypsies. Do you not think that memory can also be a curse?"

Yashim felt the blood rise in his cheeks. "Memory?"

Mrs. Satzos folded her hands on her lap and regarded him with her panda eyes. "The curse is not what is to be, efendi. The curse belongs to what has been."

"And this"—he gestured to the nail without looking at it—"revives a memory?"

"There are things that people wish to forget, efendi." She was staring at him in surprise, as if she had seen something she didn't expect. "Some disgrace. A loss. A source of pain."

She stood up and turned to one of the shelves. She selected one of the curious dolls that Yashim had disliked on sight, and opened the drawer of the little sideboard to take out a roll of lint. She cut a length off the roll and returned to the table. Pressing the nail flat against the doll's back, she began to bind it on with the lint, murmuring what sounded like a prayer.

"There!" She nodded to them brightly. "We will guard the charm, and draw its sting. If you wish to make an offering to the saint it will not be refused."

She put the doll back on the shelf. Yashim and Preen got to their feet, and Yashim dipped in his wallet for a silver kurus, which he placed in the woman's hand.

She touched his arm. "You have troubles yourself, efendi. You will come to visit me again."

"My troubles—" He was not sure what he meant to say. He shrugged. "Perhaps."

HYACINTH heard the call to prayer and automatically swung his legs off the bed onto the floor. He sat up and rubbed his hand across his face.

With a crack of his shoulders he stretched his arms, and yawned. Through the latticed window he could make out the glimmer of early dawn. He bent down and with a practiced switch of his fingers flicked out the rug that lay rolled up beneath his bed. He settled onto the rug rather awkwardly, first one knee and then the other, and began to pray.

Five minutes later he rolled up the rug, stowed it under the bed, and shuffled into a pair of slippers. His toes were long and thin and they gripped the slippers as he waddled from his cell to the hammam.

For many years, Hyacinth had recognized his hammam hour each morning as the highlight of his day.

Now, turning his long, elegant feet under the hot water of the spigot, he almost wanted to hug himself. He had not one, but two delicious pleasures to rouse him from his sleep—not to mention prayers, he mentally added, uncertain whether prayers strictly constituted a pleasure or not.

After the bath—a little further treat, why not? The valide's new slave, the woman Tülin, had introduced it to the court. The eunuchs at Topkapi were suffering a little from neglect when Tülin came to help the valide, for the luminaries of Hyacinth's restricted world clustered around the sultan in his new palace at Besiktas. Gone were the armies of cooks who worked from dawn till dusk to serve the choicest tidbits to the happy few. Gone, too, the young women, their laughter, their idle chatter, and all the gossip that their activities and moods created. Hyacinth loved his mistress, but the valide could be demanding—and there were no distractions anymore. The division of the family had brought him the only sorrow he had ever really known. He had loved the soft women. He had loved their babies.

But Tülin was like a breath from the other world! Returning from her orchestra at Besiktas, she brought gossip from the harem—why, when she talked about those women, it was almost as if one knew them intimately oneself! Poor Pembe's grief—that was just too sad. And Maral's face, when she heard the news! Pouf! What a cow—but so lovely, of course. It was the Circassian blood. He, Hyacinth, knew all about Circassians.

And Tülin was young. She made the valide happy. Sometimes, when the valide wasn't listening, Tülin would tell Hyacinth about the babies in the sultan's harem, the little ones who ran about at their mothers' knees, all their little jokes and funny names. The valide wasn't interested in them, really, but Hyacinth couldn't get enough. He used to be a favorite with the little ones, who pulled his lobey ears and ordered him about, sometimes, like sultans themselves. Quite innocent! Their sudden tempers and equally sudden smiles reminded him of—well, people like himself.

He dried himself and dressed with care. He shuffled quickly down the corridor and out into the valide's courtyard.

Tülin's door, he saw with rising expectation, was ajar. And now he could smell it, too.

"Hello, my dove!" He peered around the door, smiling, and waggled his fingers. "Am I too early for you?"

She looked up and smiled. "I saw you going to the hammam, Hyacinth efendi. And I thought—he'll be an hour! At least an hour."

She raised her eyebrows, and Hyacinth chuckled.

"So you are in perfect time."

With a bow, and the same radiant smile, she offered him a steaming bowl of chocolate.

61

"THERE." Preen flashed him a look of triumph. "I told you Mrs. Satzos was good."

Yashim nodded in sardonic agreement. "All my worries are over now, Preen. Thanks." He raised a finger and the coffee boy darted forward. "Two, medium sweet."

"She goes to the palace every week. The harem ladies can't get enough of her."

Yashim smiled. "You are a snob, Preen."

She tossed her head. "We're all snobs, one way or another." When Yashim didn't reply, she added: "It's you, isn't it? The friend—that's just what we say."

Yashim looked surprised. He shook his head. "It's not me, Preen. Not me at all."

"Oh?" She raised a painted eyebrow.

"Forget what you think. I lied, yes—but I lied in saying that he was a friend."

"An enemy."

Yashim took a breath. "I don't know, exactly."

"Rich?"

Yashim smiled wanly.

"But you told Mrs. Satzos there were no women in the house."

"Preen—you remember things too well."

The boy arrived with coffee. When he had gone Preen leaned forward. "You told Mrs. Satzos that he'd gone to sea."

"It's better you don't know," Yashim said quickly.

"The Kapudan pasha. Fevzi Pasha, right?"

Yashim ran his finger around the rim of his cup.

"Fevzi Ahmet," she said slowly. "I remember him. At a wedding, where we came to dance. It was a long time ago. One of the bridesmaids went for a walk in the garden. I saw her just as we were setting up, a country girl. I didn't know her. But something happened between her and Fevzi Ahmet, Yashim. Her brother went berserk. He said he'd kill Fevzi Ahmet, wedding or no wedding."

Angry spots had appeared on her cheeks. "Fevzi Ahmet took him for a little talk, instead, strolling about the cypress trees, and us beginning to dance." Preen caressed her neck. "When I saw him walking with the brother, at the wedding, I knew it was all arranged. Fevzi was—I don't know, sneering. He knew that no one could touch him."

Yashim bowed his head.

"They came from Erzurum, the girl and her family. I heard that she drowned there two weeks later, in the pool."

She shuddered.

Yashim bit his lip. He knew what Preen had told him would be true.

"Fevzi Ahmet was my mentor for three years," he said.

He saw her shrink back. Her voice seemed to come from somewhere farther off.

"Mentor? Like—a teacher?"

His own voice sounded harsh. "I worked for him years ago. I was at the palace school, Preen. You knew that. I ran away, like Kadri. My training was almost over, and I didn't know what they had planned for me. I didn't know what I was good for. I was afraid of being . . . inactive. I thought they might make me carry shawls for odalisques, or library books, you know. I was afraid of being trapped in the palace."

"You don't like to be trapped, do you?" She nodded. "Go on."

"I went back a few days later. My tutor thought I had been to Eyüp, to visit the tomb of the Companion of the Prophet. I don't know why. He thought it was meritorious. That's when Fevzi Ahmet talked to me, the first time. He'd been watching me, he said."

Preen hoicked her shoulders, in a little shudder. "He would."

"He offered me a job, doing something I didn't even know people could do." He cracked his knuckles anxiously. "He was the sultan's *tebdil khasseky*—his confidential agent."

Preen drew up her chin. "Like you."

Yashim ducked his head and looked uncomfortable. "I try to do things differently."

"Of course."

"I worked for others for a few years at first, to gain experience. That was Fevzi Ahmet's idea. To develop talents, skills, which he could use. Languages, for instance. He knew only Turkish and some Greek."

"Limiting."

Yashim blew out his cheeks. "I thought it sounded like a fine thing— to be the sultan's arrow, carrying his messages and his private orders. Watching over his safety. I was young and—well, Fevzi Ahmet seemed very energetic, and very sure of himself."

"So I've heard."

"He was obviously a tough bastard—even I could tell that much. But I thought that was how it had to be. Hard, but loyal. People were afraid of him because he had the sultan's special commission."

"Are you sure?" Preen leaned forward. "I thought people were afraid of him because he did frightening things, Yashim."

"Sultan Mahmut needed loyal men back then, when Fevzi Ahmet began," Yashim said. "He needed men like that. He was trying to reestablish control. The Janissary time. You remember."

"And you became his boy."

Yashim nodded. Fevzi the Hunter.

"That was our understanding. I had gained experience of the outside world. Or so I thought."

He put his hands on his knees, remembering Russia.

The bitterness of Fevzi's debt.

"It seemed like a way into the world outside."

"And was it?"

"We operated in different ways," Yashim said finally. "It took me a while to understand that. I think there is always a little gap somewhere, however hard you try to fit everything together. A small space, for something like grace, or mercy."

"Or error."

"Or error," Yashim nodded. "After that, when we both knew—we couldn't trust each other anymore."

Preen was silent. Yashim heard the coffee cup chink against the saucer as she put it down on the divan.

"He fixed it so that I could live here, like this, and for that I am grateful. But I think he did it to save his own skin, too."

On the divan Preen was sitting with her elbows in, holding her hands palms up. Preen was a dancer and her gestures were expressive and precise. Yashim recognized her pose immediately. It was a gesture as old as Istanbul itself. The Greeks had captured it here, in light, fastened to the domes of their churches; but it was common to all the city's faiths, and to the people of the city in the centuries to come.

The gesture of acceptance.

It lasted only a moment before Preen rolled off the divan and sprang to her feet.

"You owe him something," she said emphatically. "Getting you away from Topkapi."

"I don't owe him anything, Preen." Yashim gave a curious half-smile. "I think I saved his life."

She paused on the tips of her toes and whirled a finger at him.

"For that, Yashim, I think he will never forgive you."

"You will do this, Yashim, because I order it done. I do not wish to repeat myself."

"I can talk to them. I think they are only afraid, Fevzi efendi."

"Give me the torch."

"Wait, efendi. They spoke Georgian."

But Fevzi efendi does not wait.

Later, when the fire is dying down, he seems to have forgotten all about Yashim's protest. He slaps him on the back.

"This is how it must be done," he says quietly. "Permanent."

In the palace, in Bezmialem's room, Ibou gave a small cry of disgust.

Ibou had always hated mice. Topkapi had been patrolled by a small army of cats, who came and went from the harem quarters at will, padding along ledges, creeping from rooftops and the branches of trees, invading the sanctuary night after night. They were tolerated as long as they kept quiet; only recalcitrant toms were dropped into sacks and drowned. The girls were amused by their feline affairs; some of them even put out milk.

But there were no cats at Besiktas. No cats, and now—mice.

With a moue of distaste, Ibou dropped the skirt onto the floor. "Tulip!"

He heard the eunuch padding along the corridor.

"Aga?"

"This!" He pointed to the offending mass. "A mouse nest"—he dropped his voice to a whisper—"under a skirt that *hasn't been moved for days*. It is too much."

Tulip peered apologetically at the little brown heap. Then his long black face turned green, and he looked up wide-eyed.

"No, aga, it is not a nest. I cannot touch it! Allah preserve us!"

"What is it?" Ibou felt the eunuch's horror invading his scalp: it made his hair crawl. "What is it, then?"

He peered more closely, then started back as if he had been stung.

"Bezmialem—where is she?"

Tulip shrank back. "Sh-she is sewing, Aga. With the other girls."

"Keep her there, and fetch the imam."

It was not, after all, a mouse's nest: not unless mice made up figurines of wax and hair, studded with little children's teeth.

64

On the slab, in the steam room, Yashim shuddered as the heat attacked his limbs; sweat poured from his skin.

All around him, men were being soaped and sluiced, scrubbed and pummeled by the bath attendants. He could hear the clack of sandals on the stone and the gurgle of running water in the traps. He pressed his fingers to his eyes.

For most of his adult life, Yashim had struggled to put the past behind him.

What is done is done, people said. They gelded him, but he did not die. He revived to become useful: it was another way to be a man. Day by day he lived and breathed and slept to live another day, without bitterness, without remorse. That was the lesson he had learned at the palace school: not how to wrestle, or to memorize the Koran, but how to shed his regrets, how to master his memories, so that he could hold himself together as a man.

He pressed his feet against the side of the slab.

He had made himself . . . quiet.

Fevzi Pasha had detected that. Fevzi Pasha had used it.

Yashim remembered one long vigil, on a warm night, when he had begun to talk to punctuate the silence. When Fevzi wanted to know a thing he was like a fishmonger filleting his fish with a narrow blade, probing and slicing, moving from one muscle to the next. Yashim had told Fevzi everything: all the memories he'd buried.

"I'll find out who did it, Yashim."

"I—I don't think I want to know."

"Ignorance keeps you weak." He sneers. *"You don't have a choice."*

He had told Husrev Pasha the truth. They had not parted as friends.

65

IT was ten years since he and Fevzi Ahmet went to Russia. Fevzi Ahmet Pasha—for Sultan Mahmut had promoted him for the event, to negotiate a treaty with the tsar. Mahmut trusted him. Fevzi Ahmet took Yashim, his still and silent companion, as a matter of course. "Keep your eyes open," he'd said.

The snow had been monstrous that winter, with ice in the Black Sea ports. He and Fevzi had traveled by sleigh, swaddled in furs like chicks in their nest. Yashim remembered the whip cracking in the icy air, the jangle of bells, hoarfrost splintered on the pines. Once a small black bird had dropped from the sky, frozen stiff. The driver had crossed himself, and Fevzi had laughed, shortly. "Omens are for Bulgars and old women."

Yashim found the whiteness implacable. It allowed them no footholds, shattered their sense of scale. Mile after mile after mile: the same trees, the same wooden villages, rest stops in silent inns, and fresh horses that always looked the same. Fevzi was infected with a sort of snow blindness, drugged, slow, prey to fits of giddiness. In Istanbul he had made one careful step after another, always up, always pleasing. In Saint Petersburg—white river, white streets, the buildings white and interminable against a pale sky—his judgment was devoured. He blundered like a man who had lost his horizons. Yashim stood by aghast, unable to understand the change in his mentor. He remembered Fevzi sweating as he matched the Russians glass for glass in the colorless alcohol their hosts pretended to be drinking.

He remembered the girl, too.

"I heard something. I thought—I was afraid you were in trouble."

"Trouble?" Fevzi is panting. He grins and brings his face close to Yashim's, and Yashim can smell his breath.

He steps back, embarrassed. Fevzi catches him by the arm.

"A peasant. She is very beautiful. Come."

Yashim sees only the suffering.

He stands, confused, and for a long moment Yashim cannot speak.

"Why?"

Fevzi's mood changes. "What do you know? She's mine."

He brings up his hand and places it over Yashim's face. "A man would understand," he says, and pushes him back.

Among the Russians, Fevzi Ahmet expanded like a great balloon. He was grand—his gestures wider than they ought to have been, his contempt for detail exaggerated. When the Russians showed him on a map what he was about to sign away, he merely shrugged, as if to say that Batoumi, with its strategic position on the Black Sea, was a bagatelle for a sultan as powerful as his own. Fevzi Ahmet gave Batoumi away because he did not want to seem niggardly in such company; because he had compromised himself. Had it not been for Yashim he might have given away more—and the sultan's affection would not have saved him from the silken bowstring.

They returned together, in the thaw: troika, droshky, and finally an imperial barge that knocked continuously against the broken ice. Whatever trust had existed between them, too, had broken up.

Yashim did not betray his mentor, who had given everything away. It was not the casual gift of Batoumi that broke his faith, but the proof of something he had suspected for a long time. Fevzi Ahmet employed cruelty without any end in view.

Yashim did not betray Fevzi Ahmet, because he was too proud—and too ashamed. Instead, he sought permission to leave the palace and live in the city: as he explained to the grand vizier of the day, his way was different from Fevzi Ahmet's. He knocked his forehead on the steps of the sultan's throne and said: "I have learned much, but I cannot be more than what I am. I can be a *lala*, my padishah, a guardian. I see things clearer from farther off."

Surprisingly, the sultan had agreed. He must have made his own assessment of Fevzi's diplomatic gifts, because he also moved Fevzi to military duties, which he carried out punctiliously, as far as Yashim heard. But Yashim never saw Fevzi again.

Yashim blinked. An attendant was standing in front of him with a jug and a sponge. He slid from the hot slab and followed the man to the sluice.

"OH, for goodness' sake," the valide snapped; but she shifted a little uneasily on the divan.

The egg rolled across the surface of the oil.

The soothsayer drew a sharp breath. "I see . . . blood."

"Your eggs are not fresh enough," the valide sniffed.

"But it is not your blood, valide efendi," the soothsayer replied, comfortably; then, in a rapid singsong voice, she began to recite:

"This is mine eye,
the eye of fate,
the eye of seeing.
See all, break our bread, show all, and the first shall be last.
Three of three is ninety-nine
And these are the names by which we ask our way."

She passed a hand across the plate and settled back on her heels.

"Well?"

"I cannot see until it is over." As if to prove her point, the egg yolk slipped to the edge of the plate. "Ah." She studied the plate for a few moments. "There is change, but nothing for you to fear. Someone else arranges it. Not a woman. Nor a man?"

"A eunuch, *évidemment*. Everything around me is in the hands of such people."

"You have not traveled recently, hanum?"

"*Tiens!* Your question is absurd."

"What is done and what is to come can be very close—especially when I make a reading of a long life, like yours."

"Tchah! So I am to start traveling, am I? At my age?"

"Perhaps *traveling* is the wrong word. A journey, yes."

"I think I can believe that," the valide replied, drily. "I am very old. You shake your head?"

"I do not see death, hanum efendi. But it is not clear. I see someone close to you, who needs you."

The valide arched her eyebrows slightly. "My grandson?"

"Perhaps. That is all I can see."

"Pouf! It is not much. I had expected—*eh bien*. Nothing more." She plucked the shawl that lay around her shoulders. "Now I am a little tired."

She closed her eyes. A greenish vein throbbed in one of her fingers.

An hour passed. When the valide awoke, she found Tülin sitting on a cushion at the foot of the divan.

"Have I slept long?"

Tülin smiled, and put aside her embroidery. "No, valide. But perhaps you are hungry?"

The valide shook her head, and mouthed a silent "No, no." She took a deep breath. "Tülin, get rid of that disgusting plate of egg."

"I have already done so, hanum."

"Ridiculous, all that prognostication. What would a chicken know about the future of a queen? If it were the other way around, I could understand."

Tülin laughed. "Nobody ventures to tell a chicken's fortune."

The valide champed her teeth. "Of course not. All chickens go the same way, into the pot. Who put such a silly idea into your head?"

IBOU hoped that she, of all people, would have an answer.

He did not expect the answer she gave. He expected sympathy and advice, not fear.

She shrank back: "Did you touch it?"

"I rolled it into a handkerchief," he said.

"I meant, did it touch your skin?"

He tried to think. He had not wanted to touch it; instinctively he had taken it up in his handkerchief, wadding the fine lawn cotton around the object so that he would not feel its ridges and bumps.

"I d-don't think so. No, I am sure."

She had been holding her breath; now she exhaled slowly. "And words? Did you use words?"

He shook his head. "I did not know what to say."

She frowned. "Let me look at your eyes."

She stared into them for a time, then slowly she raised her hands and outlined the form of his head and shoulders in the air.

"It is as I thought. You are cut off from God, Ibou."

"I pray to God!"

She cupped her chin in her hand, and said musingly, "Yes, you pray. But can he hear you, as you are? Do you have problems, Ibou? Pains, worries, that keep you awake at night?"

He stared at her, frightened a little. "Yes."

"I guessed it."

She turned and began to rummage in a little silk bag.

"What are you doing?"

"What I can." She took something from the bag and laid it beside her on the divan. Then she took his hands in hers. "Someone has put a spell on you, Ibou. That is why when you pray, he cannot hear you."

The aga's nostrils flared. "What can you do?"

"We must find you a guide, to take you back."

"You? C-Can you guide me back?"

She looked at the frightened man levelly. "The choice does not lie with me. I cannot choose to be your guide to the light, Ibou. It is you who must choose."

"Then—I choose you."

She shook her head. "How do we know that this is the choice of your heart? You have to draw your guide to you, Ibou. Listen. This is what you must do."

THE girl had shadows beneath her eyes, no doubt about it. Her face was drawn; at the rehearsal she had played so timidly that Donizetti had almost lost his patience.

"Violins! Violins!" He had tapped the lectern with his baton. "No, no. This is not what I want." He mimed a violinist crouched over her instrument, hands feebly shaking. "No. Andante! *Forza!* Take the lead!" He swiped down with his invisible bow and glared at the violins.

The violins had looked nervously at Elif. Her eyes were downcast: she had no intention of meeting Donizetti's.

"Elif," Tülin whispered. "Are you all right? You look—" She had been about to say the girl looked ill, but it was unmannerly to be too direct. Unwise, perhaps: people said it brought the eye. She bit her lip: the word hung in the air, unspoken.

Elif looked at her nervously. "What is it, Tülin? What can you see?"

"Are you eating well?"

"Eating?" Elif hesitated, as if she were thinking about this for the first time. "Yes—no. I'm frightened, Tülin."

Tülin smiled and patted the girl on her knee. "What of? Some girl, is it? I can speak to her." She said it with emphasis: she was older, the orchestra girls respected her.

Elif laced and unlaced her fingers on her lap. "It's not what you think. Oh!" She put a hand to her lips, where it fluttered against her mouth. "Something bad," she breathed at last.

Tülin glanced around. Donizetti, the Italian, had gone with a little bow and a wave, and now the girls of the orchestra were packing up their instruments. Bright-eyed, a little flushed, they chattered together in low voices. One girl was giggling with her hand over her mouth; another was prodding her neighbor with a fiddle bow. A blond Circassian bowed myopically over her score, holding her hair back above her ear with one hand, wondering where she had gone wrong before.

For the girls this was a moment of freedom, before the tall black eunuchs stepped in and respectfully shooed their pretty charges to their chores. Respectful but firm, especially with the younger girls of lower rank whose jobs kept them far away from the body of the sultan.

Tülin frowned at the frightened girl. Elif was a kalfa, but only to a little girl: a little girl of scant importance.

"If it's something bad you must tell me, Elif," she said quietly. "I think there are many things you don't understand. You're young." She put out a hand and eased a lock of the girl's jet-black hair over the tip of her ear. "When you talk about your troubles they always seem less. Don't bottle things up." She smiled brightly and held the girl's chin. "Look! Maybe it'll turn out to be nothing at all!"

She saw the struggle in Elif's eyes, the warring doubt and hope. The girl blinked fiercely: doubt won. "This is *very* bad," she said in a thin voice, close to tears.

Tülin considered. "Come, my little one. You can tell me, whatever it is. I am quite sure you have nothing to worry about."

THE man with the knife had walked a long way.

He joined a camel train, and walked with it in silence for three days. When the camels halted at a town, the man walked on.

THE shores of the Bosphorus flushed red, then yellow as the trees turned. Small fires burned in the fields. The season expired in a blaze of heat, an Indian summer. The fishermen predicted a cold winter: the sudden blaze, and the fish running deep.

Yashim found the valide in her apartments at Topkapi. She was propped up on pillows on the divan and eating an iced sherbet.

"It's cooler now, valide. You are comfortable?"

"I was raised in the Caribbean, Yashim. The heat does not affect me. I choose to sit in the Baghdad Kiosk because it's quiet."

Yashim cocked his ear, and heard nothing.

"Yes, yes, it's quiet enough now. They're all asleep, thank God," the valide said. "Just like country girls. Which, of course, they all were once upon a time. I suppose it's a sort of second childhood."

Yashim was baffled. "Asleep, valide? Who do you mean?"

The valide gave a little gesture of impatience. "Tut-tut-tut. Really, Yashim, the ladies, I tell you. My son's ladies. I do wish you would keep up."

"The late sultan's ladies came here?"

"From the old palace. The luckier ones got married off, of course. Our sultan sent all the hopeless cases on to me. I suppose it pleased the eunuchs. They lead lives of such *ennui* at Topkapi, with only me to talk about. But now they have a flock of women to fuss over, and they are happy. As for the ladies, well. It upsets me, I admit. They are so very ingratiating. And they are all so old! Perfect frights, some of them."

"How many, hanum?"

The valide waved a jeweled hand. "I haven't counted, Yashim. I'm not a housekeeper. Dozens, I should say. Terribly aged. Some of them"—she lowered her voice, while at the same time speaking more loudly than before—"quite feebleminded now, I'm sorry to say."

"It must have come as a dreadful shock to them," Yashim ventured.

"To them, Yashim? Why? Mahmut was my son."

"Of course, valide. I only meant—"

"Marzipan, for instance. She was such a skinny, shy little thing—that's why I gave her the name." Yashim nodded: all the girls got new names when they came to the harem. Often they were mildly ironic. "Yesterday, I saw a fat, frumpy old woman sitting with her knees this far apart, smiling like an idiot. Marzipan. I couldn't believe it. Why they think to surround me with these dreadful old people, Yashim, I just can't imagine."

She glanced at him, a little slyly, he thought. He opened his mouth to speak, then closed it again. The valide had not aged like other women. She was still slender, and her face preserved in outline the beauty that had carried her into a sultan's arms. But the valide was difficult about flattery: you had to be careful.

"Age is a terrible thing, Yashim," she added, a little sadly.

He took her hand. He should have spoken, after all. Somehow the arrival of these women had disturbed the valide more than she let on; more, perhaps, than the death of her son. For years now she had been alone in the palace with her memories and dreams; and there was a certain hauteur in her loneliness, in the knowledge that Topkapi was hers. Now that she shared it with the superannuated baggage of the harem, that grandeur had dissipated a little.

He glanced about the room. The mirror that had always hung at the side of the divan had been replaced by a framed inscription.

"You, valide, are as beautiful as you ever were."

"I don't enjoy a mirror anymore," she said unnervingly. Yashim felt his cheeks redden. "I'd rather look at young people now. That's why I have my Tülin."

Tülin: it meant "poppy." "Tülin?"

"My handmaiden, Yashim. I found her the name. I think it's rather sweet."

"I hope she's as sweet as her name, valide."

"I think I may say that I am something of a judge of character. Tülin appears to me . . . almost perfect."

"Almost, hanum?"

"*Tiens*, Yashim. Only God can pronounce any woman perfect, *absolument*. And then only at the hour of her death."

Yashim gave a sigh, and smiled. The valide was always something of a coquette.

"A book for you, Yashim. Perhaps it will amuse you—I found it ridiculous. It is written by"—she glanced at the cover—"Théophile Gautier."

71

YASHIM clapped his book shut with an exclamation of surprise. "*Everything that is useful*," Gautier had written, "*is ugly.*"

Yashim contemplated the nutcracker in his hand, with its chased brass handles and polished iron jaws. He let his eyes wander around the apartment, from the shelf beside the divan, with its collection of porcelain and books, to the stack of crocks and pans in the far corner where he cooked. What sad world did this Gautier inhabit, that everything useful could be described as ugly? It was a fault of the Franks to make their slightest opinions sound like revealed laws, of course.

At his thigh were a marble mortar and the knife with *Ammar made me* inscribed on the Damascus blade. These useful things, Yashim felt, were also beautiful. With half-closed eyes he thought about Istanbul—its lovely minarets for calling the people to prayer, the scalloped and fluted fountains, which relieved the people's thirst. He considered the slender caïques, which bustled people across the water in all directions, and cracked another walnut, smiling as his thoughts turned to the sultan's palace.

The loveliest women that the empire could provide—would Gautier call them useless, then? Yashim knew the harem as a school, an arena for ambition, a human factory geared to the production of royal heirs. Many a pasha had blessed the Circassian girls for drawing a headstrong sultan away from delicate affairs of state and into their beds. The mere effort of observing the intricate etiquette of the harem quarters was enough to keep a sultan busy.

Gautier, he felt, had got it the wrong way around.

He laid the book on the divan, careful not to let his oily fingers stain the green leather binding with walnut juice.

Yashim took the mortar to his kitchen, set it on the bench, and put a small open pan on the coals. He began to pound the walnuts with a stone pestle. When the pan was hot he threw in a scattering of cumin seeds. He rattled the pan on the coals and poured the seeds into a black iron grinder. He turned the handle and ground the cumin over the walnuts. He added a pinch of *kirmizi biber*, which he had made in the autumn. He sprinkled the end of a dry loaf with water, then carried on pounding the walnuts. Eventually he squeezed the bread dry and crumbled it into the mortar between his fingers, along with a generous dollop of pomegranate molasses.

When the *muhammara* was finely pounded, he stirred a thread of olive oil into the mix. He tasted the puree, added a pinch of salt and a twist of pepper, and poured it into a bowl, which he covered with a plate and set to one side.

For the next hour he worked at his remaining meze: a light salad of beans and anchovies mixed with slices of red onion and black olives, and another made with grated beetroot and yogurt. Finally, he made soup with leeks and dill.

He was almost done when there was a knock on the door. A *chaush* in palace uniform stood at the top of the stairs, carrying an invitation on vermilion paper.

The chief black eunuch requested Yashim's presence at the Besiktas palace that afternoon.

Yashim bowed, placed a hand to his chest, and murmured: "I shall attend, inshallah."

YASHIM had not seen the Kislar aga for several months, and he was shocked by the change in his appearance. His blue-black skin had lost its sheen, and he looked tired and thinner than he had seemed in the summer; but it was his manner that most surprised Yashim.

He had developed a stammer.

"Ya-Ya-Ya-Yashim!" He clapped his skinny brown hands together. "I just knew you would come!"

Yashim bowed. "You sent for me, Ibou."

"Of course. Do sit d-d-down. Have a"—his head jerked, and he blinked—"a sweetmeat?"

He gestured to a tray, and then popped a small green *lokum* into his mouth.

Yashim settled on the divan. "How are the girls? Settling now, I imagine."

The Kislar aga passed a hand over his face and shuddered. "They're like Ta-Ta-Tatars."

Yashim pursed his lips. He thought of the Kislar agas he had known, men of terrifying girth and power, ruling the harem like cruel tyrants. At least, he had often thought them cruel: perhaps they exercised proper discipline. Perhaps that was necessary.

The Kislar aga twisted his long fingers. "They are hard to manage. Impudent and w-w-worse. They don't listen. But that's only p-p-part of it, Yashim. Some of them are a bit wild, but I could hope to settle them eventually. It's the atmosphere. The strain."

Yashim spread his hands. "A young sultan, new girls. It goes to their heads."

Ibou shook his head. "It's not that. It's as if people were a-a-a—" He blinked, jerked his chin. "Afraid."

"Afraid? Afraid of what?"

The black man hung his head. "Magic. Evil eye."

He described the little homunculus he had found, studded with a child's teeth. His own teeth chattered as he spoke. "And P-P-Pembe, Yashim. With the child that did not survive. She said it was the l-l-l-lady Ta-Ta-Ta-Ta—"

"Talfa? Bah!" Yashim dismissed the story with an angry wave. "Potions and curses, Ibou." But he could see the trouble in Ibou's eyes. "The sultan and his girls are very young. And Bezmialem . . . perhaps . . ."

"Of course." Ibou gave an angry shrug. "She is mother to the sultan. That far, she is a valide. But she is not mother to the harem."

"Talfa, then, herself? Have you talked to her?"

Ibou shook his head. "Talfa can't organize everything. She only returned to the harem after her husband's death. She's still making friends."

"Making friends?"

"I saw you talking to Talfa, Yashim."

"She wondered why I didn't live at the palace."

Ibou gave him a look of surprise—eagerness, almost. "But then perhaps, my friend—"

Yashim raised both hands. "I explained to her, Ibou, that the sultan wants me elsewhere."

"The valide at Topkapi? We could a-a-ask her to come."

It was Yashim's turn to look surprised. "She's quite frail."

The Kislar aga held up his hands, palms upward. "She has the experience, Yashim—and all the girls are terrified of her." He gave a guilty smile. "I'm terrified of her."

Yashim saw no reason to dispute the point. He said: "At her age, to move . . ."

But Ibou was shaking his head. Having taken up the thought, he seemed reluctant to let it drop. "The valide will be very happy," he insisted. "And she has a handmaiden who is very good, very caring."

Yashim raised an eyebrow. The valide had run through more hand-maidens than Selim the Grim had had viziers; she changed them like gloves. He remembered the last one, an able Circassian with a pleasant, open face. The valide had boxed her ears and sent her to the imperial laundry because, she said, her ankles were too thick.

"I've seen her," he agreed. "The flautist."

"Tülin." The Kislar aga nodded. "Very popular girl, actually. She helps to carry the ladies' orchestra—the valide allows her over to rehearse on Thursdays. She's a little older than most of the girls."

"I suppose that's an advantage."

"That's why I bought her. The valide eats the younger ones for break-fast."

Ibou's stammer seemed to have improved, Yashim noticed. "You've thought this out already, haven't you?"

The Kislar aga blinked again. "C-c-c-c-certainly not. I wanted your advice, th-th-that's all."

Yashim stared at his feet. "I'd miss her, at Topkapi."

The Kislar aga laid a hand tenderly on Yashim's knee. "We'll all miss her one day, Yashim. And you more than a-a-anyone, I'm sure." He smiled, and patted his knee. "So you will ask her?"

"Ask her?"

"Why, the valide! Ask her to come to Besiktas, Yashim. The harem needs a mother. As for Talfa—" The Kislar aga cocked his head. "What's that?"

They heard the sound of running feet outside in the corridor, and the door was flung back to admit a eunuch, who immediately hurled himself to his knees.

"Aga!" He was deathly pale. His eyes rolled in his head. Through chattering teeth he cried out: "I think she is dying! Everywhere is blood, aga. Come!"

73

THE Kislar aga rolled from the divan and clutched the babbling eunuch by the shoulder.

"Who is dying? Show me."

Yashim followed. The fluttering eunuch ran half stooped with outstretched arms along the corridor, like a startled hen. Girls clutched their hands to their breasts and pressed themselves to the wall, their mouths ovals of surprise.

At the foot of the stairs the eunuch seemed to droop, clinging to the newel post for support.

"Up there, aga! The dormitory . . ."

The aga brushed past him, and they mounted the stairs two at a time. At the top the aga whirled down a corridor. He flung a door back with a blow from his open hand and stood there, panting, turning his head from side to side.

A girl sprang from the side of the bed with a scream of fright, her hands to her ears. Ibou strode forward and grabbed her wrist; the girl winced and bent at the waist, refusing to lower her hands.

"What are you doing?" he hissed.

Yashim saw it all like a tableau from the doorway: the girl squealing, Ibou gripping her wrist in his long hand, his eyes swiveling to the bed under the window, and the bed itself, with a white satin quilt embroidered minutely with multicolored flowers.

Beneath the quilt, black hair trailing wide across the pillows, lay another girl, staring straight at Yashim. Her eyes glittered like black pearls.

As Yashim stepped forward into the room, the hairs prickling on the back of his neck, the girl in the bed moved very slightly: her jaw sagged.

"He said—blood!" Ibou shook the girl again. "Where is this blood!"

The eyes of the girl on the bed did not follow Yashim.

"She's dead," he said quietly.

Ibou turned his head and his eyes grew wide as they moved from the girl's face to the flowered quilt draped across her body.

In the center of the bed, between the shape of the girl's thighs, a new flower was blooming on the patterned quilt, growing larger and brighter than all the rest.

THE Kislar aga twitched the quilt back.

Yashim took one look and turned his head away.

The aga's jaw dropped. His grip on the girl relaxed. She wrenched herself free and blundered to the door.

Yashim made no effort to stop her.

The girl on the bed lay naked from the waist down, her legs outspread above a dark stain between her thighs. Deep welts were scored across the skin of her belly, as though she had been clawed by a great cat; fresh blood still oozed from the livid marks.

Ibou put his hand to his mouth.

"Go, Ibou. This is what you must do. Get green tea and ginger, straightaway." Yashim laid a hand on the aga's arm. "Have it sent to this room. Immediately, do you understand?"

"She's dead."

"Yes, she's dead," Yashim agreed. "The tea is for me."

He saw Ibou's color beginning to return.

"Then go and find the girl. What's her name?"

"I—I don't know." The aga yawned suddenly, flashing his gold teeth. "Her name is Melda."

"Find Melda." Yashim spoke slowly, with emphasis. "Find her, and take her to your room. When you are there, wait for me."

Yashim steered the aga toward the door. All the man's strength seemed to have drained away: he moved without protest, his head bobbing.

"Tea, Ibou. Then find Melda. I'll join you in your room."

With the aga gone, Yashim closed the door and rubbed his hands over his face.

He had no expectation of recognizing the dead girl. He knew a few of the harem girls by sight, but for the most part they were anonymous, like beautiful cattle. Naked, unadorned, only the manner of her death distinguished her from a hundred others behind these walls. He wondered what the aga could tell him; what Melda knew.

He spent some time examining the welts on her belly. He examined her hands. There were faint traces of blood on her thighs, and her skin had already begun to cool when he turned her carefully onto her side. There was a deep pool of blood on the sheet beneath her.

He plucked at the sheet. When it did not give way he looked and saw that it was the thin mattress, and the sheet had gone.

He found the sheet easily, under the bed. It was screwed into a loose ball and it was soaked in blood.

75

MELDA collapsed onto the divan, weeping.

She was dressed in the usual harem motley, a jumble of tailored and traditional costume bought in Paris and the Grand Bazaar, Turkish slippers peeping out from beneath French petticoats, a slashed and striped velvet jacket over a bodice of ruched silk, a corded girdle and a muslin shawl.

Yashim drew up a stool and perched on it, one leg drawn up, wrists dangling.

"Melda, my name is Yashim. I want to talk about what happened to Elif."

The girl covered her face with her hands.

"She was ill, Melda, wasn't she? Something inside, that was hurting her very badly. She should have seen a doctor." He frowned. "You know what a doctor is, Melda?"

Melda's shoulders heaved. Very gently, Yashim took her wrists and lowered her hands.

"Melda?"

She turned her face away.

"Tell me," Yashim urged. "Tell me what happened to Elif."

She shook her head convulsively.

"I—have—seen—the engine," she gasped.

"The engine?"

She dragged her hands free and clapped them over her ears, rocking to and fro.

"I don't understand, Melda."

Her eyes grew very wide, and she moved her hands to cover her mouth. Outside, the muezzin was calling the faithful to Friday prayers.

"How could you understand?" she burst out. "You—did you step out from a rock, or drop from a stork's beak? Did I grow like an apple on a tree? No!" Bright spots had appeared on her cheeks, and her hands were clenched. Gone was the court lisp, the fluting voice, the trembling eyelash. Melda spoke in the stony voice of the mountains where she was raised; and she evoked an ancient bitterness, as old as the pagan gods of Circassia. "Men plant children in our bellies, and we bear them until we die."

Yashim rocked slowly back.

Melda turned her eyes on him and then, like a snake, she drew back her head and spat.

"Elif was pregnant."

Yashim remained motionless, gazing at the girl's face. "The sultan chose her?"

The Kislar aga had said nothing about that, Yashim thought. Everything about a girl was carefully considered before she was promoted to *gözde*: her looks, her bearing, her conduct. To be selected to share the sultan's bed was a very high honor: from it, with ordinary luck, flowed all the rewards the sultan could bestow upon a woman—rank, and fortune, and power within these four walls.

"The sultan?" Her lips trembled. "How? How, efendi, could that be?"

She covered her face with her hands and began to sob.

Yashim murmured a few words: he hardly knew what to say. He stood up and went to find the Kislar aga.

76

"TELL me—" He hesitated. "Was Elif a *gözde?*"

The aga looked puzzled. "A *gözde?* Certainly not. Elif was a musician, Yashim. She played in the ladies' orchestra, and she and Melda were also kalfas. They look after a little girl."

"And before she came here? Three, four months ago, when Abdülmecid was still a prince?"

Ibou shrugged. "I don't understand your questions, Yashim."

"I want to know when Elif met the sultan. Perhaps while he was still crown prince?"

"She didn't meet him. Not face-to-face, not to be introduced. The only time she's seen Abdülmecid is at our concerts. We do not have the sultan roaming the corridors, meeting ladies."

"Ibou," Yashim said gently. "It seems that Elif was pregnant."

The silence between them prickled like toasted spice.

"Do you know what you are saying?" Ibou whispered. His face was waxy with—what? Astonishment? Fear?

"Elif died from bleeding," Yashim said. "What you saw, those marks, were made by her own nails. She was clawing at her own flesh." He paused. "What you haven't seen is the sheet under the bed. It's soaked in blood. If Melda is right, I would guess that Elif miscarried."

The aga collected himself. "No. Pembe was the sultan's *gözde* before he became sultan—with the unfortunate results you know about. Since then, he has taken only two other women. Leyla and Demet, both of them selected by—b-b-by me, and B-Bezmialem. To suggest that the sultan would take another woman into his bed, without protocol, is absurd. He is ruled by the traditions of the house of Osman. And Demet and Leyla would prevent it, anyway."

"To the death?"

Ibou frowned. "They would only have to speak to me, Yashim. There would be no need to talk of death."

Yashim sighed. The legitimate *gözde* would hardly stand idly by while the sultan dallied with another girl.

"This is not a house in the city, Yashim. The sultan never goes alone. Every minute of the day, every hour of the night, he is watched and cared for."

"Was Elif watched every minute of the day? At night?"

"She is with the others, Yashim. You now how it is."

"But if Elif was pregnant, and she did not sleep with the sultan . . ."

Ibou's face clouded. "Impossible."

If what Yashim implied was true, it was not just about one girl, or the lapse of a single aga. This was a taint that would spread like the blood across the quilt, but more fatal, more insidious, than either of them could imagine.

"Could she—have slept with another man?"

The aga slowly turned his head. His lips peeled back. "Is this what the girl Melda says? What to do, Yashim efendi? I cannot let her say such a thing."

Yashim had known agas who would have strangled a girl with their bare hands without hesitation or remorse; but not Ibou.

"We need to get Melda away," he said. "Somewhere she can feel safe."

MELDA startled at the water. Through the black gauze of her burka the Bosphorus looked dull and menacing, speckled with white.

Perhaps the water was to be her grave.

She entertained few illusions. The *lala* who had asked her questions had said they were going somewhere safe. She had read the expression in his eyes and thought that it could have been reassurance: but then she was not sure what reassurance looked like anymore, or how to tell the real from the false.

What had happened to Elif was real. Evidently so: the blood was real blood, the agony unfeigned. And then Elif was dead.

Her secret killed her.

And she, Melda, shared the secret.

The *lala* gestured for her to seat herself. When he smiled, did he smile with his eyes, or only move the muscles around his mouth? It was hard to tell from behind the mask she wore.

The engine was terrible enough. Perhaps there were other engines that he had prepared. Other systems.

The caïque shot forward, over the gray water.

78

HYACINTH padded softly across the polished stones, jangling his keys. Today he had started to wear his woolen slippers; he felt the cold. The valide had ordered the fires made up, and when he was called from his own snug cubicle he startled at the wind that blew down the Golden Road.

"Evet, evet," Hyacinth grumbled as he approached the little door.

Yashim, with a woman.

"Well, well," he said, blinking up at them both. "Another mouth to feed?"

Yashim said quietly: "Another mouth, Hyacinth, if you want to put it like that."

The woman stepped into the vestibule. The wind caught at her veil and she raised it with gloved hands, revealing a face Hyacinth could not recall.

The corners of his mouth turned down. "Coming, going, there's nothing regular anymore, is there?" He peered at Melda more closely. "I don't know you."

She said nothing, so he added: "You don't look well. Pretty and young, not like the rest of them here, perhaps. But not very well."

"Melda needs rest, Hyacinth."

"What does the valide say, Yashim efendi?"

"You needn't trouble the valide, Hyacinth," Yashim said firmly. "I'll look in on her now. Anyway, it's just for a short while."

"I'll put her in the old dormitory. Light the fire." He took the girl by the arm. She flinched, but either he didn't notice or he chose to ignore it. "Melda, is it? You'll be all right. Old Hyacinth will see to that."

He hefted the keys in his other hand. Yashim put his hand to his chest, and bowed.

Dogs barked and pulled on their chains as the man approached the farm.

He fingered the knife in his satchel. He was very tired and had gone two days without food.

"I am very strong," he said. "I can work."

The farmer did not understand his words, but the man showed his biceps and he nodded. He was not inhospitable.

The man worked for him for two weeks. In return he received food and a place to rest.

One morning, he was gone.

"So my grandson needs me after all." The valide plucked at an invisible thread on her shawl. "I blame myself."

"Valide?"

"My son preferred fat girls, Yashim. Imagined they lacked energy. So I picked out Bezmialem. A foolish prejudice of mine." Her silver bangles tinkled on her arm. "I thought Bezmialem was stronger than she turned out to be. More intelligent."

Yashim nodded in sympathy.

"She is merely thin, *au fond.*" The valide gave an expressive little shrug, as if to dismiss the whole affair. "One learns, Yashim. The new palace at Besiktas was, of course, Mahmut's mistake," she added. "I told him so."

"You will find it—strange," Yashim suggested.

"I am aware of that. Perhaps I should have gone before, but I am a stubborn woman."

Yashim tried to imagine the valide at Besiktas, with its gauzy windows and chandeliers, its stiff upholstered chairs and yards and yards of open, empty space.

"I shall rely on you," the valide continued. "And Tülin knows Besiktas quite well. *À cause de sa flute.*"

"You're fond of her, valide."

"Fortunately for you, she can't read French." The valide wagged her finger. "Tülin plays the flute with the other girls. The sultan's orchestra. Very pretty. And it keeps them occupied. Here at Topkapi she sees an old woman and some superstitious eunuchs. I *am* thinking of her interests, as it happens. I do not wish her to be too much alone," she added. "Isolation is dangerous in the harem, Yashim. A girl must have friends."

Yashim smiled. "You told me once that a girl needs enemies."

The valide shrugged. "Better an enemy than no one at all. To be regarded, that's something. But to be truly alone—in here, at least—it's a kind of death."

"When you first came here, hanum, you must have been isolated."

"I, Yashim? What a ridiculous idea." Unconsciously she raised a hand to her hair. "The place was positively crowded, and I was a French girl, was I not? *Espèce de merveille!* And on the way—well, I had learned more than most of the Circassians. More Turkish, certainly."

"I shall leave in two weeks, inshallah. I will ask Tülin to find out which day would be propitious." She caught his glance, and raised an eyebrow. "Not for my own sake, Yashim. I do it for the girls."

"It may be just as well, hanum. There have been—well, some disturbing incidents in the harem."

"Indeed. The Kislar aga has told me so."

Yashim looked surprised. "He has spoken to you—about Elif?"

The valide put her fingers to her temples. "Elif, Fatima, Begum," she intoned wearily. "Really, Yashim."

"But Elif—" Yashim looked doubtful. "Melda. He told you about Melda?"

The valide frowned. "My son, the sultan, does what he likes."

"Hanum?" Yashim shifted uneasily on the edge of the divan: it seemed to him that the valide's mind was drifting toward the past.

"He does exactly what he likes." The valide raised her chin and looked down her beautiful cheekbones. "He moves his court into that wretched palace of his. Everything French, he says." Yashim nodded slowly, unable to halt the confusion in the valide's words. She looked at him severely. "I don't want people thinking I am to blame. *His* father never proposed such an absurd thing, wanted us to be comfortable. I had no intention of moving myself, *naturellement*. I am perfectly comfortable where I am."

She spoke in clipped tones, not moving her head. When she had finished, she held the pose for a few seconds longer, and blinked rapidly, as though she had something in her eye.

"You have much to do, valide," Yashim said quietly.

The valide turned to Yashim with the smile that had ravished a sultan. "You are very thoughtful, Yashim. I count you among my oldest and dearest friends. Thank you so much for coming."

She held out her hand, tilted to one side, like a European.

Yashim stooped, and took it in his: her hand was very small, and mottled, and he felt the fragile bones beneath her skin where he raised it to his lips.

81

AT the door he found Hyacinth. The old man looked gray.

"Is it true?"

"True?" Yashim echoed.

"Do you, too, think I am some kind of fool?" Hyacinth whispered with sudden fierceness. "That I sleep and eat and smile like a child?"

His long fingers clamped around Yashim's arm. His hold was strong, and Yashim checked himself.

"It's a suggestion, that she should go to Besiktas. I'm sorry," he added. He had not thought of Hyacinth.

The old eunuch nodded, turning his head from side to side; his nostrils flared. "It was in the air, Yashim efendi." He spread the fingers of one hand in Yashim's face. "I felt it, here. The harem, I breathe. You understand? I watch its breath like a mother watches her child. Every breath. Every word. Each tiny glance. When they took the women—" His fingers tightened into a ball. "And now she goes."

His eyes glittered, and his grip tightened on Yashim's arm. "And will I go, or stay?"

Yashim bit his lip. The valide had spoken of her body slave, the girl— Tülin. "I don't know, Hyacinth. I'm sorry. I wish I knew."

"Ah." Hyacinth let out a ragged sigh and closed his eyes. Without another word he released Yashim's arm and turned, shaking his head. Yashim watched him shuffle away along the corridor, his slippers slapping on the polished cobbles.

82

YASHIM followed the street that dropped from Ayasofya mosque to the shore of the Golden Horn. Beyond the mosque of the valide, past the entrance to the spice bazaar, the ancient walls disappeared into a warren of haphazard wharves and boatyards that had grown up around them after many centuries of peace. Here and there one could still glimpse a section of banded brick and stone, or crenellations that crumbled above a riot of roofs and makeshift staircases, as the old defenses were gradually absorbed into the fabric of the city. Beyond the walls, the water stirred listlessly against the muddy banks.

At the Prison Gate Yashim found a caïque and crossed the Horn. The new bridge was almost complete. In summer they had cut down the great plane tree that had given the people shade, because it stood in the way of the bridge.

Without its spreading branches to protect him, the wind was keener; the crossing chilled him. At the foot of the Galata steps he stopped for coffee, and sat cross-legged with his back to the brazier, looking out across the water. The weather had finally turned. A late Indian summer had ebbed away; the storks had flown south and already white crests ruffled the Bosphorus, whipped up by a wind that blew across the Black Sea from the steppes of Central Asia.

The Turks had come from the same place, centuries ago. Nomads, shepherds, horsemen: tent-dwelling tribesmen who worshipped stones and rivers, and met beneath the spreading branches of a tree to administer justice and settle their affairs. It would have been a tree, Yashim thought, much like the great plane that had drooped its branches over the Golden Horn, festooned with rags and prayers.

He half closed his eyes. That, of course, had been the purpose of the tree: in the minds of the people it was a link between heaven and earth, a conduit between earthly troubles and heavenly justice. It was not so much a belief as an instinct: justice belonged to the sky and the open air. Justice and fairness flourished in the open, from the *kadi*, who gave his verdict in an open court, to the Turkish tribal chief, who spoke to his people sitting around the trunk of a tree.

He stared, frowning, into his coffee. How times had changed! The spreading tree had been exchanged for the palace, and its harem, where everything was effectively invisible. Nobody knew, and nobody cared, who lived there, or how they lived—or died. In a world closed and enveloped in secrecy, justice withered like a pale shoot deprived of the sun.

Yashim slapped some silver on the table and strode from the café, his cloak billowing behind him; outside he turned his back on the water and began to mount the steps two by two, dodging the porters bent double under their enormous loads, the musical instrument sellers, the sherbet vendors, and the little Jewish boys who sold paper on every landing. All Pera seemed to teem on the steps, veiled women, priests in black, foreign sailors, businessmen in frock coats and fezzes, builders in turbans. Yashim kept his head down and moved fast, not drawing breath until he reached the rusted iron gates of the Polish residency.

Dry leaves swirled around his feet as he crossed the yard. He climbed the steps and let himself into the dim hall. From overhead he heard the distant sound of a fiddle. Picking his way carefully through the gloom he reached the stairs, where the treads creaked as he mounted toward the light that streamed through the landing window.

He paused there for a moment, leaning his forehead against the glass. Outside, Marta was on the grass, pegging clothes on a line. Farther off, beyond the yellowing leaves, Yashim could make out the cobbled coach yard where the widow Baxi still lived with her two children—just another of the myriad tiny and traditional arrangements that made up the city's shape and population. He could even see the Baxi boy outside, under the pump, dangling a piece of string for a cat.

At the top of the stairs he went in, silently, and settled into a chair, relishing as ever the familiarity of these strange things: an armchair, a mantelpiece, a slender bottle of something pale and unlabeled on a mahogany side table.

Yashim lay back and listened to the notes that flowed from Palewski's violin.

When the last notes had died away, Palewski laid the fiddle on the side table. "Chopin," he said. "The Prelude in A Major."

"It's very beautiful."

"It's very short."

He opened a cupboard. "*Palinka*. Hungarian schnapps. Keeps out the cold."

"I'm quite happy with this fire," Yashim said, stretching out his hands.

"Marta had it swept," Palewski said. He poured the plum brandy into two glasses and set one down beside Yashim. "In case you change your mind," he added. "What we really want here is a stove, of course. Can't think why we didn't put one in while we still had the money."

Yashim knew that Palewski was referring to ancient history: it was many decades since any Polish ambassador had had money.

Palewski rubbed his hands. "Mediterranean people are like crickets," he said. "You never believe it'll get really cold. Your fireplaces—they'd disgrace a theater set. Flimsy, far too small. Not proper heating. And yet it snows almost every year."

"And every year," Yashim said, smiling, "you say the same thing."

"If you go on saying and believing the same things for long enough, the world will eventually come around." Palewski descended into the neighboring armchair and set his glass on his knee. "On the other hand, I have some curious news."

Yashim picked up the glass Palewski had set beside him. "News?"

"What I hear—" Palewski paused. "I hear that the admiral Fevzi Pasha has disappeared."

THE valide watched the leaves settle in the court. Now and then a halberdier, head lowered and tresses fanning out across his cheeks, entered the valide's apartment to tend the fire. It burned on a hearth beneath a high canopy that curved like folds of heavy linen; it emitted little heat. Sometimes the valide watched the soldier crossing the court, his steps heavy and cautious.

"Why doesn't someone come to sweep the leaves away?" she murmured. "That is how it always was, before."

Tülin bowed her head over her embroidery and sighed. "You are right, my valide. Of course they should sweep. Shall I send to the guardroom?"

The valide was silent for a long time, as if she were thinking of something else. But when she spoke it was to say: "No, there's no need, I suppose. They are letting it all wind down. And soon we shall be gone, too."

Tülin glanced up. "Hanum?"

"I told you, dear. The Kislar aga thinks I am needed at Besiktas."

Tülin nodded vaguely. The valide had not, in fact, told her anything; but Hyacinth had.

"The girls are getting rather out of hand. The Kislar aga is a pantaloon."

"And you are the valide still, hanum," Tülin said simply.

The valide smiled. "Quite right. I don't really wish to go, but all these dreadful old women . . . And the change would suit you, too." She shivered. "Do you read French?"

"I regret not, valide."

"No, no, of course you don't. I've asked you that before. You're a good girl, but I think you were not well brought up."

Tülin's needle paused over a stitch. "I'm afraid you must be right, valide. I can only make chocolate."

"Astonishing." The valide folded her cold fingers together, business-like. "*That* you didn't learn in Circassia."

Tülin shook her head gently, and smiled. "I think it—it just came to me, valide."

The valide gave a little grunt. "I'd like a glass of water." She closed her eyes.

Tülin looked up. The cold made her mistress tired. She laid her sewing aside and quietly rearranged the pelisse. On her narrow feet the valide was wearing woolen boots.

Tülin gingerly poked the fire, so that a flame shot up. Then she opened a little tin and took out a pinch of incense, and tossed it over the logs.

Yashim's *palinka* splashed in the glass.

"Fevzi Pasha has disappeared? How do you know?"

Palewski frowned. "I'm not entirely without resources, Yashim," he said, stiffly. "Even I have my networks."

"I only meant—" He faltered. "What does it mean, he's disappeared?"

His friend hunched forward in his chair, wrapping his hands around his glass. "I'm not absolutely sure, Yashim. According to the monsignor, the Kapudan pasha was supposed to tour the islands. They never saw him, or the fleet."

Yashim relaxed back into his armchair. "That's not such a surprise. We were all supposed to think he'd taken the fleet to the islands, but in reality he was under secret orders to go south."

"You know that?"

"I'm not entirely without resources. I have my networks." He smiled. "Husrev Pasha told me as much."

"Did he say, Yashim, that the fleet is in port, at Alexandria?"

"*Off* Alexandria," Yashim corrected him. "It's a show of force."

"That's not how it was described to me this morning."

"I'm not sure I understand."

"Who does? Your Kapudan pasha, Yashim, seems to have handed the Ottoman navy over to the Egyptians."

"I don't believe it."

Palewski shrugged. "As you like. You may be right. Even Jesuits are fallible, after all."

BUT Palewski's Jesuits, however fallible, proved right about Fevzi Pasha.

At nightfall an Ottoman cutter swept in beneath Seraglio Point to deliver a trembling lieutenant at the gates of the grand vizier's offices.

"I have urgent intelligence for the grand vizier!" he cried. "I have news of the fleet!"

The old vizier listened impassively as the lieutenant outlined the series of events, but his face grew pale.

"He took the fleet into port?"

"Yes, my pasha. We were out on patrol, so we received no orders. He sailed into Alexandria, and there was nothing. No firing."

Husrev Pasha wiped a hand across his face. "Your actions will not be forgotten, young man. You have a report in writing?"

The lieutenant produced his report, and Husrev laid it on the pile beside him.

"Tell me, lieutenant, how many men have you aboard your ship?"

"Fifteen, my pasha."

"Good men? Loyal?"

"They strained every nerve to reach Istanbul. Unswerving, my pasha, in their devotion to the sultan's service."

"Your words gladden my heart. They know, then, what you have just told me?"

The lieutenant bowed. "They witnessed it. They were as stupefied as I was."

"Of course." Husrev's fingers moved out for the bell. Reluctantly.

"Shall I bring the ship in now, my pasha?"

The pasha nodded thoughtfully. "Your cutter has not docked?"

"I've held her in the channel, awaiting your orders."

Husrev's fingers relaxed. "Rejoin your men. Isn't there some flag to run up the mast when you have pestilence aboard?"

"Pestilence, my pasha?"

Husrev waved a hand. "Typhoid. The plague. A yellow flag? I've seen it."

"The yellow flag is used for ships in quarantine, my pasha."

"That's it. Take your cutter, anchor in the Marmara roads, and fly that flag. Don't let a soul on or off your ship. I'll see that you get supplied. And rewarded, too."

Light broke on the young lieutenant's face. "We are loyal men."

"Your loyalty is not questioned. Do exactly what I have said."

When the young lieutenant—what was his name?—had gone, the grand vizier sat for a few minutes rubbing his eyes and pondering the news he had just heard.

He rang a bell.

"Send to the palace at Besiktas. Inform the sultan—wake him, if necessary—that the grand vizier has summoned the divan. A matter of urgency. His presence would be—advisable."

Years ago—in another century, another life—Husrev Pasha had spent a summer with his uncle, driving a mule train across the Balkans. The tracks were bad, often blocked by falls of stone and scree, so that young Husrev had been sure they would have to turn back. His uncle, though, had simply stamped up to the rockfalls and let his eyes wander over the mountainside, probing the ground with his stick. "The road is blocked? Then we must turn the blockage into our road," he used to say. Eventually he would wave his nephew to come on with the lead mule.

That was how Husrev came to Sarajevo, and was recruited into the army.

Now, as he sat contemplating this new obstacle in his way, he leaned over and cracked his huge knuckles, one after another, holding his hands close to his belly.

The fleet was gone. Out of a clear blue sky, if the lieutenant was to be believed, Fevzi Pasha had simply turned over his command to the Egyptians.

And I am an old Bosniac who fears the sea.

Husrev's position—perhaps his very life—hung in the balance. It counted for nothing that the decision to deploy the fleet had been taken by the late sultan. Fevzi's defection was a blow to the empire's pride, not to mention the public purse—and it had happened on his watch.

Worst of all, Fevzi's defection left Istanbul defenseless against an invader.

Husrev snorted through his nose, like a seal blowing air. The Russians had been here before. Who could say that they would not come again?

The Ottomans were afraid of Russia. She pressed against their borders, roamed their seas, bullied them, protected them and took her price. Russia's designs on Istanbul itself—Constantinople, the jewel in the Orthodox crown—were an open secret.

Husrev cracked his knuckles again.

He rang the bell. His uncle was long dead. "I want to see Yashim," he said.

Then he glanced up.

Yashim was already there.

86

OUT in the roadsteads of the Sea of Marmara the cutter strained at its anchor, meeting each swirl of the current with an almost imperceptible swing of its stern. A lantern burned at its bows; another swung from a lanyard by the mainmast, describing circles that slid shadows across the decks. Now and then a mast creaked, and the rigging gave a soft boom whenever the wind died.

The lieutenant had not yet returned when an oar splashed close to the ship, followed by a low whistle.

A rope ladder dropped from the cutter's side, and the approaching caïque slid into the deep shadow beneath the rail.

A man moved out into the light on deck. He was visible only in silhouette, and then the lantern took its turn and the darkness dropped and the man disappeared into the dark, taking the ladder rung by rung.

An oar scraped against the wooden hull of the cutter. The rigging hummed in the breeze, and the caïque's hull hissed against the current. It was barely a sound; and the oars dipped noiselessly into the water.

When the lamplight circled to the rail again, the deck was as empty as before.

87

"COME in, Yashim." The grand vizier tossed his papers aside and sat staring at Yashim. "Very bad news."

"Fevzi Ahmet Pasha has stolen the fleet."

Husrev raised his eyebrows. "You've heard? But I myself have only received the news in these last few minutes."

"According to the Jesuits, the Kapudan pasha sailed to Egypt and handed the fleet to the khedive," Yashim said. "They have a network."

The old vizier closed his eyes. "Do you or the Jesuits know why?"

Yashim hesitated. He was no longer bound by his sense of honor, now that Fevzi Pasha had defected. "In Saint Petersburg, ten years ago, he gave Batoumi away. At the time, I thought he had made an error of judgment. Now I'm not so sure."

"You think he took a bribe?"

"It's possible, isn't it?"

The grand vizier cracked his knuckles together. "Possible. Possible. I should have seen it coming, Yashim, when his dispatch failed to arrive. You should have told me. Who knows what Fevzi Pasha may do for them? Who controls the destiny of the empire, if not the Russians? For a century, they have pushed us farther and farther back. On the Black Sea. In the Balkans. The Greek debacle was a Russian affair."

"And the Russians benefit from this defection, too."

"The Russians?"

"The Egyptians gain a fleet—and can contemplate an attack on Istanbul, if they dare to make one. But that wouldn't be certain. In the meantime, with Istanbul defenseless, Fevzi's defection gives the Russians an excuse to offer us their protection, as they did before."

"We can hardly refuse, in view of the Egyptian threat," Husrev Pasha growled. "We have no fleet. It seems that Fevzi Pasha has played the sides against the center—his defection leaves us with no choice. It seems we must call on the Russians."

"Just as they intend," Yashim objected.

"What choice do we have?" the grand vizier interrupted. "We called on them before. They came—and they left. Perhaps they will do so again."

Yashim shook his head. "Last time we had a fleet, and Mahmut was sultan. Our request for protection took the Russians by surprise. This time, we're playing into the Russians' hands. Galytsin has been planning this for some time."

He thought of Fevzi Pasha's empty house—the house of a man scaling down; preparing to cut loose. It was so obvious now. He should have understood—it fitted with the Russian papers, the missing report.

The old vizier took a deep breath. "The longer we wait, the weaker we will become. The Egyptian fleet cannot move until the spring. If we talk to the Russians now, we can still negotiate, ask for guarantees. By springtime, we will be talking with a loaded gun at our heads."

Yashim made no reply. The old pasha was not talking to him—he was merely thinking aloud.

The image that arose in Yashim's mind was of the tutor at the palace school, stuffing his beard into his mouth.

"Give me two days."

Husrev Pasha glanced up. "Two days?"

"Before you speak to the Russians."

Husrev Pasha stared at him. "I must talk to the sultan, and to the viziers. I'm afraid I cannot see what you can do, Yashim efendi. But two days?" Something like a smile appeared on his fleshy lips. "Very well."

88

THE village of Ortaköy straggled out to nothing in a few hundred yards. Spiked with the wintry stems of Judas trees and hibiscus, the cliffs advanced toward the shore, and Yashim could see the road climbing its flank, deserted except for an unlit bullock cart that strained noiselessly against the gradient, laden with broom from the upper slopes.

He pushed on down the track. Certain details returned to him: the angle of a tree hiking its branches above the water; a tilted Roman milestone half sunk in furze; a long view of the Bosphorus where it slipped away between two promontories, Asian and European, etching the outline of the castle at Rumeli Hisar against the gray sky.

He had forgotten the little row of fishermen's shacks opposite the *yali*. They were built of wood and tile, single-story houses resting on massive foundations of uncut stone. Their view of the Bosphorus was uninterrupted, over the sunken wattle wall and the lurching gateway where he had said goodbye to Fevzi Ahmet years before, and shivered in his furs.

The *yali* itself was gone. Yashim pushed against the wooden gate, overgrown with the brown tendrils of a summer past; he shoved with his shoulder and felt the grasping shoots break as the gate slowly wheeled back.

Yashim wondered how Fevzi Ahmet had come by the *yali*. Armenian merchants, Greeks in the banking line, privileged governors who sojourned for a season in the capital when their own gubernatorial *konaks* sweltered in provincial deserts: these were the men who took *yali*, owned them or borrowed them, with landing stages at the water's edge and shady gardens for their ladies to sit in through the hotter months.

Yashim sometimes dreamed of a *yali* himself, a small wooden house where the water would bounce light onto the ceiling and he would fish with a line; Palewski had said it was the Greek in him. But that was only in the summer months, when Yashim's small apartment in Balat could be stifling and the breeze failed to lick through the open window. In the winter, the *yali* lost their charms. Even a *yali* a few miles along the Bosphorus could be cut off by storms and ice, no closer to Istanbul than the Rhodopes or the mountains of Anatolia. Mountain houses were snug and solid, while in winter, the airy *yali* revealed their drafts; damp seeped into their floors; cold sank through their walls. Shuttered and forlorn, the *yali* of the Bosphorus sat out the snows until the spring returned: the trees put out their leaves for summer shade, the cold retired, the damp was cleared by a few days' sun and the passage of air through rooms that had been locked for months.

But Fevzi Pasha had clung to his *yali* throughout the year: Yashim had seen the smoke rising from the chimney. And now it was gone, hollowed out like a candle in its socket, only a few charred timbers pointing wickedly toward the sky.

Yashim went along the path to where he had once stood by the front door. The building was already returning to the soil. Weeds had sprouted and withered in the ash. He stirred the ashes with his foot and dislodged a sour, acrid smell.

He took a step back. Mrs. Satzos had been right: there was always a thread to be unraveled in a man's life; a question you could ask about this house whose answer would lead ten years down the line to a Kapudan pasha sailing his fleet into the harbor at Alexandria. A question about a pile of charred wood that would explain his treason.

The day was cold and overcast. Yashim turned his back on the ruins and walked on to the next village. The fishermen had erected tiny platforms, like crows' nests, between an arrangement of poles, and between the platforms hung nets of heartbreaking length, straining the current for fish.

89

TALFA advanced to the divan and performed a *temmena*, not quite brushing the floor.

"I hope you are well, valide."

"As can be expected, Talfa." The valide took a long breath. "And you, I hope, continue in good health?"

"Inshallah, by the grace of God," Talfa replied automatically. "I grow a little every day," she added, with a giggle.

"You were always too fond of sweetmeats," the valide remarked. She glanced past Talfa, to the slender little girl who stood quietly to one side. "And who have we here?"

Talfa half turned. "My daughter, valide," she said in surprise. "Necla. I said I would bring her."

"Of course you did." The valide held out her hand, and Necla stepped forward to kiss it.

"Very pretty," the valide said.

Talfa frowned slightly. "Her skin will get lighter. Girls of her age are often a little dark."

Her eyes flickered about the valide's chamber. The valide gestured to some inlaid stools, and patted the divan.

"Please, be seated."

Conversation languished while the serving girl brought in coffee on a tray, and pipes.

"You may smoke, Talfa. I find it disagrees with me, but I quite like the smell," the valide remarked, truthfully. The whiff of tobacco reminded her of Martinique: of stinky carriages, and Creole weddings, and of her father talking business on the veranda, with a cigar. Sometimes she would creep onto his lap and fall asleep there, listening to the rumble of male conversation and laughter. In the still, dark air a lamp would be burning. The men drank rum and played bezique. Down in the lines, the African slaves were beating their drums softly. A tac-tac bird screamed in the trees beyond the garden.

She started. She opened her eyes and was surprised to see a dumpy woman sitting beside her, puffing on an amber stem held between her teeth.

"Who have we here?" she said; but perhaps she only imagined she had spoken, because the dumpy woman kept puffing away and darting her eyes about the room.

"Aimée! Aimée!" She could hear them calling for her, a long way off, but she didn't care. They would make her sit in a close, stuffy room to do needle-point with Tante Merib. It was nicer in the soft grass, once she'd kicked off those little shoes with wooden soles. She pulled off her calico trousers and chucked them into a bush, and then her bonnet, and her ribbons.

She felt the sun hot on her face and on the top of her head.

She stepped into the brown water with her hands raised.

"Aimée! Réponds-moi! Où est-tu? Aimée?" A little closer now. The water was as warm as it looked and the mud was squishy between her toes. All the little blacks played here, and Aimée knew why.

The fastenings on her bodice were the hardest to undo. She was only six, after all. She wriggled and pulled, but the dress caught under her arms and then, as she tottered forward in the water, it puffed up around her and she went off sailing . . . Sailing like a little boat!

A big black man had jumped in to get her out when she was already half sunk, and the family had arrived at the bank of the waterhole. They'd followed her trail, they said.

After, Papa used to call her his *petit paquebot.* She smiled. She'd forgotten that.

Talfa cleared her throat, and stood up.

"Say goodbye nicely, Necla."

They performed *temmena* politely, and withdrew backward.

Talfa was, in her way, a grand personage; but the valide outranked her.

"Come, Necla. Hyacinth can take us to visit the other ladies now."

90

THE road dipped behind a row of sheds that ran down to the water's edge. They were roughly planked, beneath a patchwork of tiled and shingled roofs, and from one of them a crooked pipe leaked a haze of smoke. Yashim could smell the resin in the clear air.

In a low, open-fronted boathouse, a man was working on his boat. Now and then he set down his tools and wrapped his icy fingers around a ball of dirty wool, to get them warm enough for the delicate reshellacking of the hull.

He noticed Yashim out of the corner of his eye and straightened up.

"Something smells good," Yashim said, smiling.

The workman glanced at him, and then at the pot bubbling on the brazier.

"My own recipe, efendi. Fish. Turps. The fish is mostly bones."

"It must have been the turpentine." Yashim peered further around the door, hovering.

"Are you looking for someone, efendi? Please, step inside."

Yashim had often passed these boatyards. He noticed the broom, and the dangling blue glass eyes on a peg, and the pots of brushes standing on the bench. He always liked a workshop, each ranged with tools common and special, the battered, dripped-on workbench, the perpetual fire of a brazier, the tamped-down earth floor tidy in the morning, and by nightfall cluttered with debris.

"You're repainting her?"

"I need to do it well, efendi, the paint and the lacquer. People think a boat is just wood, but that's really only the beginning, you see? It's what you do next that decides how she rides, how she looks—and how long she lasts, of course."

Yashim cast a critical eye along the black, tapered hull of the caïque.

"That's not just ordinary pine, efendi." The boatman gestured with his brush, unable to conceal the pride in his voice. "It's slow-grown, Black Sea. And a cedar keel, same as the sultan's own caïque, if you'll forgive me for saying so. That's one of the reasons she's lasted so well."

"You must have an in with the builder," Yashim remarked.

The man cocked his head. "I do, efendi. I do. I married his daughter."

"And how old is she? I mean, the caïque."

They both laughed.

"Same age as my marriage, by God! Twenty-five years I've had them both."

Yashim uttered a bismallah, in polite and indirect acknowledgment of the caïquejee's good fortune.

"Please," he added. "I'm interrupting your work."

The caïquejee shrugged, and bent over the hull of his boat to lay off the brush. Without looking up he said:

"I know you, efendi. Forgive me, I don't remember where—but I recognized your face."

Another man might have been pleased, flattered even; but Yashim frowned. Perhaps it was only the man's talk. Or perhaps as he slid into middle age, his face and bearing were settling into shape: they had become *impressionant*. Memorable.

"Forgive me, efendi. It's just a hobby of mine, faces. I see 'em all the time, rowing people around. Sad or bad or having fun. Greek or Turk. Might as well take an interest. And I remember yours."

Yashim nodded. "I understand. You're Spyro, aren't you? We met the day they took down the old plane tree."

The caïquejee gave him an odd look. "Spyro." He jabbed his thumb to his chest, then scrunched up his face and sought inspiration in the roof. "And I took you to the Balat stage."

"The bridge has come on since then," Yashim said.

Spyro leaned aside, and spat. "They'll get their bridge, now." He paused, ruminatively. "I miss the tree. Like an old face, it was." He dipped his brush into the pot and wiped the drips carefully off around the rim. "But I'll tell you something, efendi, about the bridge. People think we're sorry, but it won't be the ruin of us caïquejees, and you know why? A caïquejee built it." He laid off the brush against the lacquered hull. "God's truth."

"A caïquejee?"

"The Kapudan pasha to you and me. Begging your pardon, efendi."

"Fevzi Ahmet Pasha?"

Spyro bent his head and lifted the brush, leaning back to survey his work. "His father worked the boats. Little man. Kept the color in his hair right up to the day he died."

"He took a wife on the Danube," Yashim added.

"That's right, he did." He looked up. "You are better at this than me, efendi."

"Go on." It was like a melody heard across the water, fugitive and incomplete. Yashim had heard it before, but he wanted to hear it again.

"A girl from the Danube," Spyro said. "Fevzi was her boy. Fevzi as he was, efendi."

"That's all right."

"Nice-looking lad. Popular on the boats." He paused. "After what happened, I suppose that's what kept him together. His old father wouldn't let him work, so he found a job with some army man. New Troop."

Yashim almost missed it. "After—what? What happened?"

Spyro glanced apologetically at the brush in his hand. "Forgive me, efendi. I like to work fast—you need to lay off the paint quickly, or it dries and streaks the finish. It's the only time I'm anxious in a year, when she's out of the water, like this."

"Please, go ahead."

Spyro dipped the brush and added another streak to the stripped-down hull. Yashim could just see the top of his head. "There were two of them, efendi," he muttered. "Fevzi, and the little girl. Gül, her name was. Fevzi's little sister. Oh, she was a bright one! She and her dad, she'd make him laugh. Ride about in his caïque and pretend she was the valide sultan, do this, do that. Fevzi was popular but Gül stole the whole village, believe me. Two long plaits down her back, and her only ten or so when . . . when . . ."

The top of his head disappeared.

"Ach, what a shame. Still chokes me up, efendi, after all those years. She doted on her dad, and on her big brother, too. That's what did it. Fevzi's practicing his strokes, you see? Every evening, when his father's home, Fevzi takes the caïque out and learns to pull. Little Gül, begging for a ride. But they wouldn't let her go, see? She was only a little girl."

He stood up and waved his brush. "So one evening, the lad lets her come. She wants to go up the strait—gives her orders like an empress. There's a bit of a current above Rumeli Hisar, nasty rip. The boy knew about that, kept well out, he said, but—well. They bring the barges from Varna down, mostly timber, twenty tons, four on a line. You've got to steer clear of those because they can't maneuver much. Maybe the poor lad took his eye off the water for a moment. Panicked, steered into the rip.

"I remember coming home that night, seeing the boats out on the water, all lit up. Must have been twenty, thirty, or more. Every boat in the village. They were looking for little Gül."

"And did they find her?"

"The one that found her was her own father." Spyro shook his head. "Terrible, it was. He jumped in and hauled her out. Kept saying she was all right, just had to get her warm. 'She's sleeping,' he said. Over and over. 'Just asleep.'" He looked at Yashim. "It broke us all up. I think it was the saddest night of my life, when the old man brought his daughter back. It took him ages to understand. He wouldn't let go. Nobody wanted to be the one to say it.

"Fevzi Ahmet came in, white as a sheet. Wet, swollen-eyed. He'd been searching, too, hadn't he? He looked at his little sister in his dad's arms, and he said: 'She's dead.'" Spyro pinched his lips together, and shook his head. "Just straight. 'She's *dead.*'

"It was like the old man suddenly understood. He laid Gül's body on the ground and he lifted both his arms. I don't know what was in his head, but it was something terrible, to hear a man curse his own son. The lad just stood there and let him go on, in front of the whole village. Never said a word."

The caïquejee shook his head. "People talk about tragedy, don't they? Fevzi left. His mother died soon after that. They said it was a wasting disease, but it was what happened that night that killed her. Fevzi's old man went a bit strange. I'm sorry to say it, but people avoided him. Everyone felt sorry for him, but there was something, I don't know, just terrible about the way he'd cursed his son. And some people felt sorry for Fevzi Ahmet, too, though there were plenty of others who blamed him and said the old man had been right."

"And you, Spyro? What did you believe?"

"I couldn't say. The old man was out of his wits. And Fevzi had loved that little girl, so I suppose that drove him another way." He shrugged. "But I believed in the curse, if that's what you mean."

Spyro dabbed at the paintwork, then dipped his brush again and wiped it carefully on the rim of the pot. "Like a fish, she is. Safe in the water, vulnerable in the open air. You know how it is, with all these sheds crammed up together. And not everyone, efendi, as careful as I like to be." He began to paint.

"There was a fire at the *yali* along the way," Yashim said. "It was the Kapudan pasha's place, wasn't it?"

"That's right, efendi." Spyro paused for a moment. Yashim wondered if he was thinking about the work Fevzi Pasha did then, before he became a naval man; the way he made people afraid. "I don't know why he came back here. Perhaps—I don't know, efendi. Perhaps even he couldn't keep away, in the end. But it couldn't be like the old times. He kept himself to himself, and the family, too."

"What happened?"

"Well, the fire, of course. It was in the night, efendi—only the women in the house, too, and the little girl. And the old gentleman who was a *lala*. He used to do the shopping, so we'd seen him about. Dear old thing, my wife said." He hunched his shoulders tight for a second. "It had got ahold, to be honest, while everyone was asleep. The noise woke us—me and the wife. We had to burst the gate down, to get in. By the time we got in, there wasn't much left."

"And the little girl died."

"An eye for an eye and a tooth for a tooth." Spyro straightened up. "It's in the Bible, and it shouldn't be."

"The curse?"

Spyro nodded. "I saw him that night. Ran by me as we were coming in to help, bundle of something in his arms. He just looked at me, efendi. Cold as ice, it was, that look. I think—he knew. He sent us each a gold piece, efendi. I gave it back."

"He was never extravagant."

"That's it," the caïquejee said slowly. "Not an extravagant man, Fevzi Pasha. But I wouldn't take a piece of gold for doing what I thought right, efendi. There, I'll leave it to dry now."

He picked up a cloth and took the pot of shellac off the heat.

"It haunts me, fire," he said.

Yashim was a long time in replying. "I worked for him, all those years ago," he said at last.

Spyro turned, and Yashim could see the sullen pouches in his face. "I thought you were interested in the boat. Forget we spoke, efendi."

"I just wanted to talk." Yashim wondered how to allay the man's fears: it was like scraping mud from a boot. "I just wanted to know, that's all." He paused. "I don't have to remember your name. I don't need to know."

He could see the caïquejee working his jaws. "I'm Spyro. As you remembered. I'm a caïquejee, same as he was once."

He stared down at the hull of his boat. "That's it," he said. "I'm finished, now."

91

TALFA was enjoying herself.

One of the old lady housekeepers had bowed very low and burst into tears.

"Come, come, Ayesha, dry your tears!" Talfa smiled kindly, and reached out to take the woman's hand. "You must remember what a distinguished life you've had. What a boon you have been to us all, and to my brother, of course, especially. You should be thanking God, not crying for what is done."

The former housekeeper nodded, and dabbed a handkerchief to her eyes. "You are right, my lady. Of course what you say is true, and I must try to be happy with what God has chosen for me. But—oh!"

She crushed the handkerchief to her lips.

Necla hung her head. She found it all too sad, and dull, and awkward. With each bleak encounter she sensed her mother's spirits rise, as if the spectacle of the rejected women's grief and abandonment sharpened her awareness of her own good fortune. The sadder they were, the happier her mother sounded.

"Necla, my dear, do try to sit straight. That's better. Now, say hello to your auntie Pevenna."

Necla remembered some of them, as they flitted forward with tears and brave smiles, bowed low, and pinched her cheeks.

"How well she looks!"

"Such a treasure, little Necla! I wonder, do you remember your auntie . . . ?"

"You'll be filling out soon, little one! You will make us all so proud . . ."

Her mother, gayer than ever, ordered noses to be blown, eyes to be wiped. The valide had been something of an ordeal; but here Talfa had brought life and warmth back into these women's benighted lives.

Talfa's quick little eyes darted everywhere.

"And who is that, Hyacinth? There, beside the divan—the girl with the mandolin?"

"The mandolin? That is Melda, my lady. She is staying with us for a short while."

"Melda? Our Melda?"

"She belongs to the ladies' orchestra, mama," Necla said quietly.

"I am aware of that." Talfa sniffed. "I'm afraid, Necla, it does not explain what she is doing here."

Hyacinth bent forward. "Her nerves, my lady," he fluted apologetically. "She needs rest."

"Rest?" Talfa frowned. "Bring her to me."

Hyacinth shimmered away, and a few moments later he returned with the girl, who held her mandolin by the neck and her eyes downcast. She bowed, touching the floor.

"I know you, don't I? I set you to look after the little girl."

"Yes, hanum efendi," Melda replied in a small voice.

"Then what—?" Talfa drew herself up and swept her arm slowly around the room: "Then what are you doing here? This is not her place, Hyacinth. It is entirely irregular. If the girl is ill, she should be seen by a doctor, in Besiktas. That is where her duties lie, am I not right?"

"Quite right, hanum efendi," Hyacinth began. "But the Kislar aga—"

Talfa waved him off. "Does the valide know this girl is here?"

"I'm not sure, hanum ef—"

"That's enough. The girl can speak. She can tell me why she has come to Topkapi. Well?"

Melda's eyes flickered uncertainly toward the elderly eunuch, then down to the floor again. Talfa's expression tightened. Hyacinth wrung his hands, and his head bobbed low. "Hanum efendi, you will allow me to interject. Melda is only staying with us for a short while, until she regains her—her strength. She has had"—he fluttered his fingers in the air, looking for the permissible euphemism—"an inauspicious occurrence, a shock, exactly, so the Kislar aga and Yashim efendi had her sent to us, to recover."

"Ah!" Talfa barked, as if she had got the truth at last. "Yashim!"

Hyacinth bowed again, and said nothing. He had served in the palace for a long time.

Talfa continued to study the downcast girl. At length her expression softened, and she almost smiled.

"Come, come, little one. I don't bite, you know." She tittered, and heaved herself off the divan. "Necla, my love, I want you to stay here a little longer, on my account." She patted her daughter's hand. "It's Melda, isn't it? Let's go somewhere quiet, just you and me, and we'll have a little talk. Let's see what your auntie Talfa can do for you. Eh?"

She took Melda's hand in hers.

"Come on, my dear. I know just the spot. I was born at Topkapi, after all." She turned to Hyacinth, and scrunched up her plump face with amusement. "Don't look so worried, Hyacinth. Melda and I can have a little chat, and you can look after Necla."

Hyacinth smiled uncertainly, and bowed. It was a deep bow, because he felt that something was wrong, and when he straightened up, Talfa and the girl were gone.

92

DARKNESS was falling when Yashim arrived at the Polish residency. As he climbed the stairs he heard the sound of a violin, and when he entered the drawing room Palewski motioned him to an armchair with a swoop of the fiddle under his chin.

He sat for several minutes, eyes closed, pondering the story of Fevzi Ahmet's youth, the sister's death, the father's curse. He only noticed that

Palewski had finished playing when the ambassador flopped into the neighboring chair.

Yashim opened his eyes. "Why do you think Fevzi Ahmet chose to defect?"

"Bitterness and greed," Palewski replied, as if the answer were obvious.

Yashim turned his head. "You think he took Egyptian gold?" He sounded curious.

"I imagine," Palewski answered more slowly, "that he took Egypt's gratitude. The gold, I am afraid, was Russian. It often is."

"But why, if he was working for the Russians, did Fevzi Pasha kill the man in the well?"

Palewski shrugged.

Yashim said moodily, "Husrev Pasha thinks the same as you."

"Well, I may say that the grand vizier is not a fool. Istanbul is vulnerable without a fleet—and the Russians are very close already." Palewski sighed. "I'm afraid Fevzi Pasha's defection makes it likely that they will come, as they might say, to protect the city."

"The European Powers won't like that much," Yashim said.

"Perhaps not," Palewski said, and Yashim could hear the doubt in his voice. "And they should have thought about that twelve years ago, when they helped the Greeks get independence. I hate to say it, Yash, but your empire hasn't many friends."

"The French—or the English—wouldn't let the Russians take it over," Yashim said, stoutly.

"If it meant crowning the tsar in Ayasofya, no, they wouldn't like that. But the Russians can afford to play it softly. They've been waiting centuries to restore the empire of orthodoxy to its original seat—Constantinople. A loose protectorate might be a useful start."

He crossed to his shelves and dragged down an atlas.

"Whatever they say at the British Foreign Office—or on the Quai d'Orsay—about letting Russians into Constantinople, an independent Bulgaria would be popular with public opinion. Free the Moldavians?" He stabbed a finger at the map. "Give the Greeks a Black Sea state? Let the Walachians choose a king? Nations, that's what the British cotton millers understand. And black the sultan's eye, into the bargain? They'd love it, Yash."

"And you? You'd like it too?"

Palewski ran his fingers distractedly through his hair. "I ask only for Poland," he said. "A Russian Constantinople is not the way."

"You're sure?"

"The English cotton millers, Yashim, live far away. They stand in little danger of being spattered with the blood of the Bulgarians, or the Turks, or the Moldavians, if Russia decides to assume control. It would be very bloody. And Russia would be stronger."

He seemed to sag over the atlas. After a moment he shut it, and walked to the window.

"It would be strange, wouldn't it, if your Fevzi Pasha's defection led to women and children being hounded to death in the Balkan hills?" He spread his arms and rested his hands on the sash. "I'm beginning to think that something needs to be done."

"And yet," Yashim said sadly, "we have no friends."

"But between rulers there are no friendships. Only alliances of interest. And your empire, I'm afraid, has failed to provide them. Leaving the state even weaker than it appears."

"No one to help?"

Palewski caught his eye. "No help that I can think of, Yash. And I am sorry, for all our sakes."

HYACINTH shuffled across the frozen cobbles. The lady Talfa had gone home but the valide had been fretful all afternoon and he was feeling tired. His feet ached and the cold assaulted him when he stepped outside.

One little thing, Hyacinth thought, might cheer him up right now. The old *lala*s were drinking coffee, but coffee was always bitter, however much sugar you put in.

Tülin would never mind if he took a little piece of chocolate.

He would have asked her to prepare him some, the way she did; but there was orchestra rehearsal at Besiktas and Tülin was not due back until later.

He reached her door and turned the handle. It was almost dark inside, but the room was small and he had no doubt that he could find the chocolate easily. There would be a jar somewhere, and he could dip a finger into the dark, bitter flakes. Perhaps she would never have to know.

There was a jar. Hyacinth opened it expectantly, and shook it, and sniffed. It wasn't chocolate.

He set the jar back on the floor and squatted on his hams, surprised. The corner of the room was full of jars. Not only jars: there were packets in paper, and little wooden boxes, and clay pots, and some tiny brass containers with lids. He opened one at random: it was a sticky paste that smelled familiar.

Hyacinth's mouth turned down at the corners.

Chocolate was one thing. But as he opened one pot after another, and poked his fingers into packets and boxes, the turn of Hyacinth's mouth deepened.

It was his duty now to talk to the girl, he thought.

But his desire was to speak to Yashim.

THE man with the knife crossed the mountains in snow. He was used to the snow, to the cold, to picking his way along the mule tracks.

He did not consider the barking as he made his way down toward the valley. At this time of year dogs would be chained close to the sheep, to warn of the approach of wolves—or a stranger.

At last he lifted his head, and listened. The barking was growing closer. The man tightened his grip on his stick and loosened the knife in his belt.

With a strange dog you had to look big. Talk loud. Dogs understood firm signals. The man prepared by shifting his sheepskin coat onto his shoulders, just in case.

THE Court of the Favorites, in the Topkapi Palace, was an open and airy space surrounded by a colonnade on three sides. It was the work of the great Ottoman architect Sinan, who created the sublime panorama of Istanbul's domes, which move forward and retreat in dignified counterpoint as the traveler approaches the city by sea.

Sinan also worked on buildings that were to be seen by very few people. The fourth side of the Court of the Favorites was enclosed by a low balustrade, beneath which Sinan had constructed a delightful bathing pool as a grateful addition to the amenities of the harem. Stretched out in the sun below the balustrade, part of the pool filtered back through the old Byzantine arches into deep, almost subterranean shade.

As autumn came, and the days shortened and the air grew cool, the eunuch of the baths would test the water with his skinny elbow, until the sad day arrived when he pronounced the pool closed for the season. Then the pool was drained, to protect the tiling from frost and ice; because it stood on a hill, the draining was swift and effective. The entrances were locked, to await the return of summer, and the sultan's girls.

The girls were warned not to approach the balustrade, which was quite low; in spite of salt and gravel, the surface of the courtyard in winter was sometimes slippery with ice. But in recent years the filling and the emptying of the pool had become no more than a formality. The girls had gone. The pool became a seasonal tradition that continued because it was seasonal, and no one had thought, or would ever think, to order it stopped.

Hyacinth did not find it necessary to repeat the warning to the older women who had returned to the palace from Besiktas: they knew the danger already, and they rarely ventured out now that the frosts had come. Instead they remained indoors, clustering around the barely adequate fireplaces that warmed their lodgings, and complaining incessantly about the cold. Palewski was right: the Ottomans seemed not to reckon with winter until it was already upon them.

Thus the Court of the Favorites was largely deserted, and only Melda, who had the heat of youth in her veins, sought it out as a quiet place to sit, under the colonnade.

"HYACINTH," the valide remarked as she watched the flakes settle in the tiny court outside her window, "should order someone to sweep away the snow. I never liked it, Tülin."

Tülin smiled, and put down her embroidery. "That is because you were raised in a hot country, valide," she pointed out. "Most of the ladies are Circassians, and it does them good to see the snow again."

The valide made a moue. "I'm surprised any of them are capable of remembering that far back. If they are Circassian, which I doubt. You all pretend, Tülin."

Tülin laughed pleasantly, and stretched. The valide shot her a surprised glance. "I would like Hyacinth to order the court swept," she said.

"Of course, valide. If you are comfortable, I will attend to it right away."

Tülin gathered her embroidery and set it on a footstool, then plucked a fur-lined pelisse from a hook by the door and whirled it around her shoulders.

Outside she moved fast, one hand to the wall to steady herself over the icy cobbles. A blast of cold wind hit her as she turned into the corridor that linked the valide's court with the little suite of rooms set aside for the black eunuchs, and the cape fluttered.

She approached the door of the halberdiers. She could hear them beyond, conversing in low voices; now and then she caught the sound of a laugh, and of dice rattling on a table.

She stood and listened to the mesmerizing voices of the men. Her breath made puffs in the chill air.

The sound of a door opening in their room, and closing with a bang as the wind caught it, made her jump.

"I'm sorry, valide," she said later as she shook the snowflakes from her pelisse and hung it back on the peg. "I looked everywhere, but I think that Hyacinth has gone out."

The valide put her head on one side. "Hyacinth? Why do you want to find Hyacinth? It's cold, *chérie*. I think you might want to put another log on the fire."

It was true; the room had grown colder while she was out. Tülin reached into the basket and picked up a log. She noticed that her fingers were trembling slightly.

"There," she said with a grunt as she heaved the log into the fire. "That's much better."

"Much better," the valide echoed as she felt the warmth on her face: but she was aware that there had been something else she wanted, not fire, quite. She could not remember what it was. "Much better, yes."

97

HYACINTH had not gone out. Indeed, just as he had feared, he would never again leave the palace, which had been his home for so many years.

There was no one alive, except the valide herself, who could have remembered the stringy little African boy who had arrived at the Topkapi Palace in the cold winter of 1789. When he had first seen snow, he had shrieked with terror: for a whole day he sat in the antechamber of the eunuchs' apartments, with his hands over his funny little ears, and shrieked every time someone opened the door. The old eunuchs had found this quite hilarious; and some of the more mischievous girls had come to tease him, pretending the sky really was falling on their heads, until the Kislar aga of the day had shooed them all away, and sentenced Hyacinth to stand in the snow in bare feet until he understood what it was.

Which was also how he got his name, Hyacinth, growing most incongruously out of the snow-covered ground.

Hyacinth no longer minded the snow, of course. As it settled on his hair, and on his back, and drifted between his curled fingers, he was quite dead to the ancient terror it had once inspired.

He lay in the pool, on the tiles, exactly where he had fallen, as snow covered the lake of blood that seeped from his smashed forehead, and turned to dark ice on the frozen ground.

98

THE man with the knife saw and heard the dog before the dog saw him.

It ran howling out of the pine trees, a big mastiff with a thick, matted yellow coat. A proper shepherd's dog. When it stumbled and lurched sideways, snapping at its own tail, the man with the knife felt a tremor of fear.

He stood very still, thinking the mastiff might not see him if he did not move. Its eyes were sticky, foam lashing at its jaws, and it whirled from side to side, stumbling nearer to him across the frozen ground. But there was no purpose in its erratic course. There was a chance that the dog would simply pass him by.

When the dog was only a few yards away, the man reluctantly lifted his stick.

At no moment did the frenzied animal recognize the man, or make up its mind to attack: it seemed lost in its own suffering. But as he raised his stick, the dog flung itself at him, suddenly, with its lips peeled back and jaws wide.

The man was caught off guard, but he was strong and his aim was good. The stick connected with the dog's muzzle in mid-spring, as the man stepped back. The dog landed heavily, shook its huge head, and bared its teeth with a strangled sound.

He hit it again, a more considered blow on the side of its head.

The mastiff staggered, and seemed about to fall, but as the man raised the stick again it sprang disjointedly. The vicious jaws snapped shut on the stick, and with a heave of its head it almost pulled it out of his hands.

The man pressed the stick to the ground, lowering the dog's head, watching the saliva run toward his hands. It took great strength to hold the stick down. He wanted his knife.

The dog shook the stick a few times, then yelped and dropped back, jaws agape.

That was all the time the man needed. He plucked his knife from his belt and raised the stick, and when the dog came on again, grinding its fangs from side to side, he slammed the stick against its jaws with one hand and with the other stuck the knife straight and hard into the dog's neck, behind the ear.

He felt its hot breath against his chest; he felt the heat of its blood running over his hand. He twisted the knife and dragged down savagely, once, twice, grunting with exertion as he pulled the blade through the matted fur.

The dog sagged, overbalancing them both. The man fell back, unable to keep the weight of the dog from sinking against his chest. Blood from its gashed neck spurted out over his legs and he scrambled backward, the slippery hilt of the knife sliding from his fingers.

On the ground the mastiff jerked spasmodically, working its jaws while its hind legs scrabbled for purchase. But the man knew it was over.

He held the back of his wrist to his mouth and watched the dog die.

It died with a sort of ragged gasp. One moment it had muscles, and a form; the next, it was splayed on the ground, haunches high, the head lolling and blood staining the grass.

The man waited for a few minutes, until his heartbeat settled. He bent down and pulled the knife clear. He wiped it on the grass: he did not wish to touch the dog.

99

YASHIM woke early, groping for the quilt that had slipped from his legs. He squinted at the unaccustomed brightness and then sat up, yawning, and rubbed the condensation from the window pane. Snow lay thick on the rooftops of Balat.

He drew up his knees and leaned back against the cushions, watching his dragon's breath.

After a few moments he began to grope for his clothes, drawing them under the quilt to warm up, before he sprang with a shiver from the divan and began to dress, hurriedly wriggling his arms into the sleeves of the cambric shirt he wore over his woolen vest. There was ice in the washbasin: Yashim pulled a face, plunged his hand through the ice, and splashed freezing water over his eyes, his mouth and ears. He dried himself quickly on a towel, feeling newly awake. Over his shirt he put on a woolen waistcoat and a quilted jacket; then he tucked his feet into a pair of slippers.

Outside the door he bent down and carefully fastened a pair of galoshes over his feet. The alley was covered in snow, but once he reached Kara Davut the way was better; shopkeepers had shoveled the snow into the middle of the road. He entered his favourite café, rubbing his hands, and the proprietor nodded and put a small coffee pan on the coals.

Yashim ate his breakfast by the steamed-up window, coffee and a *corek* as usual, which is how the palace *chaush* found him a few minutes later.

Several heads turned in the café as he presented Yashim with a note, bound in vermilion ribbon; then they looked hastily away. Among the Turks, curiosity was not reckoned a virtue.

Yashim read the note, frowned, and put it into his breast pocket.

"Let's go," he said.

THE search for Hyacinth had not begun in earnest until after midnight, when the other eunuchs protested at his absence from prayers. Confusion reigned over where the old eunuch was likely to have gone; so it was not until the small hours that a proper search had been instituted by the corporal of the halberdiers.

Off-duty men had been roused from their sleep to join the search, and to confirm that Hyacinth had not left the harem earlier in the day. They looked first in the cavernous kitchens of the palace, built, like the Court of the Favorites and the pool, by the great Sinan, and then in the harem mosque. The harem was a warren of corridors and courts and little rooms, and the search party proceeded only slowly, and with many delays, as women were roused and questioned through half-open doors, and empty rooms were opened and inspected.

The harem had been home to many hundreds of women, eunuchs, and children, and over the centuries it had grown higgledy-piggledy over several levels, as rooms were extended or partitioned, demolished and rebuilt. The search party had stuck together, holding flaming torches, as they climbed and descended and followed corridors through suites of chambers and courts and little gardens. At first they had called to Hyacinth by name, but after an hour or two they had grown more quiet, alarmed by the echo of their own voices and by an increasing dread of summoning the departed. For everyone by then was already sure he was dead.

They had searched the Court of the Favorites at least twice in the night; but the light cast by their torches did not reach the pool beneath the balustrade, so it was not until dawn that someone first noticed a dark shape on the tiles below. The keys to the bathing pool were sought and produced, and at last, after the hour of the morning prayer, three halberdiers pried the body of the old eunuch off the pool floor with a peculiar sucking sound that drove several onlookers from the balustrade above.

The corporal told Yashim it was clear from the amount of snow that covered him, and from the state of rigor, that the old man had been dead for quite some time.

They had lowered him onto a sheet and brought him to the deserted hospital quarters upstairs.

Yashim pulled back a sheet to examine the body. There was little else to be learned. The old eunuch had probably died instantly when he hit the tiles. His limbs, Yashim noticed, were beginning to thaw, but he lay still with his arms outstretched over his head, as if warding off some final blow; or in a parody of waking.

Yashim spent a little more time examining the floor of the pool before he ordered the blood to be washed away. Upstairs, he stood by the balustrade, piecing together in his mind the circumstances of Hyacinth's fatal fall. Finally, he took a stiff broom from one of the halberdiers and swept at the ice and slush that covered the courtyard, peering down now and then to see if anything turned up. He found a small coin and a tiny bead of green glass; but otherwise nothing.

"And the yard was covered in snow and ice yesterday?"

"It fell heavily yesterday morning, efendi," the corporal explained.

"And was not swept? There's salt here, at least."

"We salted the open courts the night before, efendi. When it looked like snow."

"But nobody swept here yesterday?"

The corporal hesitated. "No, efendi. The order was not given."

"And tell me, corporal, who gives the orders to sweep the courts?"

"That would be the late *lala* Hyacinth, efendi. Indeed, I told the men yesterday to have the brooms ready, in expectation of his order. I suppose—" He hesitated again. "Forgive me, efendi, but it seems to me that he may have been inspecting the condition of the ground when he slipped."

"Thank you, corporal. I'd like to speak with the eunuchs now."

There were six of them, all old men like Hyacinth, sitting glumly around a brazier in the first room of the eunuchs' quarters, up by the gate to the Second Court of the palace.

"Yesterday, gentlemen, Hyacinth ate with you at the midday meal?"

They tried to remember, their eyes full of concern, nodding dumbly.

"It was the last time we saw him, Yashim," one of them volunteered in his quavery, fluting voice.

Yashim coughed gently. "And what did he talk about? Can you remember?"

The old men blinked at one another, and at the ground.

"About the snow? Did you talk about the weather?" Perhaps the corporal was right, and Hyacinth had been inspecting the condition of the courts. He could have gone to the balustrade, and slipped.

"The cold weather," one of the men said, nodding. "He never liked it, Yashim efendi."

"No. But did he say the ground needed to be swept?" Normally Yashim would have avoided such a direct question; but the old men's memories needed jogging. "Did he mean to look?"

"I don't know, Yashim efendi," one of the eunuchs replied, with a faint shrug. "But I don't think that's why he expected you to visit."

"Me to visit? Why?"

The old man shook his head. "He didn't say, Yashim efendi. But perhaps it was about the girl?"

"Melda? What was the matter?"

The elderly man cracked his long knuckles and looked unhappy. "She hasn't been doing very well," he said.

"She's been sick," another man added. "And Hyacinth *lala* was concerned. That's right. He wanted to talk to you."

"And he said I was coming? To see him here?"

The old men exchanged glances. "I thought that's what he said," the first ventured.

"Do you remember?" He appealed to the others, who considered.

"That's right," one of them said finally. "He said you were coming later on, and he'd be glad to see you."

Yashim nodded and bit his lip. "Has the valide been informed?"

The eunuchs glanced at one another. *They're rudderless*, Yashim thought. All their lives they have deferred to others, to a Kislar aga, to Hyacinth, to the valide. But the valide had grown old, and the Kislar aga was no longer there.

And Hyacinth was suddenly gone.

"I take it none of you have spoken to her yet." It was a statement, not a question. The eunuchs looked sorrowful, and faintly relieved. "I'll tell her myself," Yashim added.

The old men thought that would be best. Yashim left them all nodding solemnly and stroking their beardless faces, and went to find the valide.

HE found, instead, the valide's slave.

She put a finger to her lips and let him through the door.

"She's sleeping, Yashim efendi," she whispered.

Yashim nodded. He had momentarily forgotten the young woman's name.

"Perhaps I should wait," he said.

The girl's head bobbed. Her eyes were wide. "It's Hyacinth, isn't it? He's dead."

"Yes, I'm afraid so, Tülin," he added, remembering her name. For a moment he had felt like one of the old men. "He must have fallen on the ice. He died instantly."

"Hamdullah," the girl mumbled: by the grace of God.

"Hamdullah," Yashim repeated. "He was an old man."

She said gently: "I can tell the valide about it, if you'd prefer."

"I don't think so, Tülin. The valide has known Hyacinth for a very long time."

It came out as a rebuke, more emphatically than he'd meant. He glanced across and saw a slight flicker in the girl's eyes as she registered what he'd left unsaid. That she was less significant than Hyacinth. That she was less to the valide than Yashim himself.

He flashed her a brief, friendly smile. A girl of her age could scarcely comprehend what Hyacinth embodied: the shared experience, the years of enclosure and drama and ennui.

He turned from Tülin and stood looking into the fire that smoldered in the vestibule.

"Hyacinth was important to the valide in a way that might be hard to understand," he began. He would have added that the old eunuch was like a lovely vase given to her years ago to keep, which was now lost and broken; but at that moment a bell tinkled faintly in the room beyond.

"Tülin! Tülin!"

She brushed past him swiftly, with a glance he found hard to interpret, and before he could say another word she had gone in to the valide.

Yashim sighed, wondering whether he should stay. If he waited, it was at Tülin's pleasure: he could hardly blunder into the valide's chamber unannounced. He cocked his head. He could hear the valide muttering something next door, and the lower, soothing tones of Tülin's voice; but farther off he could hear, too, the sound of the muezzin calling the Friday prayer.

He started, surprised it had grown so late.

At the door he brushed past a damp cloak hanging on a peg; the coldness made him shudder. He noticed a pair of galoshes on the floor, surrounded by a little muddied pool of meltwater, and the sight suddenly brought tears to his eyes. It was, he thought, just the sort of little thing Hyacinth would have fussed over, in his punctilious way.

Yashim considered it the proper time to offer up his prayers.

102

THE man with the knife walked down into the valley, looking for water.

When the path crossed a stream he took off his jacket and his shirt in spite of the cold and washed his arms, his hands, scrubbing at congealed gore with his fingernails.

When his hands were clean he washed his face, drenching his neck and shoulders with the icy water.

He rubbed his wet hands over his chest, and flinched. The dog had gotten closer than he'd thought—not a cut, quite, but a red welt over one breast. He splashed it with water, and massaged it beneath his hands. He reached for his shirt and looked it over. The thick linen was not damaged: only when he held it to the light could he see a tiny hole.

He rubbed the welt again. Then he washed his knife.

103

THE little mosque of the harem was half empty, but Yashim was sure that everyone in the diminished harem population was there: the retired women weeping for Hyacinth, and the bewildered old eunuchs he had met earlier. The corporal of the halberdiers was there, too, very correct in his manner, keeping his eyes fixed to the ground. Yashim watched the women carefully, out of the corner of his eye, but he did not see Melda; nor, of course, did Tülin or the valide make an appearance.

The imam, himself very old and frail, made a short and scarcely audible reference to Hyacinth's death, and more confidently led a prayer for his soul.

Afterward Yashim found Tülin waiting for him in the vestibule.

"I guessed you had gone for prayers, Yashim efendi. I told the valide you would come." Her eyes crinkled as she smiled. "I haven't said anything, you understand. I thought—"

"Quite right, yes." Yashim nodded.

He stepped through the doorway and found the valide sitting up on the divan. She was wearing a bright silk jacket, so finely quilted that it hung loosely on her thin shoulders; under it a scarf and a fine lawn chemise. She looked exquisite.

"Mysteries, Yashim." She lowered the pince-nez with two fingers and inspected him over the rim. "Tell me all."

He inclined his head, gravely. It was just his luck to find the valide in this mood, sportive and light: she was dressed, he thought, to charm—not to receive bad news.

He approached the divan, and she held out a hand indicating that he should sit.

He took her hand. "There is no mystery, valide. It's Hyacinth. It seems that—"

"Hyacinth!" She pulled back her hand and fanned herself with it. "*La!* I desired intrigue. I'm disappointed. Go on, Yashim."

"He's dead." Yashim paused. "He fell from the balustrade, in the Court of Favorites."

The valide said nothing.

"He cracked his head on the floor of the pool," Yashim continued. "He must have died instantly, hanum efendi."

The valide lifted her chin and glanced at the window. "It's been snowing," she said.

Yashim followed her glance. "It snowed yesterday. The ground was very slippery, with ice."

"I told him to have it swept. He never liked the snow. Did you know that, Yashim? It used to frighten him, as a little boy. That's why he was called Hyacinth."

"I'm very sorry, valide," Yashim murmured.

"Yes, yes. *Et moi aussi.*" She paused. "He fell from the balustrade, you say?"

"Yesterday. They found him this morning."

"The question is, Yashim, who pushed him? An old man . . ."

Yashim shook his head. "The balustrade is low, and the ground was slippery. Hyacinth was not so steady anymore."

"Rubbish," the valide snapped. "I have never heard such a thing. When Hyacinth arrived he could barely see over the top of that rail. *C'était un nain, pratiquement.*"

Almost a dwarf? She was going a little far, Yashim thought; but yes, Hyacinth was never quite full size.

"He could have simply slipped through the gaps," the valide added. She looked thoughtful.

Yashim said nothing. Of all the ways the valide could have reacted, this was not the way he would have expected. Nor wished for, either. She was turning the shock into a kind of puzzle.

The valide had always enjoyed Yashim's investigations. He had learned not to spare her the grisly details, either, for she had the stomach for them. She liked stories about the city, about other lives, the crimes and peccadilloes of the people, and Yashim had come to realize that the valide was unshockable. But this was Hyacinth; this was a man who had shared her own life, to a degree.

It was Yashim's turn to be shocked. The dead man, he felt, deserved better.

"I thought you ought to know, at least," he concluded, a little lamely.

"Quite right, Yashim. And now I want you on the case. Who pushed him? Keep me informed."

She closed her eyes.

MELDA startled at his approach.

"Don't worry. It's me again. Yashim. I just came to see how you were."

There was no need to ask, he thought: she looked startlingly thin, the skin drawn tight over the bones of her face, her shoulders narrow and sunken. She was only twenty, but in a week she had aged like the valide herself.

Her eyes flickered toward him once, and then settled back, to stare dully at a spot on the opposite wall.

Hyacinth had placed her in the harem hospital, in a small, plain room without tiling or decoration. The high window was protected by a wooden shutter. Apart from the narrow cot on which she sat, there were two small octagonal tables and a stool with a plain woven seat.

He drew the stool closer to the girl and sat down quietly.

"Have you been eating, Melda?"

She shivered, and drew her wrists across her stomach.

"Are you cold? It's a bit cold in here, isn't it? Let's get you to a fire," he suggested gently. There must be better rooms than this, he thought.

Melda gave a jerk and looked away. Yashim bit his lip.

"You're thinking about Elif," he began slowly. "When you're alone like this, you can think things and feel things that make you more worried and afraid."

Her eyelids quivered: she was like a wild animal caught in a trap.

"I thought you would be better here," he said. "You are safe." He was about to add that she was being looked after, when he reflected that Hyacinth was dead. Had they forgotten her, in the pandemonium?

"Let's get you to a better room," he said. She needed food and warmth.

Melda gave a compulsive shake of her head, and shifted her gaze to stare down by his feet. She slowly twisted her head until she was looking out of the corner of her eye. As if she were afraid of what he would do next.

"I won't hurt you, Melda. I want to help."

She blinked. Her white lips moved.

Yashim strained forward to catch a sound. "What is it, Melda? What did you say?"

"Elif—had a baby."

"How? How could she have a baby, Melda?"

"Not—that one," Melda stuttered; her head jerked as she spoke. "A—stare-baby."

"A what? What is that?"

She glanced at him in surprise. "Elif—she—she looked. At him. That's what's happened. That's where it began."

"What began, Melda?"

"It grows inside you, just like a real baby—but it's not. It's a demon. It's from the demon in the man."

"The demon, Melda? Tell me about the demon." He took her hands in his and chafed them softly, struggling to keep the astonishment off his face as Melda explained, falteringly, what had happened to Elif: how Donizetti Pasha's glance had sowed the seed of a stare-baby, and how Elif had become sick.

"It was growing," she said. "Donizetti Pasha can't help it; he's a man, it's in his nature. But she—she wanted to get rid of it."

She covered her face and began to weep hot, real tears. Yashim welcomed them: anything, he thought, was better than that frozen impassivity.

"And then—what then?"

Melda wiped her eyes. "Then she took some things to drink, to make—to make—the stare-baby come out."

"What drinks? How—"

"They made her bleed." Her mouth twisted into a horrified grimace. "They. Made. Her. Bleed. She—said—she was on fire."

Yashim gazed at her, aghast. Elif's death had always seemed to him to be perverse, unnatural—but he had never imagined it like this.

"I'll get you somewhere warmer, and you should take something. Some soup. We can talk again later, if you like."

He stood up. She gave no sign of hearing him. At the door he turned and she was still sitting like a frightened hare, showing the whites of her eyes as she watched the place where he had been.

At the end of the corridor he tapped at the door of the orderly's room. There was no reply. He opened the door and checked: it was empty.

He let out an exasperated sigh. Hyacinth had seemed so ineffective, but his death revealed just how much the running of the harem had depended on him. Sweeping the ground, feeding a girl in the hospital, getting the other eunuchs off their backsides: since he'd gone the whole place seemed to have ground to a halt.

With a flash of anger he surged down the corridor toward the eunuchs' quarters and burst into their common room.

Within three minutes, alarmed old men were running hither and thither in pursuit of their duties. Yashim went to the kitchens, where he found a cook washing rice while another scraped carrots.

"Soup. What have you got?"

The man stirring the rice looked at him stupidly and shrugged, mouth open. The man scraping carrots jerked his chin. "The stock's all there. What do you want?"

Yashim lifted the lid and sniffed: good chicken broth.

"Can you clear the broth?"

The carrot man nodded.

Yashim had visited the kitchens before, but this was the first time he had hefted a palace pan or wielded a palace knife. He selected a small heavy iron pan.

"We use those ones for the sultan, efendi."

"The sultan is no longer here, my friend," Yashim replied. "Where are your spices?"

He laid the ingredients out on the chopping board: onion, garlic, a long red chili, and a carrot that the man had scraped clean. He set the sultan's pan on a gentle heat and covered its base with olive oil, adding a small knob of butter before he chopped the onion into very small pieces.

The knife, he noticed, was as keen as his own, and heavier: it would split a silk scarf.

Finding himself in the greatest kitchen in Istanbul, Yashim set about making one of the simplest dishes he knew: lentil soup.

He scraped the seeds out of the chili and chopped it together with the garlic, admiring the balance of the knife and the slight feathered curve toward its tip. The butter had melted; he shook the pan and swept in the vegetables, with a big pinch of cumin and coriander.

He cut the carrot into small dice, and stirred it into the onions as they began to turn.

The cook passed him a small brass grinder. Yashim smelled the fenugreek: he gave it a few twists and handed it back.

"Thank you," he said. "You have the lentils?"

The cook nodded. He handed Yashim a cup of lentils, which he poured into the pan like a cascade of treasure, stirring them around for a few moments with a small spoonful of white sugar.

The cook brought him a bowl of the clarified stock.

Yashim smiled. "When you like," he said; and then: "enough." The steam rose in a puff, and drifted into the vast cool vaults overhead. "Now, a lid—and I'll help you with the carrots, if you like."

When they were sitting together, side by side, Yashim asked him what he was cooking.

The cook gave a lopsided grin. "It's not how it is done," he explained. "I am only the peeler. But one day, I shall be a cook."

"You were a cook today," Yashim reminded him.

The man stole a glance at the man washing rice. "Yes," he said quietly. "Yes, perhaps I was."

When the soup was done, Yashim ladled it into a bowl and sprinkled it with chopped parsley.

He put a bowl over the top, to keep it warm, and carried it carefully back to the harem.

He caught sight of Tülin at the entrance to the Golden Road as she came out of the valide's courtyard. She stopped in front of him, and smiled.

"I came to ask for wood," she said. "But it seems to be taken care of, now."

Yashim bowed politely. "I hope they'll send in someone from outside," he remarked. "To replace Hyacinth. It turns out he was something of an administrator, after all. These fellows are just like chickens."

"Yes. We need a fox, Yashim efendi."

She smiled again, and Yashim smiled, too. Out in the open air, the girl was remarkably pretty: she had a freshness about her that was more than youth, or the crisp winter air.

"I'm worried about Melda, in the hospital."

"Yes." She nodded gravely. "I have been thinking about her."

"I've had her moved to a warmer room, and I'm taking her this soup, but she's—I know you have plenty to do, Tülin, but I'd be grateful if you'd look in on her now and then."

"Hyacinth didn't encourage anyone to talk to her. But I'd like to help if I can."

"That would be good. She's been too much alone, I think."

Tülin cocked her head back. "The lady Talfa spoke with her," she said. "She was very kind."

"The lady Talfa?" Yashim was surprised. "She came here?"

"Oh yes, she came over from the Besiktas palace to visit the valide. With her daughter. Later on she met all the ladies, and took Melda off for a chat."

Yashim grunted. "I'm sure she meant well."

Tülin giggled. "I am sure of it, too, Yashim efendi. She is a very— grand lady."

"Quite."

She held his gaze. "I'd better get back, now that they are bringing wood."

"Of course. But don't forget the girl. Melda."

"I won't."

Yashim shook his head. He wanted to say he was sorry for being short with her that morning; that Tülin could have told the valide the news about Hyacinth, after all. But they had an understanding now, and there was no need to say anything.

PALEWSKI glanced around a little furtively, then draped himself over the parapet of the new bridge and inhaled the scent of grilling fish.

It wasn't bad; not bad at all. The convenience of it! And a little restaurant underneath, too, to sit out in the spring sunshine and watch the boats go by.

He glanced up and down. He wasn't the only person admiring the new bridge. It was as if the whole of Istanbul had chosen that afternoon to inspect this novel adornment to the city. It wasn't beautiful. At best, with its sturdy pontoons and hefty plankwork, it was impressively functional.

And its function, Palewski had to admit, was almost sublime. He had thought of it, when it was being built, as a dreary commonplace, a purely commercial affair to allow the passage of goods and men between Istanbul and Pera. People tramping back and forth, muddying the distinction between the two: French hatters opening shops in the bazaar, perhaps; imams sallying forth to wag a finger at the more scurrilous delights of Pera.

And yet—a bridge!

He looked up and, seeing a familiar figure approaching him across the planks, he raised a finger in the frosty air. "You see, Kadri," he announced. "This bridge is already performing its essential function."

Kadri looked surprised. He bowed. "I am very pleased to meet you here, Palewski efendi." After a moment's hesitation he added: "Its essential function?"

"Yes. I was thinking, a bridge is a forced marriage, if you like. Istanbul and Pera clapped together. Pompous groom. Reluctant bride."

"But which is which?"

Palewski shook his head. "It's not altogether like that, Kadri. I see it now. Not a marriage at all. The bridge," he added, with an air of serious triumph, "is a trysting place."

Kadri looked expectantly at the older man, and said nothing.

"A trysting place, Kadri. Where the lovers meet."

"I see," the boy said doubtfully.

"Not lovers in the literal sense, of course." He waved his hand. "Air of license. Ladies out for a walk. Pashas saluting. Hobbling Sufis and swaggering tars. Jolly fellows all about. Everyone cheerful and bright-eyed, somehow. You know what it reminds me of? You should know."

Kadri looked round pensively. "The theater?"

"Intelligent boy. Forget your ragged crew, all that paint and declamation. This is the real theater in Istanbul. Long may it last!"

Kadri raised his arm and pointed. "Here comes Yashim efendi!"

106

THE man with the knife stood in the low doorway of the caravansary, rubbing his chest.

He had hoped the welt would fade; it was less than a scratch, after all, the skin scarcely broken, and there had been no blood. But it did not fade. It felt hot, instead, and around it the skin was flushed. In the mornings, when he moved his arms, the welt was sore.

The guardian of the caravansary received him doubtfully. He was not a merchant, with goods to protect; nor did men wander at this time of year, looking for work.

"Three days," he said reluctantly. "Three days, then you'll move on, see?"

For a day and a night the man slept, feverishly. On the second day he showed the guardian his wound.

A doctor was fetched. He frowned at the scratch, and prepared a hot poultice to draw the poison out.

But the man knew what happened when a mad dog bit you and drew blood. It could be weeks, or months, but in the end you went mad, too, and died.

The pasha's life hung by a tiny thread.

He had so very little time.

107

YASHIM walked with his head down, lost in the crowd and oblivious to the great stream of humanity that swirled around him as he descended to the shore of the Golden Horn.

"Fine times, efendim! It's our work, every inch—and every inch will get you closer! Bring the ladies! All safe, all sound!"

Beside him, men were shouting and laughing.

Yashim heard their words and saw their happy faces, but he made nothing of it. He could not rid himself of the possibility that Hyacinth had taken his own life. He may have slipped on the ice and overbalanced. He was an old man, after all. But he had asked, "Is it true?" Yashim had said that yes, he believed it to be true: the valide would be moving to Besiktas. And Hyacinth might not be going.

The memory turned like the wheels of the cart that Yashim was following at a cautious distance, to avoid the splash as it lurched into a puddle of dirty water freckled with recent snow. The cartwheels bounced, and began to drum as if they were running over the deck of a ship.

The traffic was busier than usual: he'd never seen or heard so many carts and porters scurrying about here on a winter's evening.

He hunched his shoulders against the wind, and looked up for a caïque.

Hyacinth fell, he repeated to himself. Hyacinth fell against the palace balustrade, in the snow.

He blinked and looked around. He saw a balustrade beside him: higher, perhaps, and made of wood.

"Try it, efendim! No charge—Pera to Istanbul!"

Happy men were standing in a knot, urging people on with their arms.

Yashim took a step forward. He glanced down, astonished to see his feet planted on wooden planks. All around him was a seething mass of people, laughing and pointing, dodging the carts that thundered across the planks.

He stopped. An old man was coming toward him, planting his stick carefully on the boards, grinning and nodding.

"See that, efendi! See that! Don't be afraid. I did it with my stick—seventy years I've waited for this day! Never left Stamboul before. Free! It's free!"

A ragged-looking man with a shock of corkscrew hair shot through the crowd. He was barefoot, and intent, and he carried a small bag in his fist.

The crowd parted automatically to let him through, and through the gap Yashim recognized two familiar faces.

They swept him up, arm in arm.

"I was just telling our young friend, Yashim, that the bridge is a splendid piece of theater. Istanbul meets Pera—the old empire and the new Europe! Preen should mount a tableau."

Yashim said nothing. Only when they had stepped onto land, and were at the bottom of the steps that led to the Galata Tower, did he stop and turn, looking back at the bridge. He shook his head. "Our navy," he said at last. "Do you know what it amounts to? Almost nothing. A few ships of the line, ill-trained crews, foreign officers. Our navy is an illusion—a costly one, for us. The grand vizier thinks that it can stop the Russians. It can't."

"Not when it's in Alexandria, certainly," Palewski said drily.

"No—never. It's not our style—we're afraid of the sea. Look at Husrev Pasha. He's an old Bosniac—what does he know of the sea? We've had two great engagements in the last few hundred years, and we lost them both. Lepanto, 1580. Wiped out. Navarino, 1827. Total collapse of the fleet."

"'God gave the land to the Turks, and to the Christians he gave the sea.' I know the saying."

They began to climb the Pera steps. "It's the sea that counts, these days," Yashim said. "We built our empire by land—because our cavalry was faster than the rest, and because we knew how to govern. All that has changed. It's ships that matter, in trade and war. With ships you can conquer distant lands, like the British in India. On land, nothing much has changed. But you can bombard a city from the sea—guns, men, drawn anywhere in the world at an instant."

"Istanbul has never been so vulnerable, that's true."

"That, too. When Mehmet the Conqueror took the city from the Greeks, he had one huge cannon dragged over the mountains to the city walls. And he attacked by land." He swept an arm across the panorama. "Today, battleships could reduce Istanbul to rubble in a few days."

"I had no idea you were such a strategist, Yashim."

"I'm not. I've been thinking, though. For fifty years or more, the empire has been crumbling around the edges. Losing possessions to Russia on the Black Sea. Losing ground to Egypt in the south. It's been like watching a bear attacked by dogs. In the end, the dogs will always win."

"Decline, decline." Palewski shrugged. "All empires, in the end, are doomed to fall."

"Naturally—unless they receive unexpected aid."

"Quite. But the Ottomans, as I've mentioned, don't have powerful friends."

"No—until now, we've simply managed our own decline, alone."

They passed below the Galata Tower.

Palewski's eyes narrowed. "What do you mean, until now?"

"It was what you said about the bridge that made me see it. Europe comes to Istanbul, is that what you said? For fifty years we've been clamped in a pincer between Russia and the Egyptians—and when the Greeks sought independence, the British and the French made sure they got it, too. No, we don't have friends. We don't even have an alliance of interests."

"Pretty tight," Palewski said. "And gloomy."

"Until Fevzi Pasha sailed into Alexandria and gave up the fleet."

Palewski frowned. "Gloomier still, I'd have thought."

Yashim shook his head. "On the contrary. I think Fevzi Pasha's defection may save the empire."

Palewski gave a dry laugh. Yashim turned.

"Britain and France, you said, don't care who governs Istanbul—as long as it isn't the Russians. But the British are very touchy about anything that crops up along their line to India. Since Napoleon's day the French feel they have a sort of proprietary interest in Egypt and the Middle East. Protecting the Catholics, for example. Both want to preserve the balance of power in Europe."

"What are you suggesting, Yashim?"

"Fevzi Ahmet may have inadvertently done what no one has managed to achieve for twenty years—least of all Husrev Pasha. He fights yesterday's battles, Palewski. Two fronts—the Russians and the Egyptians. Until now, we haven't had allies. Don't you see?"

"That by defecting to the Egyptians—?"

"Fevzi Ahmet has forced the issue. Either the Powers let it go, in which case the Russians organize a protectorate in Istanbul, and the khedive rattles his saber over the Middle East—"

"Or the British have to intervene. Yes, I'm beginning to see what you mean. The empire needed outside help—and now it can't refuse."

"It was the bridge that made me see it. You said it yourself: the bridge is theater. And so is diplomacy. Fevzi Pasha built a bridge that would bring European Pera into Istanbul. The next thing, ambassador, is a diplomatic approach to the French."

Palewski startled. "When you say 'ambassador'—?"

"It can't be Husrev Pasha. It isn't his job to spell out the weakness of the Ottoman state. I can't do it. The only Englishman I know is a third-grade secretary to the ambassador."

"Ah, yes. Mr. Compston. I can't quite see him shaping European policy for years to come."

"But you could. You're neutral and you have the rank. The French ambassador is a friend, isn't he? Just have a word in his ear, and let him do the rest."

Palewski glanced around. They were passing the mouth of the lane that led down to the British embassy. "Speaking of Compston, he dropped in earlier. Rambled on about how you saved his watch or something. Seems to feel he's under some sort of obligation to you."

Yashim waved his hand impatiently.

"Well, he was most anxious to talk to you, Yashim. Felt he owed you something, can't remember what it was about." Palewski screwed up his eyes. "A tip about some papers, I think. He said to get in touch—you'd know why."

Yashim pulled a face. "I've no idea."

"No matter. He's at the embassy, apparently—and we're just passing. Perhaps . . ."

Yashim stopped. "All right. I'll drop in, now."

THE wrought-iron gates of the British embassy were surmounted by an escutcheon that showed a unicorn and a lion pawing at a crown.

Yashim gave the unicorn a mental salute as he passed under the gate: the mythical beast amused him. On the face of it the British were a supremely practical people, interested in trade and fond—like Compston—of speaking their own mind, but the unicorn suggested a fanciful streak. Compston's obsession with the poet Byron was a case in point: the beefy English boy who appeared with a startled look at the top of the stairs was obviously not a soul in romantic torment.

He came down the stairs dragging on an overcoat.

"I say, Yashim efendi, what?" He took Yashim by the arm and steered him across the hall. "Coffee? Good little French place around the corner." He glanced around, and lowered his voice. "New boy from London. Wretched little sneak. Best not to be seen hanging about here."

A pimply young man looked up from a desk. "Going out, Mr. Compston?"

"Change of air. Been a bad smell in here these last few weeks, daresay you haven't noticed?"

Compston crammed on his hat and stepped outside. "Good dig, what? Bad smell, ha ha!"

Yashim let him lead the way to a small café on the Grande Rue.

"Messieurs? Qu'est-ce que vous désirez?" The owner was a Frenchman, stout and bald, with an elegant mustache. He had a napkin draped over his arm.

Compston ordered coffee, in his execrable French; Yashim asked for a verbena.

He watched as Compston spooned sugar into his cup and stirred it nervously.

"I say, Yashim efendi—" he began; then he seemed to check himself. "What price the new bridge?"

"The bridge? What of it?"

"Do you think it'll ever work? Fizerley says no, bound to collapse. Esterhazy—he's at the imperial embassy—says it'll stand. We've got a bet on it."

Yashim felt a twinge of impatience. "Forgive me, Mr. Compston. Our friend Palewski mentioned something you wanted to talk to me about. The bridge? I don't quite understand."

"Ah, yes, well—never mind about the bridge, efendi. Silly question." Compston flushed slightly. "My pater's not awfully keen on gambling himself. No, what I really wanted to talk about were these."

He fished in his waistcoat and brought out a packet of papers.

Yashim gave a start. "I've seen these before. But how on earth—?"

"Found 'em, efendi, just lying in the grass. The night you saved my watch, on Chalki."

He set the packet on the table and patted it, then pushed it over toward Yashim.

"I—I wanted you to have 'em. Never occurred to me you might have dropped them, but I see that now. You know what they are?"

Yashim eyed the packet. "Not exactly," he admitted cautiously. "I glanced through them. I didn't have much time, and my Russian's none too fluent anyway."

"I read Russian, Yashim efendi."

He said it with modest diffidence, as if he expected Yashim's reaction.

"You?"

Compston gave an apologetic shrug. "Never found much time for it, until I came across Pushkin."

"Who?"

"Alexander Pushkin. He's a Russian poet, dead now." Compston absently reached into his waistcoat pocket and ran his fingers up a silver chain. The watch appeared in his hand. "Killed in a duel just a couple of years ago. Affair of the heart," he added wistfully.

"Like your Byron?"

"Not bad, Yashim efendi. Put like that, you're right. Pushkin is the Russian Byron. Languages don't agree with me, but somehow Russian works." He gave a short laugh. "They're letters, written to your Kapudan pasha. I sort of pieced it together. Didn't think much more of 'em, not until we heard about the Egyptian business. Then I thought of you. Here they are."

"You didn't think about them?" Yashim could not keep the note of surprise out of his voice. "Why not?"

It was Compston's turn to sound surprised. "Well, there's not much to them, efendi, is there? Or didn't you read them? Sorry, of course . . ." He frowned. "They're nothing too important, judging by the hand. Common threats—I know your secret, a word from One Who Knows, that sort of thing. You know—your time is running out."

"Blackmailing letters? From Galytsin?"

Compston raised an eyebrow. "Galytsin? No, no. But blackmailing letters, all right. Damned obscure. Full of spelling mistakes, just what you'd expect from some Russki blackmailer. Lowest form of villainy, blackmail.

I don't say Galytsin wouldn't stoop to it, but he could never have written those letters." He pointed at the packet. "Have a look yourself."

Yashim scooped up the bundle and slipped it into his waistcoat. "Thank you."

Compston waved a hand. "Please, don't mention it. Feel much better now—one good turn, all that sort of thing. I say—" He pulled a worried face and bent to catch Yashim's eye. "As a matter of fact, you won't mention that we've met? Better not. Fizerley, well. He's a bit of a stickler."

"Of course not," Yashim murmured. He was not really listening. He was staring into the surface of his tea and wondering whether he had got everything wrong.

After a moment he collected himself. "About the bridge," he said. "I expect it'll stand, all right. Fevzi Ahmet may be a traitor, but he's no fool."

"That's just what I was afraid you'd say, Yashim efendi," Compston replied unhappily. "Oh God, it's going to be awful!"

109

WHEN the man from the mountains first saw the sea, he knelt and wept, wondering how any man could command such an immensity.

But as the day wore on, he grew more used to it; he swallowed his doubts. The pasha was a man, like any other. He would die, as a man did.

The man with the knife did not stop to look at the swollen welt across his chest. It was changing color, weeping; and darker tentacles were spreading across his skin.

He stumbled on, to the sound of the gulls mocking him over the little waves.

110

AT Besiktas Yashim asked to see the Kislar aga and was led downstairs to a Frenchified waiting room that was stuffy and windowless, furnished with two European sofas, an Italian clock, and a number of high-backed chairs that had lost some of their gilt, or a molded foot. Timid black faces he did not recognize looked in on him once or twice, before Ibou himself appeared.

He looked gray, Yashim thought; and one of his eyes was bloodshot.

The aga waited until the door had closed, and then subsided into one of the great sofas. He rubbed his hands across his face.

"The bridge," he groaned. "I wish it had never been built."

"You, too?" Yashim said in surprise.

"The opening ceremony," the aga muttered. "Tomorrow, all the ladies, in caïques. In public! The sultan on horseback. Precedence, Yashim. You can't believe."

"The opening ceremony?"

The aga's hand snaked out over the arm of the sofa. "Please, Yashim. Help yourself." He popped a sugared lozenge into his mouth. "The public ceremony is tomorrow. The real ceremony began here, today—and worse than the changeover, if that's possible. Who gets into the first caïque? What shall they wear? Do they land this side of the bridge, or is it proper to go under it? I don't know," he added, in a tone to suggest he didn't much care, either. "And now what new worries do you bring me, Yashim?"

Yashim frowned. His eye fell on an ormolu clock, standing on a shelf. It told ferenghi time, the hours spaced out impersonally between night and light. It was not how time seemed to Yashim: his hours had been as long as days. He could see its cogs and springs behind beveled glass.

He said: "What is the engine, Ibou? What does it mean?"

Ibou turned his head slowly and looked at Yashim slyly, out of the corner of his eye. "The engine?"

Yashim gazed at the clock. "Something Melda said."

"A bit of foolishness. The housekeeper ladies make it a joke among them, when new girls are brought in."

Yashim opened his hands and shrugged, nonplussed. "The engine?"

"Well, there's an old table, down in the basement. The housekeepers fool about with it." Ibou waved his hand as if it didn't matter and was beneath his dignity to comment.

"Fool about?" But Melda hadn't suggested fooling about. *I have seen the engine*, she'd said.

The aga heaved a sigh. "I should deal with it, I suppose." He wiped his hands across his eyes. "They take the novices down to look at the table. The new girls."

"Yes?"

Ibou blew out his cheeks. "The table stands on a stone flagged floor, which looks like a trapdoor. They—frighten the girls, a bit. That's what I've heard."

"The novices," Yashim repeated. "And where does the engine come in?"

Ibou pulled a face. "Pouf. I don't know. If a girl misbehaves, they tell them, she'll be strapped to this table." He stuck a finger in the air and rotated it. "They tell them never to reveal anything they've heard or seen."

"Or what?"

The aga rolled his eyes. "Or they'll strap her down, and the table will start to spin, around and around, and sink down through the floor into the Bosphorus." He let his hand drop to his lap.

"I see." Yashim was not smiling.

"It's a bit of fun, Yashim."

Yashim had seen many girls fresh off the hills enter the palace for the first time. He remembered a little black girl bought by one of the late sultan's khadins, who came into the harem with her eyes and mouth like

Os. She had gone about stroking everything and muttering, "Isn't it lovely! Isn't it lovely!" over and over again. In the evening she had thought she would be sent away; when they explained she would live there forever, she burst into tears.

He'd seen others, though, halting and shy, bemused by the form of speech they heard, dazzled by the bearing of the harem women, stupefied by the luxury. Some physically shook with fear at the prospect of being introduced. Yashim thought of Hyacinth, frightened by the first snow.

"The engine doesn't exist," Ibou snapped.

"Not here. But at Topkapi? Maybe there is an engine. Maybe, Ibou, your predecessors found it useful to have one."

The Kislar aga shrugged lightly. "At Topkapi, Yashim, I worked in the library. Nobody pushed books into the Bosphorus. How would I know? The lady Talfa is the one to ask. She showed it to the girls."

"I see." He thought of Melda, frozen with misery. "Who would Elif have confided in, when she had her trouble? Apart from Melda. Would she have spoken to Talfa? Asked her for help, maybe?"

"Talfa?" The Kislar aga looked incredulous. "They hated each other."

It was Yashim's turn to look surprised. "Why?"

Ibou groaned. "That dreadful day, when the new girls came across, Elif was very rude to the lady Talfa. She treated her like one of Sultan Mahmut's concubines."

"Not a good start."

"No. The lady Talfa gave her—and Melda—the job of escorting a little girl."

"Which they didn't like?"

"They thought it was b-b-beneath them. Elif was very, very angry. She made remarks—and did some foolish things, I believe."

"Foolish things?"

The aga rolled his eyes. "She put a rat's tail in the lady Talfa's makeup pot."

"Who told you that?"

"I didn't need to be told. You could hear Talfa all over the palace."

"And you knew it was Elif?"

"Who else? She denied it, naturally." Ibou blew out his cheeks. "You cannot believe the spite and fury of these women, Yashim."

"I wouldn't say that, Ibou."

He got up. Yashim knew that all sorts of children lived in the harem—princes and princesses, slave girls, children adopted into the imperial family for political or diplomatic reasons. "Who was the girl?"

Ibou shrugged. "We call her Roxelana. The lady Talfa took a shine to her. Very quiet little thing."

"Why Roxelana? She's Russian?"

"Either that, or it's just because she has red hair."

"And that's all you can tell me?"

"She has red hair. She didn't like her kalfas wearing their orchestra uniform. She didn't like their hats." Ibou flung up his hands in exasperation. "She's about five. Just a little girl, Yashim. Hyacinth would have been the person to ask, if you wanted."

Yashim saw the tears welling up in the aga's eyes.

"Hyacinth? Why Hyacinth?"

"Because Hyacinth was responsible for taking her into the harem. It was Hyacinth who gave her the name."

SNOW was falling in scattered flurries as Yashim strode away from Besiktas. His head throbbed. He tore off his turban and walked on bareheaded, grateful for the cold and the thin wind and the darkness that all but hid the buildings around him.

He swung his arms, sucked at the cold air. He knew now precisely why he had chosen to live outside, away from the palace; precisely why

Talfa's insinuations had made his flesh creep and his ancient fears rise up. Preen was right: he could not bear to be trapped. He beat his arms over his chest and thought of Ibou's subterranean rooms, of the women who dragged out their lives within the confines of a harem, of Kadri bursting his constraints and vaulting the walls of his palace school.

Shadowed, muffled figures slipped past him in the gloom. Now and then he shivered, like an animal discovering its limbs after a long sleep: ever since that ceremony of the birth he had been laboring under a burden of dread. And dreadful things had happened. At Besiktas, a girl had become possessed by a demon: a demon of the mind that created the demon in her belly. Hyacinth's fear of abandonment was a demon, too, which plagued him remorselessly until he died falling from the balustrade. Yashim was oppressed by thoughts of Fevzi Ahmet, the mentor whose example he had rejected, whose memory he had thought buried and contained.

Yashim stepped almost automatically into a caïque. Later he could remember reaching the landing stage, but not how he had crossed the Horn, nor how he had come home.

Images floated unbidden into his mind: a little boy standing frightened in the snow; Pembe, the mother of the sultan's ruined child; a bloodstained sheet; Hyacinth's frail body in the pool. He shuddered: for a few moments he had felt that he was seeing with another eye. An evil eye, which roamed from Besiktas to Topkapi, picking out its victims, sapping their will to live.

Back in his apartment he riddled the stove, angrily, and added a scoop of charcoal. He stood for a moment warming his hands above the glow, then he wiped them and stripped the skin from a pair of onions, which he split on the board. He sliced the halves in both directions, and let the tears well in his eyes. One day, Ibou had said once, you will mourn the valide yourself.

He put a shallow pan on the coals and added a slick of oil. He smashed the garlic with the flat of a blade and swept it from the board with the onions into the pan. They began to sizzle on the heat, and he wiped his eyes. He peeled a few carrots, potatoes, and a knob of celeriac, then pulled the chopping block toward him and began to slice the vegetables, first into strips, then into little dice.

He shook the pan.

The valide had once told him that a long life inside the harem depended on intelligence, not good health. But the valide was not well.

The onions were soft; he stirred in the vegetables, turning them in the oil.

It took a man or a woman to cast the eye. And there was one woman in the harem whose bitterness was active—and corrosive. Talfa was the senior lady in the sultan's harem. Talfa had intuitively divined Yashim's own fear of being pinned down in the palace, and played upon it. Talfa was bitter, and ambitious.

Perhaps she had frightened others? Pembe claimed that Talfa put the evil eye on her. Bezmialem had become a cipher. Elif had died at Besiktas, Hyacinth at Topkapi—but thanks to Tülin, the valide's handmaiden, he knew that Talfa had gone to Topkapi only days before, and talked of nothing while the valide dozed. Talfa had insisted on meeting all the sultan's ladies, so that they might meet her daughter, and then she had spoken to Melda. Taken her apart. Taken her aside for a little chat.

He sprinkled some sugar over the pan and threw in a couple of bay leaves. He covered the vegetables with water, and left them to come to the boil while he cleaned the mussels.

Talfa knew Topkapi very well, from top to bottom. She had been born there, after all. Talfa would know all about the engine. It didn't matter whether the engine really existed or not. He might spend hours in the palace, searching for a contraption that whirled people to their doom— and all he might find would be a dusty table in a neglected room.

Ibou said that Talfa and Elif hated each other.

But Talfa had a knack for divining people's fears, and playing on them. Elif's stare-baby—where had that come from? Perhaps Talfa had suggested a desperate remedy.

It made her bleed.

By taking Melda to Topkapi, Yashim had thought he was protecting her.

Instead, he had isolated her. What was it the valide had said? *To be truly alone—in here, at least—it's a kind of death.*

Yashim tapped a mussel on the board. The mussel closed, and he tossed it into the bowl. Eventually he tipped the bowl and drained the juice into the pan. After a few minutes he stirred in the mussels.

Had Melda confided in Hyacinth? Talfa had something on Hyacinth that would make his heart sink, too.

Yashim took a bunch of parsley and chopped it on the board. He imagined Talfa dripping with feigned concern: "Poor Hyacinth. With the valide gone, there'll be just you, won't there? You and the old women at Topkapi?"

Yashim raised his head, with a jolt.

It had happened so slowly, so inexorably, that he hadn't really noticed how Talfa had made herself queen of the harem. It was she rather than Bezmialem or Ibou who created and enforced the rules.

But if the valide moved to Besiktas, Talfa's influence as the senior lady of the harem would be eclipsed.

Yashim picked up the *pilaki* and moved it off the heat, to the table. He scattered the parsley over the mussels.

Then he washed his hands and wound the turban around his head, and went out into the night.

THE valide looked at Yashim with her bright eyes.

"Am I going to Besiktas, Yashim? I can't remember."

Yashim took her pale hand in his. He found the question difficult to answer.

"Perhaps, valide hanum. When you are feeling stronger."

She closed her eyes, and smiled faintly. "I wonder. I wonder what Dr. Sevi would suggest." Her eyelids flickered, and he felt the pressure of her hand relax.

Yashim stooped and put his ear close to her lips. A silver carafe, fluted like a swan, stood on a small inlay table. Yashim grabbed at its neck and went to slosh some water into a glass. But the carafe was empty.

He thrust it into Tülin's hands. "Fetch water. Fill it."

She took the carafe and ran with it to the outer door.

Yashim turned back to the valide. He smoothed a skimpy lock of hair from her forehead. She was papery to the touch; papery and thin. At his touch her eyes flickered, and moved slowly toward him.

"Papa." Her word was scarcely a breath, just a shape on her lips. "Papa." Her eyes fixed on him now, watery and old and very deep. *"Je me suis perdue,"* she murmured. I am lost. *"Mais—ça va bien."*

He read the question in her eyes: the old question that always lay in the eyes of the dying. Her look was full of tenderness, as if the answer were already known, like a secret between them—the secret by which all men and women were bound, as long as men lived and died.

He could not betray that look by moving his own eyes until the girl came back and Yashim heard the sound of water in the glass.

He bent forward carefully, and brought the glass to the valide's lips. The water ran across her tongue and he heard her throat catch. He brought the glass to her lips again. She swallowed slowly, closing and opening her mouth.

He let her breathe, then tried again.

After a while her eyes closed. The glass was almost empty.

He looked into the valide's face, noting the veins in her eyelids and the translucency of her skin. Bending very close, he caught a faint sigh from her lips.

"I am going to fetch the doctor." He went out into the courtyard. In the eunuch's room he scribbled a note for the doctor, advising him to come with all possible speed, and handed it to a halberdier.

"Not Inalcik," he added. Inalcik was young, courteous, and French-trained; he was always consulted by the ladies of Besiktas. "You must ask for Sabbatai Sevi. Do you understand? The old Jew."

"Sevi the Jew." The halberdier bowed.

But it was young Inalcik who came, smooth and serious in a black frock coat, stepping very precisely over the old stones of the courtyard with his bag in his hand.

He went into the valide's chamber and remained there for twenty minutes, listening to her chest through a stethoscope, examining her eyelids, writing notes in a yellow book with a fountain pen.

When he emerged he looked solemn. They met Sevi at the gate to the harem. He wore a long coat, edged with velvet, and a blue skullcap. Dr. Inalcik looked surprised, and amused.

"A second opinion, Dr. Sevi. I approve, heartily." His eyes twinkled as he outlined his own diagnosis to the Jew, who stooped to listen. "I hope you will be able to do more than I have achieved," he added.

Sevi opened his hands. "I am very old, doctor. So is the lady."

As Yashim led him to the valide's room, Sevi stayed him with his hand. "The mind?"

"Wandering," Yashim explained. "It has been like this for—" He screwed up his eyes, casting back. "A month, maybe more. Now, I think, she spends more time at home—her childhood home."

Sevi nodded. "Perhaps she had a very happy childhood. Can she walk?"

"I haven't seen her walk in weeks."

"Then why not a visit to her childhood home? It's easier on the feet."

He came without a bag, or instruments of any kind. He knelt by the divan and took the valide's hand in his own. After a while he peered more closely at her fingers.

Yashim felt a twinge of doubt. In Sevi's day, the doctor often examined a woman through a curtain. Childbirth, disease, all manner of conditions had to be treated by the doctor without actually touching, or even inspecting, the woman's body; it was the tradition, it maintained propriety.

"Modern medicine," Inalcik had remarked, as he clipped open his bag and retrieved his stethoscope, "goes rather deeper to the sources and the causes of discomfort and illness."

The old Jew remained on his knees for some time, watching the valide's face, absently rubbing her hand in his.

He seemed to have gone into some sort of dream. Yashim gave a discreet cough and the old man sighed.

He unfolded slowly, and stood up.

"Poison?" Yashim asked.

Sabbatai Sevi looked at him sadly. "Poison? No. The valide sultan," he added gravely, "is extremely thirsty."

ROXELANA dreamed. She dreamed she was all dressed up like a big bear. Furry boots. Furry hat.

"You must catch it this time, silly!"

"I will try, my precious!" The kalfa smiles at the little girl. But it is hard to catch a ball made of snow when the light is beginning to fade.

Roxelana knows this. It is what makes her laugh.

She says: "You may sit in the arbor. I am going to play." When the kalfa crouches down to put a shawl around her, Roxelana tells her about the bear. The kalfa is Elif.

The kalfa laughs, smoothing her hair, but her eyes go out toward the garden.

Roxelana runs to the tree, taking big steps in the snow, like a bear. She is a bear and can hide behind the thick black trunk. There is not as much snow on the ground here.

Peep-o! Her kalfa is Melda now, sitting in the arbor, on the stone seat where they have put the cushions. Peep-o!

Silly Melda! She is not looking. She doesn't know there is a bear so close.

She glances around. The trees at the end of the harem garden are tangled, and black and white with snow, and the snow between is quite fresh and smooth. She sets off, planting her fur boots into the white coverlet one after the other. Counting. Melda cannot see her; the tree is between them.

One step, two step, three step, four.

The trees are close. She can see between them now, into the shadows. For a bear those shadows would be a good hiding place.

Roxelana stops. She turns her head and looks back with a dubious frown. Of course she cannot see her kalfa, because of the big tree. What she can see are her footprints in the snow, and for a moment she wonders how they got there, those footprints coming after her across the shrouded lawn. They have swerved from the big tree and chased after her, dark sockets running across the whiteness. They are headed right toward her. To where she is standing.

And before she can turn her head she knows that the bear is on the other side, in the shadows behind her. The little girl opens her mouth to scream, but nothing comes out.

She hears the kalfa calling, and sees herself running back toward the big tree, running too slowly, willing her face forward, with the footprints always just a step behind her.

She woke up, gasping, wide-eyed in the dark.

The quilt had slipped onto the floor: it made a shape in the dark, and Roxelana was cold and afraid and all alone.

IN snow, Istanbul transformed itself from a city of half a million people into a fantastic forest running down to an icy shore: its domes were the earthworks of a vanished race of giants, its minarets gaunt boles of shattered trees, its roofs, blanketed under a rippling veneer of snow, terraced fields marked only by the arrowed tracks of birds and the dimpled pawprints of hungry cats. The rattle of porters' barrows, the clatter of hooves, the usual hum of markets and muezzins and street hawkers were muffled. Some lanes were blocked; now and then great slides of snow would precipitate themselves from the roofs and land with a *whump!* on the street below.

Yashim glimpsed lamplight as he reached the water steps at Balat. He had left the valide in the care of two elderly eunuchs, who were to give her sips of lukewarm water whenever she awoke. Tülin had retired to the girls' dormitory, taking her instrument with her. He had gone back down the stairs with the sound of Tülin's flute blowing in his ears.

She played beautifully. She played, perhaps, as a consolation. But the music had needled him.

Lanterns hung from the mooring poles; two caïquejees were keeping warm by knocking ice from the base of the poles with the ends of their oars. Yashim had heard that the Golden Horn might freeze.

He stamped his feet and one of the caïquejees grabbed a lantern and swung it up.

"Fare, efendi?"

"Pera stairs," he said. "How's the ice?"

The man blew out his cheeks. He reached down into his caïque and scattered the cushions, which had been piled up beneath a tarpaulin. "If it gets any thicker, I'll carry you on my back," he said cheerfully. "At your pleasure, efendi."

The boatman picked up the oars and with a deft flick of his arm sent the fragile craft racing into the deep, still waters of the Golden Horn. Overhead a few stars shone among the drifting clouds, and on either bank the snow showed pale against the hills. Something was alive in the back of Yashim's mind; something that wanted to be remembered, but lurked there, shy of the glare of his thoughts as if it feared the eye.

The boatman set him down opposite the steps that climbed the hill to the Galata Tower. Yashim was relieved to find that they had been swept and even scattered with ashes. His breath cooled on his cheeks as he climbed, pausing now and then to admire the snowy hills of Istanbul. A dog, whimpering on its cold paws, slunk past in the shadows. Yashim skirted the shacks that had spilled out around the base of the tower, and pressed on up a sloping street to the Grande Rue.

At the Polish residency, someone—Marta, perhaps—had scraped a path across the frozen carriage sweep to the front steps. As he slithered on the ice, Yashim wondered if it might have been better to leave the snow.

He thumped on the door and felt the frame quiver. A chunk of snow fell from the roof of the porch. Without waiting for an answer, Yashim pushed inside.

Inside it was even colder, but Yashim knew better than to linger in the darkened hall. He took the stairs gingerly, two at a time, using the rail to guide him.

He paused at the top. Palewski would be reading in his comfortable chair by the fire, perhaps working on his translation, surrounded by sheets of paper, a glass at his elbow. A band of light showed beneath the door.

Long ago, when they were new to each other, there had been courtesies on both sides, bows, salaams, even little speeches in the proper Ottoman style, and in good French. Yashim would have found it unthinkable that he should slip in unannounced, and unacknowledged; but years of friendship and understanding had knocked off the courtesies like so many rococo embellishments.

Yashim entered without knocking.

A comfortable heat radiated from a crackling log fire. The shutters were closed, the candles were lit, and across the room an oil lamp cast a pool of yellow light across a small round table covered with a green chenille cloth.

Palewski was sitting at the table, both hands laid flat on the chenille cloth. Opposite him sat his housekeeper, Marta. She too had her hands on the table.

A thread of blood was trickling from Palewski's nose.

Behind Marta stood a man with a rifle, and the muzzle of the rifle was pressed against the nape of Marta's neck.

Behind Yashim the door closed.

A voice he knew all too well spoke in his ear.

"So, Yashim. After all these years."

115

"I am sure you can appreciate your friends' position," Fevzi Ahmet said. "The ambassador made an effort to rearrange it, but you see I was able to change his mind."

Palewski spoke without turning his head. "I'm sorry, Yashim. I thought it was you earlier, on the stairs."

Yashim tasted bile in his mouth.

The pasha smiled. "I won't detain them longer than necessary."

"Necessary for what?"

"Securing your cooperation."

Fevzi Ahmet folded his arms. In ten years his face had grown thinner, and his hair was gray. He had lost some of the thuggish beauty that had attracted the late Sultan Mahmut to him, but his black eyes were as deep and cold as ever.

What do you want?"

"Just put your hands up, over your head."

Yashim glanced at Marta. Her eyes flickered toward him as he lifted his hands. He saw her jaw clench, and her eyes rolled upward. She blinked slowly, then looked at Palewski, and forced a little smile.

Palewski rubbed the tablecloth with his fingertips and held her gaze.

"You wonder why I have risked coming back to Istanbul?"

"Of course."

Fevzi Ahmet considered him for a while.

Yashim glanced back at Marta. Kadri: Kadri wasn't here. He was upstairs. Asleep.

"Just before I left with the fleet," Fevzi Ahmet said, "one of Galytsin's agents came to see me. He brought me some unwelcome news."

"A Baltic German, blond, scarred. He was blackmailing you. You killed him."

Fevzi's eyes were like snow holes. "Four out of five. You're losing your touch."

Fevzi Pasha sat down in Palewski's armchair, making Yashim wince. He picked up the poker and riddled the fire. A log crashed down, emitting a shower of sparks. "I need your help."

"You seem to have help already," Yashim said, nodding to the man with the gun.

"Oh yes, the caïquejees. Splendidly loyal, I must say, to one of their own. But I'm afraid this is rather beyond them. Beyond any man, except you."

Yashim frowned. "Why me?"

Fevzi Ahmet let out an exasperated sigh, and stabbed the fire. "Four years ago, when I was promoted to Kapudan pasha, the Russians approached me with an offer."

"I thought it was earlier than that," Yashim said drily. "Saint Petersburg? Ten years, at least."

"Saint Petersburg, Yashim." Fevzi Ahmet frowned. "The Russians gave me a whore . . . ?"

Yashim looked at him. "You gave Batoumi away."

"Batoumi was already lost. My job was to let it go."

"What do you mean, it was your job? To exchange Batoumi for a woman?"

A flash of irritation crossed Fevzi Ahmet's face. "I took my instructions from the grand vizier. They didn't involve you—and I thought you were too green. Perhaps you still are." He fixed Yashim with a stare. "Ironic, isn't it? Now I need your help."

"So you say. Four years ago, what offer did the Russians make?"

"Galytsin made me an expensive offer, in return for news. My inactivity." He shrugged. "All that matters is that I turned them down."

"Oh?"

"The Russians are hard, Yashim. I didn't reckon on the cost of ignoring them. A few weeks later my home was burned to the ground." Fevzi

Pasha clinked the poker against the grate. "My wife was inside. A concubine, and the old *lala* who looked after them." He paused. "And my daughter, too."

Yashim looked away.

"But I saved her, Yashim."

Yashim glanced up quickly. Fevzi Pasha's eyes were bright with triumph.

"Yes—I saved her. The *lala* dropped her into my arms."

KADRI opened his eyes in the dark and wondered what had woken him.

He glanced at the window; it was a dark night, and he could not tell what time it was.

He pushed his blanket aside and swung his bare feet onto the floor, cocking his head, listening to a faint murmur from somewhere downstairs.

Perhaps Yashim had come?

He was about to get back into bed when he realized that he was thirsty.

He would go down to the kitchen and fetch a glass of water without disturbing the two men.

He pulled on a woollen coat the ambassador had lent him, and padded to the stairs.

Somewhere below, a floorboard creaked.

Kadri had lived wild in the hills of Cappadocia, and he was not afraid of the dark, but he paused at the sound.

"All ready?"

Kadri was suddenly alert.

Someone had whispered on the landing below.

He bent over the banister, listening.

117

FEVZI Pasha rested the tip of the poker against the grate. "The fire taught me that as long as I had a family, I would never be safe. The Russians might try again, and next time they would use my daughter. So I gave her up."

Yashim thought back to the horrible doll in Fevzi Ahmet's house.

"The sultan had appointed me to command the fleet, and to build a bridge across the Golden Horn. I had to put her somewhere safe."

"The sultan's palace," Yashim murmured.

"I arranged for her to enter the sultan's harem, yes. Only an old eunuch would know who she was. So I thought."

"Hyacinth?"

"Full marks, Yashim. But then you know the story, don't you? It was me and Hyacinth—until someone told the Russians, after all."

He was staring at Yashim, but Yashim was aware only of something unlocking in his mind—something about Hyacinth, and the harem, and the dead girls.

"Someone who wished me harm," Fevzi Ahmet added. "In the circumstances, I imagine it was you."

Yashim blinked. "Me?"

"'Me'! You can do better than that, Yashim. But I don't have time to listen to your outraged innocence. You wouldn't think it, ambassador, would you?" Fevzi Ahmet called over his shoulder. "Yashim sold my little girl to your old friends. Quite Galytsin's confidant, I hear."

"You should have stuck to rowing," Palewski said glumly.

Fevzi Ahmet's face twitched as he faced Yashim. "You will bring my daughter here. Hyacinth will find a way."

"Hyacinth is dead," Yashim said.

The pasha looked pale. "It is happening . . ." he muttered. He sprang to his feet and went to the door. "That complicates things—for you. For the sake of your friends, I imagine you can find a way."

"A way?"

"To get my daughter out of the harem."

Yashim shook his head. "I can't just walk out of the sultan's harem with a little girl."

Fevzi Pasha whistled into the dark, and two men entered the room: caïquejees both, to judge by their swinging gait.

"These men are going to take you to your cellar, ambassador. Marta—is it?—will accompany you. I'm afraid it won't be very comfortable, but it depends on your friend how long you will remain there. Tie them."

The last words were spoken to the caïquejees. They lifted Palewski's hands and bound them behind his back.

Palewski kept his eyes on Marta, and she on his, even when they tied her hands behind her back. Neither of them spoke.

The door closed behind them. "I don't know how you plan to get away with it," Yashim said.

"Interesting, isn't it? Neither of us can tell how the other will lay his plans. I only hope, for your sake, that yours will be as effective as my own."

"I'm afraid you overestimate my talents," Yashim said. "I didn't know you had a daughter."

"So you say. It doesn't matter, does it? You know now—and your friends downstairs." He stood up. "You will bring her here. If not I will kill the ambassador, and his woman. And I will kill you, too." He paused, and flung back his head. "For you, however, I actually have a little gift. An incentive, if you like."

118

KADRI saw the drawing room door open, and the two caïquejees go in.

He was about to go down and find out what was going on when the door opened again, and the men came out holding candlesticks. Between them came Marta and Palewski. Kadri could see that something was wrong; he checked his impulse to call out, but moved noiselessly down the stairs to the half-landing.

He heard the cellar door open, and close.

Frowning with anxiety, he darted down the second flight of steps and listened by the door.

He recognized Yashim's voice, and another one he didn't know.

119

"THERE'S nothing I could possibly want that you could ever give me, Fevzi Ahmet."

The pasha smiled. "No? Think of your father, Yashim. The governor. Poor old man. He died, I'm told, still trying to find out who brought such dishonor on his family."

A stubborn look came into Yashim's eyes. "What do you mean?"

"Well, well. His wife—the lovely Greek girl? Manhandled, shall we say, before they slit her throat? At least she got to see who gelded her only son, before she died. I'm told she was allowed to watch."

Yashim's lip peeled back.

"The governor's son," Fevzi Ahmet went on, in the same musing tone. "Not quite a son, anymore. Very sad, for everyone. And embarrassing for the old man, wasn't it? With all his power, not knowing who. Not knowing why. His wife dishonored and dead, and his son castrated. Who did it? He never found out. Too much grief. Some people said it pushed him into an early grave."

Yashim closed his eyes. "I don't care, anymore."

"If I thought about the wife I never had, the children . . . I think I would still dream about that cave. My mother's screams."

"My mother's screams?" It took Yashim a violent effort to control his voice. She hadn't screamed, the woman with the laughing eyes. But he had been forced to watch her die.

"I find things out, Yashim. I knew years ago." He stepped closer: just not quite close enough—he had measured the distance carefully. "So if you can rescue my daughter—and help me get away—I'll tell you."

He opened the door. "I hope you can find your own way out, Yashim. I'd give you a candle, but in the circumstances it would be foolish, don't you think?"

"What do you mean?" Yashim had hardly spoken when the stench rolling up the stairs answered his question.

Paraffin oil.

On the landing he could hear one of Fevzi Pasha's men, sloshing fuel across the floorboards below.

"Just in case you thought of mounting a daring rescue," Fevzi Ahmet said. "A fire is very effective, and leaves nothing behind—as I well know. It took the *yali* ten minutes to burn to the ground. The bodies went up in smoke. My wife's coffin, as it happens, contained a quantity of ash and a piece of bone. Her silver bangles had fused to it. That's how I knew."

120

KADRI had just time to back up the stairs when Yashim and the stranger came out onto the landing.

He heard them talk, and then they went downstairs.

For some reason he could not understand, Palewski and Marta were imprisoned in the cellar; only Yashim had been allowed to go.

He heard the front door close, and a breeze laden with paraffin wafted up the stairs.

It would take only a spark, and the whole place would go up in flames—just as the stranger had said.

Kadri knew he did not dare go down. If he met the man with the spark . . .

He thought of trying the empty drawing room, but the windows would be closed, and he would make too much noise opening them.

Very quietly he went back to his room and eased the window open.

It was a long way down to the yard.

121

"M arta?"

"I am here, kyrie." Her voice came out of the darkness behind him.

"Can you move?"

"Not very well, kyrie. I can move a little—but it is cold."

"Yes." Palewski tried to remember how Marta had been dressed, but after a while he gave up. All he could remember was the trusting look she had fixed on him earlier, in the drawing room.

He shifted slightly on his knees, to ease the discomfort; his kneecaps crackled against the damp stone. Already his knees hurt; in an hour, they would be worse. He imagined the cold, and the cramps shooting up his thighs.

"Marta, have they made you kneel on the floor?"

"To kneel, kyrie? I am sitting down, but I cannot move my arms. They have tied my arms behind my back."

"You can move your legs?"

He heard the sound of her skirts rustling against the stone floor. "Yes, kyrie."

"Could you—stand up?"

"I—I think so." He heard her move again. "I can push myself up against the pillar."

"Reach out with your foot, Marta. As far as you can, but gently. Perhaps you can reach the wine racks, with your foot?"

"Just, kyrie. I think I brushed it with my shoe."

"That's good. That's very good."

"Kyrie?"

The sweat beaded on his forehead. "I'm thinking, Marta, that we need a knife."

In the next ten minutes, too, he thought: I don't think I can stand this, on my knees, much longer.

KADRI landed safely on the cobbles, and at once drew back into the shadow of the wall.

He needed to find Yashim. If Yashim had gone home . . .

He bit his lip. Yashim lived far away, in Balat, across the Golden Horn.

He crept to the front of the residency and looked around. He could not quite see the front door. If someone was watching . . .

He doubled back, and left the compound through the courtyard at the back, making no noise.

Out on the street he ran, weaving from doorway to doorway, keeping to the darkest shadows.

He did not want to run into the stranger he had heard on the stairs.

"YASHIM!" Preen put a hand to her mouth. "You look terrible, darling—what happened?"

Yashim shook his head.

"Fevzi Pasha came back," Yashim said heavily.

"Tell me," Preen said. "Sit, and explain. I don't understand—Fevzi Pasha? How can that be?"

"I barely understand it myself," Yashim admitted. He told her what had happened, and how Palewski and Marta were being held as hostages against the recovery of the girl.

"Kadri?"

"I don't know. I think he was asleep, upstairs."

"If he wakes up—if he comes downstairs—"

"Yes, what can I do? Fevzi Ahmet doesn't like surprises. He'd kill him."

"What about—the others?"

"I'd trust him to do what he says—or worse. He'd kill them both without blinking." His shoulders sagged. "Perhaps he already has."

The door opened and both of them started.

"Kadri!"

Kadri stepped in and closed the door. "I heard you on the stairs, Yashim efendi. I came to find you."

"How did you—" Yashim began.

Kadri explained how he had climbed down, trying to quell the note of pride in his voice.

"Marta and Palewski efendi—they're in the cellar."

"And Fevzi Ahmet has left a man to watch." Yashim did not repeat what he had said to Preen. "If we make a move—"

He left the idea hanging in the air.

Kadri leaned forward. "I went down there for Palewski efendi's wine. That was last summer, when the weather was so hot. He said it would give me an education."

Yashim frowned, and glanced at Preen. The young thought only of themselves—and this was hardly the moment to discuss Kadri's education.

"When I was living in the mountains there were caves where you could go to get out of the sun. Some of them were very deep, and they were always cool. The best one always had a wind blowing. Like the cellar. I found a funnel in the rocks which took me down to a ledge on the side of the hill. There was a small pool there, and I think the air somehow got sucked up. I don't know why."

Reluctantly Yashim gave Kadri his attention. "Why was it like the cellar?"

"There was a hole in the cellar floor, right at the back. I thought it must be a well, but it wasn't."

"Why not?"

"Because when I looked in I got hit by a wind. A really cold breeze. Just like that cave—only it was very dark. I meant to go back and have a better look, but I never got the chance."

"Did Palewski know? Did you tell him?"

"He said we'd have a go at exploring it one day. He said—" Kadri screwed up his face. "He said there must be lots of tunnels under Galata Hill, from the old days. He wouldn't have been surprised if we found an old road going down to the waterside, that had got built over and forgotten about."

Preen gave Yashim a warning look. "Even if there was a tunnel, and you could find the opening, you'd have to get into the Tophane arsenal to find it."

"The arsenal is built on reclaimed ground, Preen," Yashim said thoughtfully. "If Kadri's tunnel exists it would have come out at the old waterline. At the bottom of the hill, where the city walls used to be."

"Long gone, Yashim."

Yashim shook his head. "That's what everyone thinks. The towers have gone, and the walls along the Golden Horn aren't there anymore—" He paused. "I'll think of a way of getting Fevzi Pasha's little girl, but first I have to get Marta and Palewski out. Kadri's given me an idea."

Kadri jumped to his feet. "Yes, Yashim efendi. Yes. Are you going to explore?"

"No—we are. We may find a use for your special talent, after all. Preen—if the theater could spare some rope?"

PALEWSKI, too, was thinking about rope.

He had done his best to tense his wrists, but the men only cinched the ropes tighter. At the foot of the cellar steps they had bound his ankles, too.

They had run the rope through the loop of his arms, drawn it tight, and fastened him to a square pillar, leaving him on his knees with his feet drawn up painfully behind him.

He thought about rope as he knelt on the gritty flags.

"A knife, kyrie? But I do not—ah! I understand."

"Some people, Marta, think that I drink too much wine. I'd very much like to tell them that wine has saved my life."

He heard the rasp of a bottle against the wood.

"I—just—can't . . ."

"Take off your shoe, maybe. Try with your toes."

"Oh, kyrie!" A thud as she dropped a slipper to the floor. "That's better—but I can't reach so far!"

"Very well, take a rest." He frowned in the dark. "How high did you raise your foot?"

Marta considered. "I think, up to my waist. A little lower."

"Good." Palewski bit his lip. Marta had touched the top of a bottle with her slipper, just. He imagined that she could describe an arc with her foot, and that arc might just make contact with a bottle in the rack. Like a circle inside a square: one small point of contact.

"Use your toes. Whatever you do, don't push the bottle. Maybe next time, if you can, just twist a little to one side. It may help you stretch a little farther."

Marta responded with a deep intake of breath.

"I've been a complete fool," he muttered, as he listened to Marta kicking her skirts aside. She was reducing the weight on her leg, and he heard her groan as she twisted to one side, dragging on her wrists.

"Aaaah!"

The bottle dragged slowly up the rack, clamped between Marta's toes.

At the last minute she jerked her foot and the bottle flipped out. Palewski heard her cry and the sound of the glass splintering on the stone floor.

He took a deep breath. He sniffed, momentarily distracted: Petrus, damn it, and almost certainly the '04. But it was the glass that interested him; the broken glass, and Marta.

"Marta, when we're out of this—?"

There was total silence in the cellar.

"Kyrie?" Her voice sounded cold.

Palewski swallowed. He'd been about to say something else, but he was warned now. "When we're out—you won't forget?"

125

"IT might be here," Yashim murmured, running his hand across the beaten iron surface of the gate. "The question is how to get in."

Kadri stepped back into the roughly cobbled street and glanced up. A thin crescent moon hung in the black sky, and by its feeble light he assessed the wall.

"Let me take the rope, Yashim efendi."

Kadri slipped off his shoes and slung the rope across his shoulders. He approached the base of the wall and raised his hands, feeling for a hold.

Kadri climbed swiftly, barely pausing to establish his grip on the stones: he swarmed up the wall as though it were covered in net. He had learned in boyhood that falling took time, and effort, so he moved fast instead, fingers and toes loosely flexed. Yashim saw him pause when he reached the projecting tiles, then whip out and over the eaves like a snake.

A moment later, Kadri was peering down into the inner court, formed in the ditch that separated the double walls of Genoese Pera. The walls themselves were velvety with soot from the forges, and by the time Kadri had descended, more cautiously, he was black from head to toe.

He went to the gate and called to Yashim through the latch.

"I'm in."

A street dog rose from the shadows and gave two hollow barks, before settling down.

Yashim passed a candle through the little opening. "The watch is coming. I'll be back in ten minutes."

He melted into the darkness of a side alley, waiting for the familiar tap-tap of the watchman's staff on the cobbles. When it did not come, he waited another few minutes before he went back to the gate. There he smelled charcoal, and the faintly acidic odor of cut metal. A nearby dog whimpered and whinnied in its sleep. Yashim listened for sounds in the courtyard and heard nothing. He moved from one foot to the other, feeling the cold, so that when Kadri spoke close to his ear he jumped.

"Three tunnels," Kadri whispered urgently. "One's small, more like a pipe. It goes in about twenty yards and then bends up sharply."

"Maybe drainage," Yashim suggested. "What about the other two?"

"The first one could just be some sort of cellar—it hardly slopes at all, and the air is musty. But it'll take time to explore them both."

"There isn't much time," Yashim pointed out. "The second tunnel?"

"Lower than the other one. It doesn't seem to go upward but it smells fresher inside."

"I'm sure that's the one," Yashim urged, with a confidence he didn't really feel. Istanbul was a honeycomb of tunnels, cisterns, and holes in the ground; blanked-off cellars, disused waterways, the foundation arches of Roman buildings. Where they ran, or how they were linked, nobody knew. They composed a dark mirror image of the city above, an impress of the centuries that had passed since Constantine first planted his standard on the banks of the Bosphorus and named the city for himself.

A sound at his back made Yashim turn his head. Kadri melted from the gate, noiselessly; but still Yashim stood, ears cocked, listening.

A dog detached itself from the base of the wall and crept a few yards along the street toward Yashim, where it sat and scratched its fleas. It stuck its muzzle on its paws, and went back to sleep.

Dogs did not willingly shift about at night, Yashim thought.

MARTA said: "How shall we use the broken glass?"

"I was rather counting on you to come up with an idea."

He heard her sigh. "I have," she said.

She carefully drew the shard of glass toward her, with her toes.

She tucked her foot beneath her. Her fingers were cold; her feet were cold; she did not feel the glass in her fingers until the blood ran.

Palewski heard her give a gasp.

"Are you all right?"

"I have a knife, kyrie." He heard the triumph in her voice, and said nothing.

At the same moment he heard the sound of the cellar door swinging open.

127

KADRI had gone about thirty paces into the tunnel before the ground dropped away.

The breeze was faint, but it flowed steadily up the tunnel at his back. Carefully shielding the candle, he moved to the side of the tunnel and held the flickering flame out of the wind. He was standing halfway up a vaulted chamber thickly festooned with cobwebs that hung from the ceiling in hanks, spinning in the breeze. He shuddered, and peered down.

He wriggled forward on his belly.

128

A shape broke from the shadows down the street. It was not the shape of a dog, but of a man.

Yashim edged to the side of the gate and put up his hand to feel the stones. His fingers found a crevice and his arm tightened.

Had the moon been any brighter, Yashim might have recognized the bow-legged walk of Akunin; had he stopped to watch, he would have seen Shishkin step out from a doorway farther up the street, blocking his escape.

But Yashim did not stop to watch. With a sudden grunt he dragged himself up on his fingertips and scrabbled for a foothold on the wall.

Everything Kadri had told him about climbing vanished from his mind as he dug his toe into a crack and reached up.

The man on the street started to run.

Like Kadri, Yashim moved quickly, barely pausing to check his holds, using vertical fissures as well as horizontal, flinging hand over hand and using his feet to flail upward against the rough surface of the wall.

Akunin reached the base of the wall and lunged: Yashim felt fingers close around his ankle. He was gripping the stones above with one hand, the other searching wildly for a hold as he tried to break the pressure rapidly increasing on his ankle. But he could feel his fingers slipping from the stone and with it his balance beginning to move, driving his body away from the wall.

His free hand found a crevice between the stones and clutched at it: but it was almost too late.

Akunin held tight and dropped his weight behind his arm.

MARTA and Palewski froze as they listened to a heavy tread descending the cellar steps.

Two thoughts ran through Palewski's mind. The first, that one of the men had been sent to kill them. Or that the sound of the breaking bottle had brought him down to check.

About the first possibility, he could do nothing—unless Marta could pass him the shard of broken glass.

Palewski felt Marta's hand close around his wrists, searching for the cord.

The man stopped. Then they heard him tramp upstairs again, and the door closed.

Palewski climbed slowly from the pillar, flexing his fingers.

Marta laid a hand on his arm. "They are coming back."

He cocked his head, and heard the sound of someone scraping nearby. He tightened his fingers around the glass and put Marta behind him, covering her with an outstretched arm.

In the dark they strained their ears.

Palewski frowned, incredulous.

One of his favorite pieces was Chopin's tiny mazurka, the prelude in A major. He had practiced it all summer, with fairly good results.

It didn't sound too bad right now, whistled by Kadri between his teeth, from the far end of the cellar.

YASHIM felt the savage yank on his foot. Rather than tumble to the ground, he used his outward-falling momentum to spin in the air. Akunin had stepped back, face raised. He received the full weight of Yashim's knee on the bridge of his nose.

The *crack!* of the cartilage breaking loose was lost in the sound of both men crashing to the ground.

Wrestling training at the palace school had saved Yashim's life before. Leaving Akunin on his back instinctively cradling his broken nose, Yashim rolled with the fall and came up about six feet short of the running man. Shishkin eased back, but not fast enough. His last faltering step halved the distance between the two men: Yashim closed the gap with his lowered head.

As Shishkin doubled up, Yashim sidestepped and chopped his neck with the side of his hand. The Russian fell to his knees, coughing.

Akunin had got to his feet, but he was in no mood for fighting—one hand was clamped to his face, the other flailing drunkenly in the air.

Yashim placed a knee on Shishkin's back and took hold of his chin in both hands.

"Why were you following me?"

Akunin began to back away.

"Stop. Tell me, and you can take your friend."

Akunin hesitated. "The Fox," he said thickly. "He thinks Fevzi Pasha is back—and he wants to talk to you."

"Fevzi Pasha back?"

Akunin tilted his head. The blood was black under his hand. "I saw him, at the Polish residency."

Shishkin groaned. Yashim said: "Go on."

"He went in, about an hour before you came. Galytsin guessed you were meeting him there. He told us to pick you up."

Yashim released his hold on Shishkin, who sputtered and sank to his hands and knees. "Where's Galytsin now?"

"At the embassy, efendi."

"Tell him I'll meet him there for breakfast."

131

TEN minutes later, Yashim heard a low whistle from the yard. He put his face to the bars.

"Yashim!"

He recognized the voice, even in a whisper. He thrust a hand through the bars and gripped a well-known hand.

"Incredible!" Palewski's excited whisper cut through the night like steam escaping from an engine. "We'll have to rethink the whole story!"

"Yes. It's not Talfa—"

"Talfa?" Palewski dropped his hand. "I'm talking about the Genoese settlement, Yashim, prior to the Conquest. Those tunnels? Greater continuity than anyone realizes. Gibbon, von Hammer . . ." His whisper trailed off. After a moment he said: "If this gate is locked, how the devil do we get out?"

It took almost half an hour with ropes, and muffled curses, to bring Palewski and Marta over the wall.

She descended with solemn grace, holding her skirts tight.

"It would be better for you not to go back to the residency just yet," Yashim explained as they made their way up the open lanes toward Galata Hill.

Twenty minutes later, when everyone had told their story, Preen looked at Yashim.

"You've been very quiet, my dear." She turned to the others. "Yashim is thinking up a plan to capture Fevzi Pasha," she said, rolling her eyes. "Bring the bastard to justice."

Yashim shook his head. "I thought that. But no. My plan is—to send him to Egypt, with his daughter."

Preen stiffened. "You'd do that for him—after everything?"

He caught her look: it chilled him.

"You said—you promised me—you'd seen through him, Yashim. And now—you work for him, like that!" She snapped her fingers.

"Do you remember, Preen, when I said there is always a gap, however tightly we try to fit the pieces together?"

"For mercy," Preen sneered. "For a man who would give none!"

"It's not for him. Not exactly."

"Who, then?" Palewski said.

Marta smiled shyly. "He means his daughter, of course."

Yashim cast her a grateful look. "I can't play God, Preen. If we don't move now, I'm afraid the little girl will die."

Preen tossed her head. "She's in the harem, you said. Safe—and secret. The safest place in Istanbul."

Yashim slowly shook his head. "It's secret—but it isn't safe. Not safe, at all."

"What do you propose, Yashim?" Palewski yawned. The night had been long.

"I propose, my friend, that you get some sleep. As for you, Kadri, I want you to find a caïquejee called Spyro, and bring him here."

132

YASHIM found Galytsin at a table laden with patisseries.

"Join me," the prince suggested, pouring Yashim a cup of tea.

Yashim sat down opposite him, and ripped a croissant between his fingers. He had been tired, but now he was only hungry. "You were closing in on Fevzi Ahmet Pasha, weren't you? Threatening him?"

"Is that what he told you?" Galytsin shrugged. "Threatening him with what?"

A question for a question. Yashim took a side step: "Three years ago you burned his *yali*—as a warning."

"I have good reason to remember that." Galytsin smiled, showing a row of perfect teeth. "Try the jam, Yashim efendi. But no, believe it or not, that was his concubine."

The tea burned Yashim's tongue. Galytsin pushed the jam toward him. "It seems to me, Yashim efendi, that you know very little about the pasha."

Yashim tried the jam. Galytsin leaned back and stuck his foot up on the next chair.

"Pervyal." He twisted his hand in the air and a liveried footman stepped forward with a box. "Fevzi Ahmet bought a concubine on the Black Sea coast," the prince remarked, selecting a cigar. "Smoke?"

Yashim shook his head.

"Pervyal," Galytsin repeated, putting the cigar into his mouth. "She was beautiful, and clever, too, in the Circassian way." The footman presented a match to the end of his cigar, but the prince ignored him. "More beautiful than his wife, naturally. In Istanbul, she would have fetched thousands—and the imperial harem would have taken her."

Yashim put a smear of jam onto his croissant. "So how did he buy her?"

"A very good question, which Fevzi didn't think to ask."

The footman struck another match, and this time Galytsin presented the tip of his cigar to the flame. He drew on it, turning it fussily this way and that, until the flame was almost touching the man's fingers.

"I imagine Fevzi Ahmet thought the dealer was doing him a favor. He brought her back, and installed her in his harem—he told her he would marry her when she produced a son. His wife had given birth to a daughter. Pervyal was very helpful. A very good second mother to the child."

"So—?"

"Pervyal got pregnant. It was a boy. He was dead when she gave birth."

"And Fevzi Ahmet—"

"Didn't marry her, no. He wanted a live boy. But Fevzi Ahmet told her next time, it would be all right." He blew a ring of smoke into the air. "She miscarried. She became—difficult. She spent a lot of time with the little girl, but the wife didn't trust her."

"I can understand."

"Fevzi Ahmet became Kapudan pasha. Mahmut told him to build the bridge." Galytsin dropped his hand toward his cup, and the footman reached forward with the teapot. "He was less often at home. Two women, a child, a eunuch attendant—you might say it was a combustible situation. And Pervyal had a flaw."

"A flaw?"

Galytsin leaned forward with a look of amusement. "That's what the dealer had recognized. I don't know if you are a superstitious man, Yashim efendi, but some people would say Pervyal was a witch."

Yashim shook his head. "I don't understand—you talk about this woman as if you knew her."

"Oh, yes." He examined his cigar. "I am—or rather, I was—her employer. Her dealer, I should say. It was me who sold her, Yashim efendi."

Yashim reached for his cup and drained it. "You sold her to Fevzi Ahmet?"

Galytsin chuckled. "I was rather better than that. I sold her to the sultan."

Yashim stared.

"It's good to see your face, Yashim efendi! I knew nothing about Pervyal myself, until she set fire to the *yali*. We had warships in the Bosphorus then, and she came to us. A very good-looking young woman, with subtle accomplishments. Not a virgin—but there are, apparently, ways of remedying that. We used them." He waved a hand. "We restored her purity, and arranged her sale—at a distance, of course. Quite a coup, wouldn't you think? But we overlooked one thing."

"What?"

"The sultan's harem is an enclosed world. Pervyal was supposed to report to us—we had arranged a drop-off at the bazaar. When she sent for anything, she was to give the eunuch who shopped for her a purse and he would leave it at the shop. The eunuch and the shopkeeper supposed she was sending money to her family. It was a perfect system, except that she never made a report."

Yashim sat back, considering. "Once she was in the harem, she broke the connection?"

"Completely. She was an intelligent woman, and she'd got where she wanted. She used us, of course. We don't even know her harem name."

Yashim could not resist a smile at the irony of it. "But why are you telling me this?"

Galytsin drew on his cigar and then, with a curiously vulgar expression, sent a smoke ring wobbling across the table.

"I don't like being used, Yashim efendi. But I am generous to my friends. I want you to consider it. Fevzi's concubine tricked me, and you might say she is tricking you. Your people. You could take it as a tip."

Yashim stood up. "Thank you for the breakfast. If I may ask—when you say 'subtle accomplishments'?"

Galytsin spread his hands. "Well-trained. Elegant manners."

Yashim smiled. "They all have elegant manners, your highness."

Tü LIN stepped to the window and looked out over the gray leaded roofs and curving domes of Topkapi, here and there touched by pockets of melting snow.

Her face was grave; she had not slept well, visited by dreams in which the valide was dead, or trapped in a room engulfed in flames. She had woken from one such dream beating her hands on the quilt, surprised to find herself in a cold room, the morning already advanced.

Quickly she broke the ice on the washbasin, and splashed her face. With a grimace she let her shift slip to the floor, then stepped forward and cupped the water in her hands and dashed it over her neck and breasts.

She dried herself carefully with a towel and picked up the shift, which she folded and laid on the bed.

She rummaged in the bags hanging against the walls, finding a pretty patterned jacket she didn't recognize. She held it up. When she tried it on, it fitted well; she smoothed her hands down the sides and wished she had a mirror.

After a while she grew bored of staring out over the Topkapi rooftops. It was only in one corner, beyond a dome, that she could discern the outline of the land beyond: the Galata Tower and the trees of Taksim, where they kept the water.

134

THE wind had dropped. On the Bosphorus, the water ran black and smooth; the waters of the Golden Horn were oiled like old steel. Sultan's weather, they called it, for the official opening ceremony of the bridge.

It had snowed before dawn, and by midmorning, when the sun came out, most of the alleys and thoroughfares of the city were a laced tangle of mud and standing ice; the air was clear, and the skyline of the seven hills was picked out sharply against a cold blue sky.

The bridge cast a crisp black shadow on the water. Its planks were swept, and glistened darkly in the frosty air; its parapets were entwined with glossy leaves, with here and there a spray of yellow flowers.

Crowds thronged the shoreline on the Pera side, and spilled through the gates that opened in Istanbul's Byzantine walls, their appetite whetted by the scent of roasted chestnuts and corncobs grilling on little fires. A man with long mustaches raked stuffed mussels over a brazier. The *simit* seller wandered through the crowd, with his distinctive bread rings on a tray on his head. The sherbet seller followed him, clinking two glasses between finger and thumb, and the water man, with his tank on his back. Boys darted through the crowd with roasted chickpeas in paper bags, and the *sahlep* men pushed their trolleys along the waterfront, offering their concoction of sweet orchid root sprinkled with ginger and cinnamon.

The kebab houses and the cafés were busy, and the frosty air was full of music, too, played by bands, by gypsies, by wandering musicians with bagpipes and flutes, stringed ouds and mandolins. A team of Africans who had arrived in the autumn were knocking out unfamiliar and catchy rhythms on their drums; gypsy girls were tinkling their tambourines; grave Sufis chanted the ninety-nine names of God, for charity.

In spite of the cold, Yashim could see that it was a larger crowd than had turned out for the accession of Abdülmecid only a few months before. That had been a more private affair, conducted swiftly upon the old sultan's death in the presence of the Ottoman family, the sultan's pashas and his slaves. The ceremonial opening of the bridge marked the sultan's gift to the people of Istanbul, and it was generally understood that Abdülmecid would bring his ladies.

Cannon fire announced the departure of the sultan's suite from Besiktas. Everyone turned expectantly to the water and watched the mouth of the Golden Horn; people leaned from balconies in Pera and crowded the crumbling walls of Istanbul.

The *corps diplomatique*, including the ambassadors of Russia, France, Britain, Austria, and the United States, was assembled in an edgy silence on the Pera side of the bridge. The Polish ambassador was there, too, looking tired but talking amiably to the Sardinian consul; his presence was noticed by certain members of the crowd. Only the junior members of the ambassadorial suites chatted and laughed among themselves.

"Admit it, Compston," Count Esterhazy was saying as he waved a smoldering cigar. "The Ottomans have done it. They have built their bridge after all, and you fellows have lost the wager!"

George Compston adopted a mulish expression. "The bet says the sultan has to get across the bridge. Isn't that right, Fizerly?"

"I grant you they built it," Fizerly added. "But will it stand? That's the question, Esterhazy."

Esterhazy's pale face betrayed the hint of a smile. "I think you will pay the forfeit, gentlemen. Look!"

A vermilion eight-oared caïque appeared, flying brave pennants, carrying important dignitaries of the empire: the grand vizier, Husrev Pasha; the mufti of Istanbul; the military chiefs of Rumelia and Anatolia.

Behind it came the imperial caïque itself, with young Abdülmecid and two veiled women; it was rowed by twelve men, who barked like dogs in the traditional manner, so that the sultan's conversation would go un-heard.

As the cavalcade approached along the Bosphorus, ships anchored in the roadstead dipped their colors. Six caïques, vermilion and eight-oared, bore the ladies, who turned their veiled heads regally this way and that, to appreciate the lively scene. Among them could be seen some of the harem children: little boys in silk jackets, little girls in furs.

The sultan's caïque passed momentarily from sight, then swept out of the shadows below the bridge and into the basin of the Golden Horn. The crowd began to chant its approval: *"Hu! Hu!"*

The third, then fourth caïque slipped beneath the bridge. As its prow passed under the parapet, two garlanded caïques that had been milling in the lower basin shot forward and fell into flanking positions, one on each side of the caïque as it went under the bridge.

Eight seconds later, straddling a crossbeam of the bridge's superstruc-ture, Erkan, the Strongest Man in the World, took hold of Kadri's ankles and lowered the boy toward the water.

The ladies in the caïque gasped as the swinging figure of a boy jostled against them. Then he was gone.

The caïque shot out into the Golden Horn. The ladies looked about them, uncertain what had happened in the fifteen seconds it took them to go underneath the bridge. The rowers blinked—and kept on rowing, for there was nobody aboard to change their orders.

Invisible from the shore, Kadri, Erkan, and the little girl they had just snatched from the harem caïque scuttled along the gantry below the planked surface of the bridge and made their way to the far side. The girl was lowered into a waiting caïque. Low and black, it had not been spotted moored up against the pontoon.

Spyro the caïquejee twitched a blanket over Kadri and the little girl and applied himself to his oars. They came out from beneath the bridge, heading to the open water, as the last imperial caïque emerged on the other side.

Erkan scrambled through the final span of the bridge and stepped onto land, where he was soon lost in the crowd.

Spyro rowed vigorously toward the Tophane stage. "There you are, princess," he said, swinging her out of the caïque.

Kadri took Roxelana by the hand.

She dragged slightly. "Where are we going?"

"Come on," Kadri said. "I'll race you up the hill."

135

"I think I feel a little better, Tülin, now."

Tülin folded the shawl and laid it tenderly on the divan. "Yes, valide. I'm glad."

"When this business of the bridge is over, would you send to the Kislar aga? I think he and I need a little talk."

"Yes, valide. What do you want to talk about?"

The valide let her eyelids droop. "What about? Oh, your future, my dear. And mine, too."

Tülin stood respectfully at the foot of the divan. "The Kislar aga is expecting us at Besiktas tomorrow, valide. Perhaps you should talk to him then?"

The valide cocked her head. "Tomorrow, is it? *Tiens!* Time flies so fast."

"Yes, valide. Would you like a tisane, now?"

"No, thank you, my dear. I'm quite comfortable." Her eyes roamed around the room she knew so well. "I'm very comfortable, right here. You'll send for the Kislar aga, won't you?"

Tülin turned to the fire and put another log on the blaze.

"Tülin?"

"Yes, valide. Yes, I'll send for the Kislar aga, right away. Just let me light the lamps before I go."

136

THE outing had made everyone slightly hysterical. Many of the girls had seen more in one afternoon than they could quite take in. Crowds of men, for a start.

"Did you see the dragoon, by the bridge?"

"The man lolling in the window, showing his private parts!"

"Go on!"

"Never!"

"I told you to look, but by then he'd disappeared."

"I only saw the sultan. So handsome, in the landau."

"Oh, yes!" Their voices were shrill with agreement: everyone wished that they'd said it first.

"So handsome!"

"So imperial!"

Ibou, the Kislar aga, moved uneasily among the chatter. "Has anyone seen Roxelana?"

"The little girl?"

"She's upstairs asleep, with all the kiddies."

"Somebody pushed her over the side."

"Watch what you say—young men dangling all over you, under the bridge! Whoo!"

"I told you, aga—somebody lifted her off the caïque."

"What?"

"I didn't really see. It was all dark under the bridge, after the sunshine."

"That's right, aga. There was something funny under the bridge."

"And Roxelana was gone?"

"How could I tell? She wasn't with us when we got into the carriages. Maybe she'd run on ahead. Children! In the carriage, I peeped!"

"You didn't!"

"You would!"

Ibou gave up, in despair. Everyone had their version. No one had been remotely interested in the child.

And yet no one had seen her all afternoon.

He was worrying about nothing, he thought to himself.

YASHIM stood listening to the sound of the muezzin calling the Friday prayer.

Only a fortnight, he thought, since he had gone to Friday mosque at Topkapi, to escape his awkwardness with the valide's handmaiden. The day, of course, that Hyacinth had died.

He remembered the sound of the muezzin rising and falling as Melda told him that Elif had been pregnant.

That, too, had been Friday.

Hyacinth and Elif had died a week apart. Hyacinth had been trying to talk to him, the old eunuchs had said.

Hyacinth had died in Topkapi; Elif in Besiktas.

Yashim leaped, as if he had been stung.

"Hats!" he exclaimed. "Roxelana never liked the hats!"

138

THE Grande Rue was still full of people, many of them in a holiday mood after the ceremony of the bridge; many of them from Istanbul, visiting the European quarter for the first time. Loafers sizing up the opportunities; knots of veiled ladies peering into the unfamiliar vitrines of the European shops, with their regimented displays of hats or pastries or upholstered chairs; dignified gentlemen astonished by the height, and apparent solidity, of the stuccoed buildings.

The crowd moved like treacle: Yashim dodged and weaved, veering around the groups of visitors and diving between startled families. The road seemed longer than it had ever been, but eventually it began to slope downhill. He raced, panting, past the base of the Galata Tower, and flung himself down the long flights of steps leading to the waterfront.

He had saved Roxelana, for the moment.

But with Roxelana gone, everything was changed.

139

HE heard pounding footsteps behind him, and glanced back.

One of Fevzi's caïquejees was vaulting the steps three at a time.

At the bottom of the stairs Yashim skidded out onto the icy thoroughfare. The caïquejee behind him gave a piercing whistle, and suddenly the roadway ahead was full of men, bare-fisted and bowlegged, stringing themselves out across the way that led to the bridge.

Their caïques rocked unattended at the stage.

Without a second glance, Yashim dashed to the stage and flipped the painter on the leading caïque. He snatched up an oar and drove it against the wooden jetty. With a heave he shot the fragile craft out into the Golden Horn.

The caïque gave a lurch. Water splashed over the gunwale, and Yashim very nearly overbalanced: his arms flailed and he sat down abruptly in the stern. He fitted the oars to the rowlocks, and pulled—almost tumbling over again as the fine-keeled caïque, improbably light, began to twist through the water. He drew it in line with the central arch of the bridge, dipping his oars too deep; at the next stroke his blades scudded over the surface like lifting teal.

But he had it now: two firm bites of the blades, and the caïque was skimming toward the bridge.

He glanced up. Some of the caïquejees were racing to the bridge, others piling into caïques waiting at the stage. One, two, then three shot forward, and slipped into his wake.

Yashim battled against the nervous movements of the boat. The shallow gunwale dipped and the caïque shipped water again. With an effort he steadied his stroke, forcing himself to slow down. He glanced up: the caïquejees were gaining on him now.

As he slid into the shadow of the bridge he began drawing firmly to the right, zigzagging so that the men above would misjudge the point where he emerged. As he shot out on the other side he looked up—his maneuver had not been wasted. A man on the bridge dashed to catch up with him, and seemed ready to jump; but it was too late. Yashim had cleared the bridge by a boat's length.

He leaned to the oars, and felt the current of the Bosphorus take him as he moved out of the Golden Horn. It was sweeping him slowly toward the opposite shore, toward Seraglio Point, where the very tip of Istanbul jutted into the strait, and he bent with it, willing it to whirl him toward the little jetty that stuck out beneath the walls of the seraglio.

For a few moments, with the help of the current, he left his pursuers trailing; but once they emerged into the stream they began to advance rapidly. One hundred and fifty yards. One hundred and twenty. One hundred.

One of the pursuing caïques began to pull in toward the shore. There were riptides and eddies all along the shores of the Bosphorus, and no doubt the caïquejee knew exactly where to find one that would speed his pursuit.

Yashim could only keep rowing, grimly, back cracking, hands raw against the wooden sculls.

140

"I—don't—think I—can take much—more—of this," the young man gasped. A wavelet slapped his face and he swallowed another spoonful of the Bosphorus.

"Think of Byron—Compston—old man."

"Byron did it—in summer." The acting third secretary at the British embassy kicked out with both legs; but his energy was waning. His lips were blue. Compston could hardly remember why he was here, slowly freezing to death in the gelid waters of the Bosphorus.

"Damn—that wretched—Esterhazy."

Compston could not have believed he could ever be so cold. Before they waded into the water, he and Fizerly had smeared themselves in a liberal coating of mutton fat until Fizerly said they looked like prize porkers from his father's model farm. For the first hundred yards or so, the fat had done the trick.

"Damn—that—blasted bridge!" Fizerly glanced around. In the dusk, he could see only the glowing disk of Compston's face in the water. "Keep—going, Compston. Old man? Compston?"

"It's late, Tülin. I feel tired, I want to sleep."

Tülin hovered. "Yes, valide."

The valide turned her head. "You can go now. Leave a lamp."

She gestured to the lights.

"The Kislar aga did not come?"

"No, valide. I sent the message."

"Well, well. No doubt he is busy."

"No doubt, valide. Perhaps you should tell me what you wished to talk about, and then—"

"And then?" The valide's glance was quizzical.

Tülin shrugged. "He has many calls on his time."

"Ah, yes." The valide turned over and rested her face on her pillow. "I suppose you are right." She closed her eyes and nestled down. "I wanted to tell him I can't go to Besiktas."

"Valide?"

"Too old, Tülin. Too much change. It makes me ill."

Tülin's fingers twisted the button on her jacket. "Once we've made the move, you'll feel much more comfortable."

"Nonsense." The valide munched her lips. "Let's talk about it in the morning."

"You promised me, valide. You promised the Kislar aga, too."

"Promised? I promised nothing, Tülin. I made a plan—and now I have changed my mind. You may still go to the orchestra, every week."

But Tülin didn't want to go to the orchestra every week.

For months she had sat at the feet of the woman who had been—still was—the most powerful woman in the Ottoman Empire. Old as she was, and frail, her memories had been instructive.

Tülin certainly had made plans.

She twiddled the button very fast, between her fingers; and her eyes grew narrow.

The valide lay back on her cushions, her eyes closed.

Tülin picked up a pillow, and very slowly she crept toward the divan.

142

YASHIM closed his eyes, and closed his mind: he was a machine, an automaton, back, forward, back. His lungs were ready to burst. Back again!

His mind was fixed on the old jetty beneath the seraglio gardens. Once, in former years, it would have provided him with an instant sanctuary: two Janissaries at the gate, a couple of hefty bostancis to guard the imperial caïque. These days the jetty was likely to be deserted; the gate sealed. It was many years since the valide had expressed a wish to go scudding across the Bosphorus.

And the water gate was now his only hope.

His pursuers were almost on him. Two caïques running almost side by side, twenty yards behind him. He could see the muscles bulging in the rowers' necks. He glanced back, over his shoulder.

It would never work. He still had two, three hundred yards to go.

He grunted, and dragged the sculls through the water. They had to board him first, of course. Yashim set his mind to the coming fight when something quite unexpected occurred.

The caïque nearest to him gave a sudden lurch, and the rower was almost hurled overboard; at almost the same moment the second caïque swung around with such force that spray flew into the air. It was as if some unseen hand had reached out from the depths and taken both caïques in its iron grip.

As they bobbed and dipped, Yashim could hear shouts of anger, or surprise. One of the caïquejees stood up and appeared to be driving his oar into the water.

Yashim pulled hard, not letting up, almost superstitiously eager to get away from the commotion that had overtaken his pursuers.

He cleared another hundred yards. Over the icy waters he could hear the shouts of the caïquejees. One of them, indeed, seemed to have regained his stroke: but the distance was on Yashim's side.

He turned his head and saw a lamp at the landing stage, with a knot of men around it.

His heart sank.

They'd beaten him to it.

And then, with a second glance, he saw something else: the bobbing prow of an imperial caïque, with its boxlike pavilion, tethered to the stage like a thoroughbred in its stable.

He pulled up. A man bent down to gather in the painter, and Yashim half crawled from the pitching craft onto the stage.

"On the sultan's service," he gasped. "Yashim, for the valide."

143

NOT far away two very cold, very unhappy young men crawled out of the icy water and sank down in the mud.

Fizerly's knuckles were covered in blood. He thought he'd lost a tooth.

"Blasted caïquejees!" Compston spat. "Think they'd want to save a life—almost killed us!"

Dark figures approached, gingerly, over the slippery ground.

"Towels, gentlemen. And my congratulations!" Esterhazy snapped his fingers. "I have brought rubbing spirits. My man will see that you get warm as quickly as possible."

"Rubbing be damned," Compston gasped, and shot out a trembling arm. "Good man!"

The bottle rattled against his bloody mouth.

YASHIM reached the garden door of the harem and crashed on it with his fist.

A startled eunuch stood in the open doorway.

"Yashim!" he squeaked. "But how—?"

Yashim brushed past him and began to run down the Golden Road. He darted out into the court of the valide, and swerved to his right.

He heard a noise like a champagne cork being popped.

He dived at the valide's door and flung it back.

In three steps he crossed the vestibule and entered the valide's apartment.

Tülin was standing by the divan with a pillow clenched against her chest.

On the divan the valide was half sitting up, half lying, on her elbow.

She held a little gun in her hand, and the gun was pointed at Tülin.

BOTH of them glanced at Yashim as he came in.

But when Tülin turned her head, she kept on turning. Her eyes swept glassily over the valide, over the little gun, over Yashim standing in the doorway, and then, without another sound, she subsided onto the floor.

Yashim sprang forward and the valide reached out, dangling the gun from a slender finger.

"Take it, Yashim. I won't be needing it again tonight."

Yashim took the gun mechanically. "She was going to kill you," he said.

"*Incroyable.* And with that pillow. You have to be firm, Yashim, as I have always said."

Yashim glanced down at the dead girl.

The bullet had got her just above her eyes.

"I have spent a great deal of time with my *vieux papa*, these last few days, Yashim," the valide said wearily. "Or is it weeks? Long ago, on Martinique, he taught me how to shoot. I suppose it's one of those things you don't forget."

Yashim's legs felt weak. He sat down on the divan. "Where did you get the gun?"

"I've had it for years, Yashim. The sultan gave it to me. *My* sultan, of course—Abdülhamid. I think it amused him to watch me shoot. He was rather a dear man, in many ways." A filmy look came into her eyes; then she tossed her head, and said: "You can put it away now. The case is under the divan."

The pistol case was made of red leather and bore the *tughra* of Sultan Abdülhamid on the lid. Inside was a yellow silk lining, and the pistol's twin, nestling in its groove. It bore an English label: *J. Purdey, London.*

Yashim slotted the pistol back into its case and closed the lid.

"You might ask someone to take her away," the valide said. "I'm feeling rather tired, and these days I prefer to sleep alone."

Yashim stood up. "Of course, valide."

"We'll talk in the morning, Yashim." She yawned. "I expect I'll have . . . rather exciting dreams."

He bowed.

And went to find the colonel of the halberdiers.

PALEWSKI stood by the fire with his elbow on the mantelpiece.

"And so," he concluded, "they sped across the frozen lake, the prince and the princess, to the gates of the ice castle. And when the ice maidens flung back the gates to welcome them, they went in, and sat down to the most beautiful banquet there ever was."

"What did they eat?"

"Yes, what did they eat? They ate, um, tiny kebabs."

"Why were they tiny?"

"They were tiny because that way they could eat more of them," Palewski said.

The little girl nodded, as if that made sense.

"Ah, here's Marta!" Palewski cried. "And that, Roxelana, is the end of the story."

Roxelana nodded again, and looked serious. "I'd like tiny kebabs," she said.

Palewski cast a hopeful look toward Marta.

"If the young lady will come with me to the kitchen . . ." she said with a smile.

Roxelana slipped off the armchair. She bowed gravely to Palewski and slipped her hand into Marta's.

At the door she gave a little shiver, and turned. "I wouldn't like to live in an ice castle forever," she pointed out.

Palewski nodded. "It's unlikely, Roxelana, that you ever will," he said, thinking of Egypt.

When the door had closed he turned to Kadri, who was sitting in a window seat, and said: "Any sign?"

Kadri shook his head. "I enjoyed the story, too."

Palewski ran his hand through his hair. "Good, good," he said absently, and moved toward the sideboard.

"Here he comes," Kadri said.

"Yashim?"

"I don't think so. No. It must be Fevzi Ahmet Pasha."

Palewski sighed. He picked up a pair of candles from the sideboard.

He heard the sound of someone yanking on the bell; the dry slither of the bell chain in the metal eye, then muttering.

He went downstairs and opened the door.

Fevzi Pasha was standing on the steps, frowning down at the bellpull, which had come away in his hand.

"Please, do step in."

Fevzi Ahmet dropped the bellpull to the ground. "Where's my daughter? Where's Yashim?"

"If you'd be so kind as to follow me," Palewski said, holding up the candles. "Just mind the first step," he added, as he reached the stairs.

In the drawing room he introduced his visitor to Kadri. Fevzi Ahmet looked suspiciously around the room.

"Tea, my dear fellow?"

Fevzi Ahmet scowled and shook his head.

"Perhaps—if you'll allow—a little brandy?"

The hunted man turned and stared at Palewski.

"Yes."

"Capital! Capital! Do you know, efendi, I think I'll join you."

THE man with the knife stood in the shadows, watching the lighted window.

He did not think the doors would be locked. He was not expected.

He shivered, though the sweat sparkled on his forehead. He felt the ice on his face, and the fire in his chest.

So many doors, so many windows! Istanbul was bigger than any town he had ever seen. At first he had been bewildered; even afraid. But he could track his prey through a maze of alleys and squares more easily than hunting in the hills.

And now, standing there fingering the blade, the man with the knife swallowed and smiled a small, sad smile of satisfaction.

A pasha, too, was only a man. He would beg for mercy. He would bleed.

And then he would die.

148

YASHIM came slowly up the dark stairway.

At the top he paused.

The light was drifting from beneath the door, and he could hear voices beyond.

"They say that the Greeks did have a bridge," Palewski said. "Under Justinian."

"Maybe. Maybe not. There was an Italian, later on."

"Leonardo da Vinci. It was never built."

Fevzi Pasha spat. "I saw the plans. Too complex. It would never have worked."

Yashim pushed the door. "Good evening," he said, with a bow. "I'm afraid I was detained at the palace." He advanced into the room. "Where's Roxelana?"

Palewski came past him, to the door. "Marta!"

149

ROXELANA came in reluctantly, her eyes on the carpet. As she advanced she glanced once over her shoulder, and at the door Marta nodded with an encouraging smile.

Roxelana bowed, lowering her hand to the floor.

"Efendim," she whispered. She did not look up.

Fevzi Pasha took a step toward her. "You—you know who I am?" He grinned awkwardly and thrust his head forward. "Your baba!"

The little girl shrank back. "I'm Roxelana," she whispered. "I'm big now. I'm five."

Fevzi Ahmet dropped to one knee and opened his arms.

"My—little—girl," he said.

Yashim and Palewski both turned their heads and looked at each other; but out of the corner of his eye Yashim saw the little girl take a hesitant step forward, twisting her fingers.

"Baba?" Her whisper was scarcely audible.

Fevzi lunged and snatched her up. Then he took her off, toward the window, whispering something in her ear.

"It's a cold night," Palewski said. "Have a glass."

Yashim declined. "Too many surprises in one day," he said, and dropped into the armchair. "I've come from the valide."

There was a silence. Marta spoke from the doorway.

"The little girl was just eating her dinner," she said.

Fevzi Ahmet let her down. "Finish your dinner."

When she had gone, Fevzi turned to the window. "Long ago," he said, addressing his own reflection in the glass, "I lost someone very precious to me. Never again." He glanced around. "My daughter comes to Egypt. With me."

Yashim considered him. His enemy. His mentor.

"My men are waiting."

They went downstairs, Yashim holding the candles. In the hall Marta came through with Roxelana, who climbed sleepily into Fevzi Ahmet's arms, and wound her own around his neck.

Fevzi Ahmet stroked her hair. Over the top of her head he said, "We had a deal, Yashim. Or have you forgotten?"

Yashim shook his head.

"Then you are afraid?"

"Yes. I am afraid."

Fevzi Ahmet bent and peered into Yashim's face. "Why do you think I chose you, all those years ago? Why?"

"Because I spoke Greek and—other languages," Yashim answered. He looked into Fevzi Ahmet's face, watched the shadows flicker across his scars. "Because I can be invisible."

Fevzi Ahmet gave a dry laugh. "It takes some courage, Yashim efendi. I think you have some. That's why I chose you."

Yashim said nothing, but for a moment the candles dipped in his hand.

Fevzi's voice was a whisper. "Shamyl."

Yashim stood woodenly at the door.

"Shamyl? That's not possible."

"The Lion of the Caucasus," Fevzi said. "The great hero."

Yashim blinked. Almost single-handedly, Shamyl had fought the Russians to a standstill in the mountains of Georgia. He was a figure of myth, pure and beyond reproach.

It made no sense.

"Ask Shamyl." Fevzi laughed. "A promise is a promise."

He wrenched at the door and flung it back. The candles guttered in the sudden draft, and Yashim heard his boots on the stone steps. He heard him cross the graveled courtyard. He heard the sound of men assembling on the road outside. He saw a lantern, and its feeble light swinging in the air; and then the light and the pasha were gone.

The candelabra was still in his raised hand.

He lowered his hand, closed the door, and made his way back, slowly, treading carefully up the dark stairs.

150

PALEWSKI stood in front of the fire, rubbing his hands together.

"The trouble with the pasha, Yashim, is that he has no manners. I rather noticed it the first time he visited us."

"Manners?"

"A word of thanks, I'd have thought. Well, well." He put two glasses on the mantelpiece and poured the brandy. "The little girl goes back to her father, in Egypt. Tülin gets her just deserts, thanks to the valide. The English have begun negotiations to return the fleet to Istanbul, too. It's only a beginning, but I rather think the Ottoman Empire has found the outside help it needed."

Yashim nodded.

"And Mickiewicz wrote from Paris, to approve the first few pages of my translation."

"I'm very pleased," Yashim said.

"You don't seem awfully pleased." Palewski set the brandy on the sideboard. "Go on, what is it?"

Yashim sighed. "The only people who could have known about Fevzi Ahmet's daughter were Hyacinth, who took her into the harem, and Tülin, who recognized her there. Galytsin had set up an elaborate method for receiving Tülin's reports—but apparently she never filed one. She broke off communications with him at the very moment she discovered that Roxelana was still alive. So how did the Russians know?" Yashim glanced up at his friend. "Or more precisely, who told Galytsin's agent about Roxelana?"

Palewski frowned. "Don't tell me you think it was Hyacinth?"

"A quiet old man who scarcely left the harem in his life? Hyacinth was loyal."

"Impasse, Yashim." Palewski sighed.

But Yashim shook his head. "Unless Tülin did file her report. Not to Galytsin, but to someone else."

"Who?"

Yashim patted his fingertips together, concentrating. He remembered Tülin playing her flute as he descended the stairs, and how the music had nagged at him. Not only because it seemed so dismissive—there had been something else, some idea at the back of his mind that had failed to emerge.

"When I asked Galytsin why Pervyal had been so cheap, he said that was a question Fevzi Ahmet should have asked."

"What does that mean?"

"At the time, he meant to say that Pervyal was a witch. The dealers couldn't wait to get rid of her. But there's another explanation. We know that the Russians fixed it up so that Tülin could enter the sultan's harem. What if it wasn't the first time? What if her entry into Fevzi Ahmet's household was a setup, too?"

"Arranged by the Russians?"

"Not necessarily. After the fire, Galytsin couldn't believe his luck when Pervyal—Tülin—turned up on his doorstep. He should have realized that it *was* too good to be true. The whole event was cleverly fixed so that even if someone suspected her—and why should they?—the trail would lead to the Russians."

Palewski looked interested. "I can take a lot of this," he said. "Misleading the Russians."

Yashim went on: "Inside, by a stroke of fate, Tülin became the valide's handmaiden."

"Which allowed her to steer clear of Roxelana."

Yashim studied his friend absently. "Yes. But it also meant that she wasn't sent away with the other women when Sultan Mahmut died. She stayed with the valide, while the harems changed over."

"You mean that whoever put her there knew the sultan was about to die?"

Yashim nodded.

Palewski said: "Who?"

"You keep asking me," Yashim said. "But you already know. Who would want a spy in Fevzi Ahmet's house? Who would be most threatened by Fevzi Ahmet's promotion to three horsetails—so much so that he would get Tülin to burn his house to the ground?"

Palewski shook his head. "I don't see—"

"You do! You do!" Yashim was excited now. "It was you who pointed it out in the first place. You said he needed a crisis, to stay in power."

"Husrev Pasha? The grand vizier?"

"Husrev Pasha was always afraid of Fevzi Ahmet," Yashim said. "And terrified of losing power. He needed access to the valide, to the sultan, everything. Once Abdülmecid came to the throne, he and Tülin saw their chance. They planned to let her reach the sultan's bed."

"So he and Tülin worked together?"

"She was a Bosniac—like Husrev Pasha. They both come from Bosnia."

"You mean Husrev Pasha told the Russians about Roxelana? Granted he wants power, hates Fevzi Pasha, all that—but why would he tell the Russians anything?"

Yashim hunched forward. "Not the Russians, Palewski. Just one Russian. One Russian greedy and gullible enough to think that he could use the information for his own, private ends."

Palewski raised an eyebrow.

"At the outset of this . . . investigation, I made two guesses. The first, that Fevzi Ahmet murdered the man in the well. The second that the man in the well—let's call him Boris—was working for Galytsin."

Palewski shrugged. "The *Totenkopf*, Yashim. My contribution."

"And a very good one—only it misled me. Boris was blackmailing Fevzi Ahmet because he knew his daughter was alive. He knew where she was, too. But Fevzi Ahmet didn't kill him. He may be a monster but he's not so stupid that he'd drop a body where it was bound to be discovered."

"Who did?"

"Galytsin. Not personally. He sent his thugs—who are not reliable. Later, when the body was recovered, Galytsin was at pains to get the branded piece of skin, which could identify the man. First the little man on the ferry, then the invitation to take a carriage—an abduction, in effect."

"But—you went to see him, later that morning."

"Yes—but it was too late to have me disappear. I'd spoken to the grand vizier. And anyway, I gave him what he wanted."

"But why would Galytsin want . . . Boris killed?"

"He had him killed because the man was working privately, on his own account. He was using information to blackmail Fevzi, instead of sharing it with his nominal employer."

Palewski whistled through his teeth. "Is that why you let Fevzi Ahmet go?"

"Partly that. Partly because his treason is more complicated than it looks. He defected because he knew his career was finished once Husrev had taken power. But also because he had to get away, and save his little girl. Egypt is the safest place for her."

Palewski stood up and went to the windows. "Why did Husrev tell Boris about the girl?"

"I think he had two reasons. First, he wanted to cultivate Boris himself—to provide himself with a friend on the other side. Also, to terrify Fevzi."

He stared for a long time into the dark.

"If anything you've told me is true, Yashim, I hope you plan to keep it to yourself. That little gap, after all."

Yashim gave a curious smile. "You surprise me." He stared at his friend's back. "If I keep quiet, we'll never know for sure."

Palewski turned around. "You'll be dead, Yashim."

Yashim nodded. He thought of the Ceremony of the Birth: the dying child, the mother's grief. He thought of how he stood apart from the central mystery of life.

"That wouldn't be so terrible either, in the scheme of things," he said.

"Fevzi Pasha gave me a way to serve—all that." He waved a hand. "The sultan. The empire. Its people, too, I hope. It's what I do."

He smiled again, remembering Kadri on the banks of the Golden Horn.

"It's the only thing that makes any sense of my own life," he added. "And in the end, it isn't about people, or sultans, or corruption. It's about the truth. The little gap, in this case, is for me."

Palewski looked at him without speaking. Then he gave an imperceptible bow.

"Of course, Yashim." Tears stood in his eyes. "Forgive me. I was only thinking selfishly."

Yashim took his hand in his.

"Truth is the only protection we have," he said. He glanced at the dark windows. "Husrev always works late."

"Now?"

"Now is as good a time as any."

Palewski accompanied him to the front door.

"Be careful, my old friend."

Yashim nodded, and went out into the dark.

151

"Yashim?"

The old pasha raised his eyes to the door, but the shadow was deep, and his eyes were ruined by years of scrutinizing papers.

"Yashim? Is that you?"

A figure stepped into the lamplight.

"Who are you?" The pasha was not afraid. Not yet. "What do you want?"

Whatever he expected, it was not that voice.

"You won't remember me, Husrev Janovic. Why should you?" The stranger used the language of Husrev's youth; the language of the mountains of Bosnia. "I saw you when you came to our village. Your village."

Husrev's hand moved slowly toward the little bell. "Our village?"

"Polje, Husrev. The family home."

"You want money?" Husrev Pasha growled. "Or work? Why are you here?"

The man stepped closer. "I want vengeance, for the girl you stole."

Husrev Pasha blinked hurriedly. "Girl? What girl?"

"Janetta. The woman you stole to be a sailor's whore."

"Janetta—?" The grand vizier frowned.

"My wife."

Husrev's yellow eyes flickered to the shadow that stood before him. "She will become a queen," he said, slowly. "You are—what? A shepherd? What can you give that woman now?"

The man hesitated. Husrev Pasha's hand closed around the bell.

"My wife is dead. She died. In a fire at the sailor's house."

"No, no." Husrev Pasha lifted the bell and shook it.

The peal startled the man.

He saw his journey coming to nothing. His vengeance unappeased.

But he was swift with a knife. He had always been good with the knife.

Husrev Pasha caught the spark of metal in the light.

The man with the knife knew how to kill.

A weight caught him below the knees. He was a big man and he fell back, seeing the ceiling spin, and the raised knife in his hand—and then the room was full of voices.

He let the knife drop.

He could not remember if he had killed the pasha or not. He thought, after all his trouble, that he would feel something. Elation, or satisfaction. Even disappointment. Instead, he felt only very tired.

152

"A long time ago, when I was a boy, there was a man in the village who had the evil eye. He was not a bad man, Yashim. He was a good man. But bad luck attended him, everywhere. Cattle became sick when he looked them over. Women dropped things as he went by." Husrev shrugged. "He stopped going to the church, because twice his presence made an icon fall. He carried bad luck with him. But you—you are lucky."

Yashim rubbed his chin and contemplated the grand vizier.

"Perhaps it's you who has the luck, Husrev Pasha," he said. He had expected to find the vizier alone. Instead, he had heard the peal of the bell, and had hurled himself upon the deranged man. Now that the assassin had been taken away, the room was still. Husrev Pasha, he noticed, remained seated on the divan, just as he had been when the killer drew his knife.

"Tülin is dead," Yashim said.

The heavy lids sank. "Tülin is dead," Husrev repeated. He worked his jaw. "But I am the grand vizier."

The silence hissed in Yashim's ears.

"Tell me, Yashim. In the harem is a little girl—"

"Roxelana."

"She is—well?"

"She is well. But not in the harem anymore."

"Not?"

"Roxelana is on her way to Egypt."

Husrev's eyes were the color of old parchment.

"You will be making a report?"

"No. No, I will not be making a report. You have enough paper as it is."

Something approaching a smile moved on the pasha's lips.

"You are good, Yashim efendi. Thank you."

PREEN took Kadri's chin in her hand.

"What was it, darling? Theater life too dull?"

Kadri smiled, and ducked away. "Too exciting, maybe."

"I was about to teach you to juggle," Preen said, with mock reproach. "Juggling's another whole two kurus a week."

"I'm going to try it on my own," Kadri said. "Will you give me a job when I'm finished at school?"

Preen waved a hand. "Oh, you'll be on your way by then. Grand vizier by thirty."

They both glanced at Yashim, who stood at a discreet distance pretending to read a playbill tacked to the wall, his hands clasped behind his back.

"Not my idea," he announced, without turning. "The Great Kadri! The India Rubber Man!" He swept his hand across the playbill. "Dropped from a roof! Fired from a cannon! It's safer than politics," he added.

As they were leaving, he took Preen by the hand.

"That party," he said. "Where you saw Fevzi Pasha—and the girl."

"Hmm?"

"Husrev Pasha wasn't there, too, by any chance?"

Preen frowned. "As a matter of fact—why do you ask?"

"I just wonder—I don't know. Perhaps we all had Fevzi Pasha slightly wrong."

"Wrong? The man's a monster, Yashim."

"Of course. Of course. I know that."

She gave him a curious look. "You're not going soft on him now, darling? I don't know what it is about you and that man—if he's not the devil, he's got to be an angel. But that's not the way it works."

Yashim nodded. "I know. I met him—" He shrugged. "I suppose it was an impressionable age. Kadri's got you, luckily."

"Kadri, Yashim, is not a fool." She smiled. "Go on. Take him back to the school."

"IT'S too extraordinary," the valide said. "I put the whole thing down to that wretched Kislar aga. The one you recommended, Yashim."

Yashim shifted uncomfortably on the divan.

"Ibou was hardly to blame," he said. "The dealer tricked him. Perhaps even the dealer didn't know."

"Pouf! A dealer always knows. It's his business, Yashim. Like horses, like girls. She must have had a crooked pedigree. I never much liked her myself. Valide this, valide that. And desperate to get to Besiktas, of course. I saw that straightaway. But I enjoyed her magic. It reminded me of Martinique."

"Martinique?"

"Where I grew up. Chickens. Trances. We called it voodoo. Brought back happy memories."

"She denied you water," he said. "She pushed Hyacinth over the parapet, too. It wasn't magic."

The valide waved a hand, and her bangles chinked.

"It's always magic, if you want." She shrugged. "Talfa believes in it. So did the girl you brought here—Melda. What happened to her friend?"

"Elif believed she was pregnant," Yashim said. "She thought Donizetti Pasha had given her a baby."

The valide clapped her hands together. "That's it, Yashim." Her face was serious. "He is round, like a mushroom—but she was very young. He twirled a mustache. He caught her eye."

"Tülin gave her something," Yashim said. "A potion."

The valide shivered. "It was very cruel," she said.

"Melda believed it, too. She believed she had a secret that was too dangerous to reveal."

"Tsk, tsk." The valide shook her head. "These girls from Circassia! It is the mountains, Yashim. It makes them stubborn, and leaves them ignorant."

"And this—" Yashim gestured at the walls. "This harem . . ."

"Encourages them to be silly, too. I know it, Yashim. Almost alone of all the women who come here, I have the benefit of an education. *Ne t'en souviens-tu pas?* Between you and me, Yashim, it's like catching snowflakes. They have desires, hopes, plans, secrets. And they wear them on their faces, like *maquillage.*"

"And die, as a result?"

"Of course. Death is a secret, like any other."

She touched a hand to her cheek, and smoothed it back.

"Tell me, Yashim, what did you make of our friend Monsieur Gautier?"

"*'Everything that is beautiful is useless,'*" Yashim quoted. "It seemed insincere."

"Very silly," the valide agreed. "It could have been written by one of our girls."

"If any of them knew how to write," Yashim pointed out.

"Or understood French, Yashim."

ACKNOWLEDGMENTS

For a recipe for the Greek fishermen's stew with tomatoes on page 32, go to my website at www.jasongoodwin.net.

Western writers tend to imagine the harem as a perfumed bathhouse full of naked odalisques. In fact it was much more like an old-fashioned girls' boarding school, run as a department of the civil service; the baths may have been hot but the food was usually cold. Having been brought up with four sisters, a mother, a stepmother, grandmothers, and innumerable aunts and great-aunts, it took no great leap of the imagination to people the harem of Abdülmecid. My thanks and love to them all.

I drew on several excellent accounts of harem life, including Leyla Saz Hanimefendi's memoir *The Imperial Harem of the Sultans* (from which I borrowed the Ceremony of the Birth); *Arabesque*, the 1944 memoirs of HRH Princess Musbah Haidar; and Douglas Scott Brookes's invaluable *The Concubine, the Princess and the Teacher: Voices from the Ottoman Harem*, from which I took the terrible engine.

While *An Evil Eye* is a work of fiction, Fevzi Ahmet happens to be a real person who rose to be Kapudan pasha and did make the astonishing career move with the Ottoman fleet described in this book.

Thanks to Richard Goodwin for his own patient and indulgent reading; to Sarah Crichton at FSG and Julian Loose at Faber for forbearance and wise comment; to Charles Buchan and Sarah Chalfant at Wylie; to Krista Kaer for taking Yashim (and me) to Estonia.

As for the harem, my wife, Kate, is as trenchant a critic as the valide herself: I am grateful for all her suggestions. Harry, my youngest son, is among other things a skillful and prolific writer. I do my best to discourage him from pursuing that path, but he comes up with wonderful ideas and I plan to steal some of them for the next Yashim story. Especially the banditry.

This one, meanwhile, is for him.

A NOTE ABOUT THE AUTHOR

Jason Goodwin fell under the spell of Istanbul while studying Byzantine history at Cambridge University. Following the success of his book *A Time for Tea: Travels Through China and India in Search of Tea*, he made a six-month pilgrimage across Eastern Europe to reach Istanbul for the first time, a journey recounted in *On Foot to the Golden Horn: A Walk to Istanbul*.

He later wrote *Lords of the Horizons: A History of the Ottoman Empire*, described as "a work of dazzling scholarship" in *The New York Times Book Review*. His books featuring Investigator Yashim have been translated into more than forty languages; the first, *The Janissary Tree*, won the Edgar Allan Poe Award for Best Novel in 2007. He lives with his wife and their four children in Dorset, England.